Never Too Late

Books by Michael Phillips

Is Jesus Coming Back As Soon As We Think?
Destiny Junction • *Kings Crossroads*
Make Me Like Jesus • *God, A Good Father*
Jesus, An Obedient Son
Best Friends for Life (with Judy Phillips)
George MacDonald: Scotland's Beloved Storyteller
Rift in Time • *Hidden in Time*
Legend of the Celtic Stone • *An Ancient Strife*
Your Life in Christ (George MacDonald)
The Truth in Jesus (George MacDonald)

AMERICAN DREAMS

Dream of Freedom • *Dream of Life*

THE SECRET OF THE ROSE

The Eleventh Hour • *A Rose Remembered*
Escape to Freedom • *Dawn of Liberty*

THE SECRETS OF HEATHERSLEIGH HALL

Wild Grows the Heather in Devon
Wayward Winds
Heathersleigh Homecoming
A New Dawn Over Devon

SHENANDOAH SISTERS

Angels Watching Over Me
A Day to Pick Your Own Cotton
The Color of Your Skin Ain't the Color of Your Heart
Together Is All We Need

CAROLINA COUSINS

A Perilous Proposal • *The Soldier's Lady*
Never Too Late

CAROLINA COUSINS

Never Too Late

A NOVEL

MICHAEL
PHILLIPS

BETHANY HOUSE PUBLISHERS

Minneapolis, Minnesota

Never Too Late
Copyright © 2007
Michael Phillips

Cover photography by Steve Gardner
Cover design by The Design Works Group

Scripture quotations are from the King James Version of the Bible.

Published by Bethany House Publishers
11400 Hampshire Avenue South
Bloomington, Minnesota 55438

Bethany House Publishers is a division of
Baker Publishing Group, Grand Rapids, Michigan.

Printed in the United States of America

Paperback: ISBN-13: 978-0-7642-0043-4 ISBN-10: 0-7642-0043-7
Hardcover: ISBN-13: 978-0-7642-0237-7 ISBN-10: 0-7642-0237-5
Large Print: ISBN-13: 978-0-7642-0271-1 ISBN-10: 0-7642-0271-5

Library of Congress Cataloging-in-Publication Data

Phillips, Michael R., 1946-
    Never too late / Michael Phillips.
        p. cm. — (Carolina cousins ; bk. no. 3)
    ISBN 978-0-7642-0237-7 (hardcover : alk. paper) — ISBN 978-0-7642-0043-4
(pbk. : alk. paper) — ISBN 978-0-7642-0271-1 (largeprint pbk.) 1. Reconstruction
(U.S. history, 1865-1877)—Fiction. 2. Freedmen—Fiction. 3. Plantation life—
Fiction. 4. North Carolina—Fiction. 5. Young women—Fiction. I. Title.
    PS3566.H492N47 2007
    813'.54—dc22   2006036463

To those young people I have been privileged
to teach and coach in track and cross country
through the years, from Winship Junior High to
Eureka and Fortuna High Schools. You have
enriched my life in many ways, and I thank you
for the pleasant memories of wonderful
experiences and friendships.

CONTENTS

PROLOGUE

⊰ ✳ ⊱

It's mighty strange how you think you know folks so well, when you really don't know them as well as you thought.

Everybody's got more thoughts and feelings going on inside than you realize. People have pasts too, whole lives you don't know about, and might never find out about either if you don't take the time to try.

I reckon that's what makes getting to know people so interesting, almost an adventure you might say. The stories people have to tell—even just about themselves and what has happened to them and where they've been and what they've seen and what they've learned—are some of the most interesting things there are in life. Maybe that's why they say that everyone's life is interesting enough to write a book about if you just knew how to go about it.

That's probably why I've enjoyed telling stories ever since I started spinning yarns for my kid brother Samuel. Back then, when we were slaves, I just made them up to pass the time. Or, I'd retell the old tales I'd heard around the fire—the ones about Mr. Rabbit and Mr. Fox were my favorites. But later as I grew, I discovered that the best stories of all were about people—true stories about what happened to them. Maybe they're not really "stories," then . . . I'm not exactly sure about that.

But they're still fascinating, and I still enjoy telling them just the same.

⇗ ✳ ⇖

FIRE

1

ENRY PATTERSON WAS A MAN WHO HAD NO enemies. At least that's what people thought.

Why danger would stalk such a peace-loving soul was a mystery no one in Greens Crossing ever quite understood except those involved. And they were not the kind of men who talked.

The previous day had not been unusual. There were a couple visits from men Henry did not recognize asking for the owner of the livery stable. When told that he was not there, they had looked about in an odd sort of way before riding off. Henry thought little of it at the time. Yet the peculiar exchanges played on his mind long afterward, and kept him from sleeping soundly that night.

He was awake as usual at daybreak the next morning. Most of the rest of the Rosewood family were talking around the breakfast table about going into town that day too. But as Henry and his son Jeremiah both had to be at their jobs early, they were the first to ride away from the plantation house about half past seven.

The secret men's vigilante club known as the Ku Klux Klan had spread rapidly throughout the South after the War Between the States, dedicated to the preservation of white supremacy and Southern tradition. Its members viewed it as their sacred duty as loyal Southerners to exact retribution on whites who embraced the new order . . . and on blacks who did not know their place.

The Klan was not the only such vigilante group that roved the counties of the South, tormenting and killing what they called "uppity niggers." But it was the most powerful and the most feared. The very thought of the silent night riders—clad in white sheets and hoods—awoke dread and terror.

The Klan's weapons of choice were three: the gun, the torch, and the rope.

In the North Carolina communities of Greens Crossing and Oakwood, some twenty miles from Charlotte, a number of prominent men had been initiated into the mysteries of the Klan. Although there had been one attempted hanging, their mischief in the area had thus far produced no deaths. That seemed, however, about to change.

On this particular day in the fall of the year 1869, the local KKK had decided to modify their tactics. They would strike in broad daylight and in plain sight, in order to teach a lesson none in the community would forget. Their target was a black man every one of them had known for years. If the truth were known, none had any personal quarrel with Henry Patterson. He knew his place, spoke respectfully, and never gave any trouble. But he was also involved with people who didn't seem to know the difference between blacks and whites.

It was what he represented. He had been the first free black to settle in the region before the war. Now with unsettling changes taking place everywhere, it almost seemed as if he had been the start of it all. The fact that he now lived out at the Daniels place made killing him the easiest way to get back at the whole pack of them—whites and blacks together.

And so as the fifteen or more white-robed riders galloped toward Greens Crossing a little before noon, the burning torches in their hands were not to light their way, as would have been the case had the raid come in the middle of the night.

They intended to put the fire to another use.

Mary Ann, Templeton, and Ward Daniels, Kathleen Clairborne, and Josepha Black had all arrived in Greens Crossing sometime after eleven o'clock, and were now about their own business. The two Daniels brothers had gone to the bank. Josepha was in Mrs. Hammond's general store picking up Rosewood's mail and a few supplies. Mayme and Katie had gone to the shoe and boot shop.

The thundering approach of the riders, coming from the far end of Greens Crossing where the livery sat as the last building in town, did not at first attract the attention of any of the townspeople.

Inside the livery, the moment Henry heard the angry shouts, he knew they were meant for him. He started to walk outside. Several gunshots at his feet stopped him in his tracks.

"Get back inside, Patterson," called one of the hooded riders, "or you'll be a dead man!"

Several more shots followed rapidly to enforce the threat.

The livery was quickly surrounded by the horsemen. Escape on foot would be impossible. The first torch landed on the roof before the echo of the last shot had died away. It was followed by over a dozen more lighting the wall. Within seconds, the small building was encircled in a ring of fire.

Henry heard the crackle of flames and smelled the smoke the instant the first torch landed. He ran to the stables to free the three or four horses inside. Their wide nostrils had also smelled the smoke and they had begun to whinny and rear in growing fright.

With effort, Henry got them loose, then unlatched the rear door and kicked it wide. A blast of heat from five-foot flames sent him staggering backward. He shouted and kicked and whipped at the terrified horses, until at last, shrieking in panic and confusion, they bolted through the smoke and flame to safety.

"Look out!" cried several of the riders, hurriedly getting their own mounts out of the way.

"Don't let him through!" shouted another. "Keep the circle tight . . . shoot him if he tries to make a break for it!"

The instant the horses from inside stampeded past them, they closed ranks, guarding every inch of the perimeter so that no human could follow the horses and escape.

The explosions of gunfire, followed so quickly by a plume of smoke rising from the livery—a tinderbox of straw and dried wood—brought everyone running out of stores and homes looking about to find the cause of the commotion. Mr. Watson was one of the first men into the street. Glancing toward the livery, he shouted for the fire brigade. Within seconds a dozen men were running toward the scene.

In the bank, someone shouted, "The livery's on fire!"

At Watson's mill, Jeremiah Patterson had been working inside. He too heard the shouts and was only seconds after his boss into the street. Ward and Templeton ran up to join him from the direction of the bank. The instant he saw where the smoke was coming from, Jeremiah sprinted ahead of them toward the livery.

People were running and shouting from everywhere now.

Inside the burning building, the dense, suffocating smoke was so thick that Henry could see nothing. All was blackness about him. He grabbed a bucket half full of water from near the anvil and doused it over his head and shirt, then dropped to the floor, avoiding the smoke and trying to breathe the little air coming through what openings it could find beneath the flames. Any possible route of escape was gone.

Already flames from the front of the livery rose crackling into the sky. The building was too far gone for the makeshift fire brigade to hope to accomplish anything. Though men were shouting and running from all corners of town, one look at the place and they knew it was too late. Whatever they might have tried to do otherwise, most slowed down as they drew closer, intimidated at the sight of a circle of hooded men surrounding the blaze. No livery stable was worth getting killed for by *that* crowd—they would probably be crazy enough to start shooting if someone made a move to help. All they could attempt to do now was keep the fire from spreading.

As more and more people reached the scene, no one held out much hope that life would be found inside once the flames began to subside.

⌒ ✳ ⌒

I don't suppose Negroes in the United States of America would ever be able to think of themselves apart from slavery.

It was slavery even more than the color of our skin that defined who we were—as individuals and as a race. Some of us were lighter (like me, because I was half white). Some were darker. But all of us who had been bought and sold before the War Between the States had been slaves together, whatever the shade of our skin.

Of course there were lots of free blacks in the United States, mostly in the North. There were free blacks like Henry in the South too. Some of them had had kind white owners who had freed them on their own. Others had managed to buy their freedom. And then some, like Henry—though I doubt there were too many like him—who had won their freedom on a bet over whether or not Henry could break a wild horse. When he'd accomplished the feat, Henry's former owner was mad as a March hare thinking Henry'd honey-fuggled him. But because he'd made the bet in front of another white man, he couldn't back down. So Henry gained his freedom and had eventually wound up in Greens Crossing.

But what I was fixing to say was that I doubted even free blacks in this country could think of themselves apart from slavery either. To be a Negro in those days was either to be a slave yourself, or to hurt from the sting of slavery for the rest of your race. We were all free now, several years after the war, thanks to Abraham Lincoln. But we all still hurt from the memories.

Probably blacks in the United States would always hurt from it, no matter how much time passed. Maybe slavery would always be part of what it meant to be an American Negro.

I had only known one black person in all my life who had never been a slave ever. His name was Micah Duff and he'd come from up North. He had recently married our friend Emma and they were now on their way out west. Micah hadn't been a slave, but now he was married to Emma, who had been. They'd lost Emma's little boy William because of slavery. And so even free Micah Duff would always know the pain of slavery too.

Since I'd grown up as a slave, I had only learned to read a few years ago—thanks to my friend and cousin Katie Clairborne—though I still wasn't that good a reader. I hadn't had much schooling either, because slaves weren't taught much of anything except how to work hard. Everything I knew about what I reckon you'd call the bigger world out beyond Rosewood (that's the plantation where Katie and I lived) I'd learned from books or from Katie or from my papa, Templeton Daniels. But I still didn't know much about history or the rest of the world and other countries, or even other places in this country.

But I was about to find out about somebody who'd grown up a long way from North Carolina, just as far away as Micah Duff had been in Chicago—although in the other direction. She was from a place not far from New Orleans, down where the Mississippi River empties into the Gulf of Mexico. It's a place where the weather can get mighty severe sometimes.

⤛ ✳ ⤜

A WORLD LONG BEFORE
THE WAR
2

A N AUTUMN BONFIRE HAD ALMOST BURNT ITSELF
out under the Louisiana night sky.

The remaining embers glowed dull orange in a bed of
ash. The black revelers from the slave village on the De
Seille plantation who had gathered after dusk to sing
hymns and spirituals had mostly dispersed to their cabins.

A black girl of six or seven still sat staring into the
dying fire, her back propped against a tree in drowsy content, eyes nearly shut. The words of the last hymn echoed
again in her brain.

> *When we's in that glorious place*
> *All dem tears gone from our face*
> *We be free.*

A rustling in the brush roused her. She opened her eyes
to see a tall boy three or four years older. He crept forward,
then crouched over the dying embers and prodded them
with a long stick.

"What you doin', Mose?" asked the girl.

"You still here, Seffie?" the boy said, glancing around.

"I got sleepy."

"I gots me some nuts for roastin'," said Mose. "Want one?" He held out a plump pecan in its shell.

She shook her head. "I ate enuff already."

"Den you'd bes' be goin'," said the boy she had called Mose. "I heard yo' mama axin' 'bout you."

Slowly she rose and wandered toward the fire.

"You really gwine roast dem nuts?" she asked.

"Why not?"

"It's too late."

"Not fo me. Da fire's jes' right fo roastin'."

He tossed three or four pecans from his pocket into the edge of the ashes, then stirred at them with his stick to keep them from bursting into flame.

"Where you git dem nuts?" asked the girl.

"Off de groun' where dey fell off da trees ober yonder."

"Will you git me a stick, Mose, so I kin play wiff da fire too."

"I ain't playin', Seffie. I's roastin' dese nuts. 'Sides, you's too young ter play wiff a fire like dis. Fire's dangerous. Ain't nuthin' ter play wiff nohow."

Seffie sat down and stared into the red-orange embers, mesmerized by the glow, as Mose continued to poke and prod at his little stash of nuts, whose shells were now blackening and smoking.

After another minute or two, he rolled them out of the fire toward him with the end of his stick, then anxiously waited for them to cool.

"You shore you doesn't want one er dese nice nuts, Seffie?'' he said, picking one up and tossing it back and forth in his hands as he blew to cool it down enough to hold.

But his young companion had grown sleepy again.

Slowly she rose, leaving Mose alone with the dying fire and the treasure of his few nuts.

When the girl called Seffie reached the row of shacks, a big black woman swept down on her and hustled her inside one of the smaller cabins.

"Seffie, where you been?'' scolded the girl's mother. "I been lookin' all roun' fo you! Come on, git in here. Hit's long past time you wuz in yo bed.''

The child came in and was soon asleep in the corner with her older brothers and sisters. She awoke only an hour or two later from loud shouts and pounding feet.

When she opened her eyes, flickering shapes and a strange glow filled the cabin. Smoke stung her eyes and throat.

"Mama! Mama!'' she cried. "What is it?''

"Hurry, chil', git on yo feet an' follow me,'' said her mother, snatching her hand and yanking her to her feet.

The little cabin was full of people. The youngest children, two toddlers and a baby, were crying, and Seffie's mother and a crippled toothless old woman they all called "Aunt Phoebe'' were trying to save what few possessions they had in case the cabin went up in flames.

Hurrying out into the chilly night air, the cause for the uproar was immediately visible. The woodshed and a large pile of dried chunks of oak waiting to be stacked inside were on fire and sending flames twenty or more feet into the air. Tiny hot glowing cinders sprayed upward and floated on a southerly breeze ominously toward the slave village. All the black men were running with water buckets from the stream and dousing the walls and roofs closest to the blaze. The master and several of his men from the big house were there, boots hurriedly pulled on over night-clothes, shouting out orders to make sure the fire did not spread.

Early the next morning, while a few wisps of smoke still rose from what had been the pile of split oak and the wood-house, the overseer shouted for all the slaves to come out from their cabins.

"That fire last night wasn't no accident," he said in a stern voice as soon as they were gathered. "The master gave you permission to have your bonfire and sing your songs and now look what's happened. Our next winter's wood supply and the woodhouse—they're all gone. You're going to have to cut and haul us a whole new batch of wood, and that's after your regular work is done. The mas-ter's mighty upset with all of you and he told me to thrash every one of you unless I bring him the name of whoever let that fire spread, 'cause he knows it came on account of that fire of yours and wasn't no accident. So unless you want whippings all around, he wants to know who it was."

He stopped and stared around at the thirty or forty silent black faces with a look that said he secretly hoped no one would speak up so that he could have the pleasure of whipping every one of them.

A long uncomfortable pause followed. A young black boy of eleven or twelve suddenly stepped forward.

"Well, speak up, Dominique," demanded the overseer.

The boy shuffled his feet where he stood.

"Speak up, boy, unless you want a taste of my strap!"
said the overseer.

"It was dose two," said Dominique, pointing. "Dat
Mose an' dat Seffie kid what belongs ter Aunt Phoebe. I
seen dem sneakin' roun' after everybody lef' las' night. Dey
wuz pokin' at dat fire till sparks flew up."

The overseer glared at the two accused offenders.

"So it was you two nigger brats," he said.

"No, massa, please!" cried Mose. "I didn't spread no
fire! Dominique done tol' you a lie!"

The overseer approached and looked down at the girl.

"Were you playing with the fire?" he asked.

"No, suh," she said, looking up with wide eyes of
dread.

"What were you doing, then?"

"Jes' sittin' watchin', suh."

"Was he playing with the fire?" he said, nodding
toward the boy.

"He wuz jes' roastin' nuts, suh."

"Was he stirrin' up the fire?"

"Not much, suh—jes' enuff ter git da nuts out."

"Did he have a stick?"

"Jes' a little one. He didn't make no fire wiff it."

But by now the overseer's mind was made up. He
didn't care as much for facts as he did that retribution was
made. It was the one law of dealing with slaves his boss
wanted enforced above all others—that *somebody* pay for
every slightest infraction. It didn't much matter who.
Whether the actual guilty party was the one punished was
of but minor concern. Even in a case like this, which was
likely just an accident, someone must be punished. Justice

didn't matter, only retribution—that *someone* suffer in full view of the rest of the slaves. It was the only way to keep fear as the dominant element of rule on the plantation.

He stared at them all in silence for several long seconds. Then at last he spoke again.

"Stand up, girl!" he said.

Trembling in terror, Seffie rose to her feet.

"Mose, boy," he growled, "come up here. Come and take your punishment like a man. It will be fifteen strokes for each of you at the whipping post."

He grabbed the boy by the arm and reached for the little girl. "Oh, please, massa, no!" screamed Seffie's mother. She pushed her way through to the front where the overseer stood.

"Please, massa," she said desperately, "she didn't know what she wuz doin'! She's jes' wooly-headed. She don' mean no harm. She's neber been one ter start trouble afore."

The overseer considered a moment. Then he nodded his head slowly. "You have a point. Trouble of this magnitude merits more than a whipping. I can't keep slaves who may set fire to the master's house."

"What you gwine do?" cried the child's mother, clinging to the girl even tighter and suddenly more afraid than before.

He gave a sudden jerk and wrenched Seffie from her mother's grasp and pulled her screaming toward the big house.

"I'll let the master decide," he said. "He may just tell

me to sell these two monkeys for all the trouble they've caused."

"No!" wailed the woman behind them as he dragged the girl away. Mose followed, compliant but also terrified at what might be waiting for them.

Strange New Home
3

S EFFIE WAS TOO YOUNG TO HAVE TO EXPERIENCE A
broken heart.

Torn away from her mother and the only home she had
ever known, could her heart ever heal? Or would a hard
scab grow over the wound and prevent her from loving
again?

Mose told her to cling close. He would say she was his
sister, and that a master would get more work out of them
if they could stay together.

When Peter Meisner, a wealthy German immigrant,
saw the two at the New Orleans slave market, however, it
was the girl who attracted his attention. She looked about
the right age. She was obviously frightened, but her eyes
looked bright and intelligent.

He walked toward them. The girl glanced down at the
ground, but the boy held his gaze.

"She your sister?" he asked.

"Yes, suh," said Mose.

"What's your name?" asked Meisner, turning toward her.

"Her name's Seffie, suh," Mose answered for her. "I's real good wiff horses, suh."

"How old are you, Seffie?" asked the man.

Seffie glanced up at Mose, too scared to speak.

"Answer me, girl," prodded the man.

"'Bout seven, suh," said Seffie.

The man knelt down. "Do you know how to read, Seffie?"

Again she glanced toward Mose and hesitated.

"Don't worry," said Meisner. "I won't make you leave your brother. If I decide to buy you, I'll buy you both. Now . . . can you read?"

"No, suh," said Seffie timidly.

"Would you like to learn?"

Again Seffie looked at Mose, wondering what she should say. He gave an imperceptible nod. Already he could tell this man would be a good master to them.

"Yes, suh," said Seffie.

"Good, then—I will see what I can do."

Neither of the two black youngsters knew it yet, but Peter Meisner had come to the slave market hoping to find a companion for his eight-year-old daughter. He and his wife had been in Louisiana for only a few years. Two years before, their daughter Grace had contracted scarlet fever. The long battle for her life left her blind and with a weakened heart. But Grace knew how to read and loved to learn. If she could not read for herself, she could be read to. They hired a governess, but the woman, though a good enough teacher, did not have a nurse's compassion. Grace gradu-

ally quieted. Her governess grew distant, and the school-
room became quiet and depressing. Grace's father had
gone to the slave market in hopes of finding a bright young
slave girl for Grace to play with and learn with and hopefully bring some cheer back into his daughter's life.

It did not take long for both Grace's parents to realize
they had made a wise choice. How different it might have
been had Grace been able to see her new friend's dark
brown face, none of them would ever know. As it was, the
two girls hit it off immediately. Seffie's aptitude for learning proved as much a boon for the governess as her presence was for Grace's spirits. Not that she had been hired to
teach a slave girl, but, as she read to Grace, Seffie came in
for her own share of the learning. Within six months, and
much to Grace's delight, Seffie was reading to Grace herself. Trying to model her own speech after Grace's—with
occasional correction from the other two—gradually Seffie
began to lose some of her slave dialect. Listening and paying attention and asking questions as Miss Walker tutored
Grace in the subjects her parents had set, within another
year Seffie knew how to write and had begun to learn math-
ematics.

"All right, girls," said Miss Walker one morning,
"today we shall practice our sums again. Grace," she
added, "do you think you can visualize the numbers in
your mind like we did yesterday?"

"I will try, Miss Walker," said Grace.

"It be all right if I's write—"

"Will it be all right if I write them," corrected Grace.

"Thank you, Miss Grace," said Seffie. "Will it be all

right if I write dem on dis paper, Miss Walker?" asked Seffie.

"Certainly, Seffie. You write them and try to do the sum with the pencil while Grace does it in her mind. But you mustn't say anything until Grace has a chance to say the answer. Then you can see if it is the same as what you have written down."

"Yes'm."

"All right, here are the numbers I want you to add together—sixteen plus three plus eight."

"That's easy," laughed Grace, "that's . . . let me see . . . it's twenty-seven."

"Very good. Is that what you got, Seffie?"

"I didn't get nuthin' yet."

"Let's do another one. This time, Grace, give Seffie time to get her answer too.—Eleven . . . plus thirteen . . . plus ten."

It was silent a minute. Seffie wrote the three numbers on the paper and then began to add up the first columns as Miss Walker had taught her. When she had the sum completed she glanced up.

"I think I got it," she said.

"How about you, Grace," said Miss Walker. "What is your answer?"

"Thirty-four."

"That's what I got too!" exclaimed Seffie.

"Very good, girls. Let's do a few more. Then I have a surprise for you."

"What surprise, Miss Walker?" asked Grace excitedly.

"Let's do our sums first, then I shall tell you."

Fifteen minutes later, the governess set aside the sheet of arithmetic problems.

"Now for the surprise I promised. Your parents want you to begin learning another language, Grace."

"What language?"

"They said I could let you decide. Since there are only two languages other than English I know, you can choose either Latin or French."

"Say something in them so I know what they sound like."

"All right . . . hmm, let me see . . . *Salve—si vales optime valeo. Meum nomen est Marie Walker.* And then . . . *Enchanté de faire votre connaissance. Je m'appelle Marie Walker.*"

"Which was which?" giggled Grace. "I liked the second one much better. It sounded soft and nice."

"That was French."

"Then I want to learn to speak French."

"It sounded like I used to hear people talk on the plantation where I come from before," said Seffie.

"That was probably Cajun French," said Miss Walker. "Many people in Louisiana speak it."

"What is that?" asked Grace.

"It is a dialect of French, brought here in the 1700s by the French Acadians when they were deported from their homeland, which is now a province of Canada."

"May we begin today, Miss Walker?" said Grace excitedly. "I want to learn to say what you just said."

"In a little while, Grace, my dear. But right now, you look a little pale. I think perhaps you should take a rest. Come, Seffie, help me get Miss Grace to her bed."

Unfortunately, the fever had taken a greater toll on Grace's strength than the doctor had realized. Slowly its effects began to return. They had not progressed but two or three months with the new French lessons, which Seffie seemed to have more aptitude for than Grace, before lessons had to be suspended for two weeks.

Seffie was told nothing except that Grace was sick and there would be no more lessons for a while. She was kept busy around the house doing other jobs. When Miss Walker returned and they resumed lessons, Grace looked thinner and more pale than before. She could hardly sit up in bed.

This time the lessons lasted only a week and were discontinued again.

Again Seffie was told nothing. But from the whispers and worried expressions and silences, the coming and going of the doctor, and the look of sadness on Mrs. Meisner's face, she knew the situation was serious.

Then came a day of closed doors with sounds of crying behind them. People she had never seen came to the house. Everyone was solemn and sad.

The next day a wagon came, all draped in black. Some men carried a long thin box into the house. The mistress and most of the slaves were crying. At last Seffie knew that she would never see Grace again.

Her heart broke in a second place, and another scab grew over yet another wound of loss.

FRIENDS
4

A SLAVE GIRL OF TEN WALKED SLOWLY FROM THE kitchen of the large plantation house to a vegetable garden which stood at the edge of a planted field. In her hand she carried a large basket full of the carrots and beans she had been sent to fetch.

In the distance, at the far end of the field, two dozen Negro men and women worked bent over under the hot August sun, hoes in hand, whacking out weeds from the soft earth between indescribably long rows of growing cotton. As the girl went she glanced toward the workers. No feelings of kinship arose in her heart as she did. She had no mother, no father, no brothers, no sisters, no cousins, no aunts, no uncles at this place where she had been for three years. She had one friend, but no family. That one friend had made her uprooting three years earlier, if not bearable—what in a slave's life could be said to be bearable—at least tolerable. They saw each other only occasionally over the years, since she lived in the big house and he in the slave village. But still, that they chanced to be here together was nothing short of a miracle. But no one she saw in the field caught her eye with feelings of kinship or affection.

Mercifully she had been attached to the kitchen after Grace's death, mainly to wash dishes. So she had not had to endure the fields under the hot sun, but had recently grown accustomed to the hot, sweaty, endless, thankless work of a kitchen slave, laboring so that a privileged few might never have to lift a finger for any provision they might want. Now at the mere age of ten, her intuition with food and baking had already begun to manifest itself. She was occasionally told to make a batch of bread or mix up a fresh pot of soup on her own. Neither her white master, nor any of his family, nor the Negro house mammy had yet been disappointed.

She reached the garden, opened the wire gate, went inside, and proceeded to gather the vegetables she had been sent for.

Twenty minutes later she left by the same gate, closed it carefully, and headed back toward the house. She was not exactly a dreamy sort of girl, though she often gave the impression of being lost in faraway thoughts, for she said but little. The fact was, she had never recovered from being cruelly ripped away from her family at the tender age of seven, nor the death of her young mistress a few years later. Since then her life had been a dull, mechanical tedium of work for which she had little interest, among people she did not care about and would never care about and who did not care for her. Some were kinder than others. But no one really cared who she was or where she came from or probably whether she lived or died. To care brought pain in the

life of the slave. Though she had not stopped to think
about it, and was too young to do so anyway, the pain she
had already suffered had scarred her too deeply to care
much about anything. So she kept to herself. Even the
threat of the whip, which she had felt at her previous home,
was not sufficient to arouse her from lethargy. She had been
torn from her mother. Death had torn her from Grace.

She cared for nothing anymore . . . except her one
friend.

Lost in the uncaring boredom of hour that followed
hour, day that followed day, she did not hear the pounding
hooves coming toward her. Even had she glanced up and
seen the horse, she would not have known it to be a runaway from the stables, and no sense of danger would immediately have registered itself in her brain.

But at length she did hear the pounding, paused, and
glanced toward the sound. A horse was coming straight for
her along the narrow road from the house to the field.
Behind it ran three or four men, yelling. Maybe they were
yelling at her—she couldn't tell.

Her legs froze in panic. It was the same fear she felt
when getting a whipping or being on the slave block. Her
mouth went dry and she might as well have been mute, for
she could not utter a word.

By now the words coming from the men were plain
enough.

"Get away . . . get out of the way . . . get off the road!"
they continued to shout at her.

But she could run no more than she could speak. She
was frozen to the spot as the huge black horse with fire in
his eyes charged straight toward her. Ever since that day

after the fire, fear had been capable of paralyzing her into a statue of stone.

The basket fell from her fingers to the ground. But still she stood unmoving.

From out of the corner of her eye there was a swift movement. She was not even capable of turning toward it, yet was somehow vaguely aware of it. A figure was sprinting at a speed unseen on the plantation before that minute. He was just a boy, but he was running faster than any of the men about the place, white or black, could have run.

When the horse, wild-eyed and as heedless of its danger as the girl of hers, was nearly upon her and seemed sure to trample her under his pounding hooves, from across the meadow flew a black blur diagonally between them. He did not even slow as he slammed into the girl and knocked her to the ground and off to one side of the path. A second later the horse thundered by, crushing the basket and vegetables under his mighty hooves.

The men came charging up and ran past, shouting out a few derisive words as they passed at the girl who had nearly gotten herself killed. But they were soon gone, for they cared more for the horse than they did her.

The boy stood, then pulled her back to her feet.

"Why didn't you git outta da way, Seffie?" he asked. "Dat blamed horse coulda killed you."

"I don't know," she said. "I jes' saw it an' got plumb scared. When I gits scared, sometimes I can't move."

"It's a good thing I saw you when I did."

"Thank you, Mose. You saved me, like you always does. I don't know what I'd do ef you didn't always take care ob me."

"You take care ob yo'self jes' fine, Seffie!" laughed
Mose. "You take care ob yo'self in da kitchen."

"Dat's different. In dere I knows what I's doing. Dat
reminds me—I brought you something, in case I saw you."

She dug her hand into the pocket of her dress and
pulled out a handful of pecan nuts.

"De're shelled an' everythin', Mose."

"Thanks, Seffie!" said the boy. "Dey really all fo me?"

"I brought dem fo you."

"Wuz you s'posed to?"

"I don't know. I just did. Dere wuz a whole bowlful ob
dem. Dere can't be no harm in you havin' a few."

"Thanks, Seffie," said Mose again, biting into a large
pecan with eyes full of satisfaction.

"Oh, but look at my basket and the vegetables! They'll
scold me somethin' awful."

"I'll tell 'em what happened an' 'bout da horse an'
everythin'. Meantime, let's pick up dose things an' git a
few fresh carrots and beans for dose da horse trampled an'
den I'll go back to da house wiff you. Ain't dat much harm
dun dat I kin see."

But Seffie didn't want Mose to go in and tell what happened for fear of what might happen to him. So she went
in alone. Seffie got no whipping, just a scolding for being
late with the vegetables and for breaking the basket. They
all knew the sadness she felt after Grace died and had been
patiently waiting for her to get her spirit back. She said
nothing about Mose's part in the incident, and it was soon
forgotten by all but the two friends.

One-Eyed Jack
5

A YEAR LATER, ONE OF THOSE HOT SUMMER DAYS came when it didn't seem that anyone had energy to lift a finger, much less a cotton hoe. It happened also to be a Sunday, so the slaves were free to do as they pleased and most of them, especially all the children, wound up down at the river trying to cool off. By midafternoon the shouts and laughter from the swimming hole were gradually fading to sounds of exhaustion from hours of continuous play.

Mose, meanwhile, after a swim with the others, was on the back of an old plough horse that had nearly outlived his working life. The overseer let Mose ride him when neither was wanted for anything else. Mose had shown himself useful with horses and had turned into one of the main young stable hands. On this day Mose was trying to get old one-eyed Jack, so called because he was blind in one eye, to swim across the river with him on his back, something neither had ever done before. But Jack would not take a step beyond the water's edge despite Mose's yells and kicks and threats and promises, not a word of which the horse understood anyway.

"Whatchu doin', Mose?" asked eleven-year-old Seffie, walking along the river's edge, her bare feet up to her ankles in the water. She had lapsed almost completely back into the slave talk of her childhood. The looks she'd had from the other slaves in the kitchen told her clearly enough that they didn't take to an uppity slave any more than whites did. It was different when she was with Grace. But that was over now, and it was time she acted like a slave along with the rest of them.

"Tryin' to git dis blamed horse ter take me across ober ter da other side," said Mose in frustration.

"Why won't he go?"

"I don't know—he's jes' an ornery cuss, I reckon.— Why ain't you swimmin' wiff da others?"

"I don't know—I's too fat ter swim."

"Whatchu sayin'? Anybody kin swim, an' you ain't fat anyway."

"Well, why ain't you swimmin', den?"

"I wuz. See . . . I's all wet. But den I thought ob ridin' Jack across da ribber, but I can't.—Hey, I got me an idea," said Mose excitedly. He threw one leg over Jack's back and jumped to the ground.

"You git up on him, Seffie," he said. "Den I'll pull him across wiff da reins. Den when he's deep enuff, you jump off an' I'll jump on."

"I can't ride no horse, Mose. I never been on a horse's back. An' I can't swim neither."

"Ain't nuthin' ter either ob 'em. You jes' git up an' sit on his back. You jes' sit dere."

"What'll I hang on to effen you's got da reins?"

"His mane. Jes' hang on to his hair."

"I don't know, Mose . . . I's kinda skeered ter git up dat high. What ef he runs or somethin'?"

"He won't, cuz I got da reins."

"But what about da swimmin'? You ain't really gwine make me git off him where da water's deep, is you?"

"How 'bout ef you get off where you kin stan' up on da bottom."

"But not too deep? I'd be skeered ter git too deep."

"Not too deep, den.—Come on, den . . . git up on Jack's back."

"But, Mose, I don't know how."

"Here, jes' take hold up here—grab a fistful ob his mane an' da reins . . . dat's it. I's keep hold ob his bit."

"But how I git all da way up dere? I can't jump up dat high!"

"Here, I'll kneel down . . . now put yo foot on my knee, dat's it . . . now give a jump up an' git across his back wiff yo belly."

Timidly Seffie tried to do as he said. But she only succeeded in reaching halfway up Jack's flank before sliding back down to the ground. The horse gave a little snort and shuffled his feet about in the dirt.

"I can't do it, Mose! He's too high!"

"You kin do it, Seffie. Come on—you jes' gotta jump harder off my knee an' pull yo'self up. Try it agin . . . dis time I'll give you a shove."

"Oh, Mose . . . do I have to?"

"Come on, Seffie—you kin do it. Anybody kin ride a horse."

With a groan, Seffie approached again, reached up to clutch the reins and mane in a single mass, then stepped on

Mose's knee and lunged upward. At the same moment, Mose stood and shoved at her rump, pushing her up over the top of Jack's back.

"Ow!" she cried. "What do I do now!"

"Swing one leg over and sit up."

Awkwardly she did so. A few seconds later she was seated atop Jack's back, beaming in triumph, though still holding on to hair and leather for dear life.

"Dat's it, Seffie! I knew you cud do it!" said Mose. "Now let me hab da reins, while you keep hold er Jack's mane."

Gently he reached up and eased the reins from her.

"You want ter take jes' a little ride first," Mose said, "afore we go into the ribber—jes' ter see what it's like?"

"Do you think I kin do it?"

"Shore, ain't nuthin' ter it. Jes' sit there . . . lean forward a bit an' keep yo knees in tight against Jack's back . . . an' keep hangin' on. I'll lead him myself."

Slowly Mose walked to the front where Jack could see him, then with reins in hand gently pulled him away from the water and along the edge of the river.

A little cry went up from behind. Mose turned to his rider with a grin.

"You's doin' it, Seffie! You's ridin' a horse. I told you dere wuzn't nuthin' to it!"

"It's a mite fearsome, Mose! What ef he kicks or runs or somethin'?"

"Den I reckon you'd fall off. But he ain't gwine do dat. He's jes' an old tired horse who don't want ter do nuthin' but walk real slow."

On they walked, as Mose said, very slow. Gradually

Seffie became more comfortable with the movement beneath her.

"Now, Seffie," said Mose, "I's gwine han' you da reins."

"No—I can't do dat!" yelled Seffie in terror.

"You kin . . . here!"

Her eyes wide in fear, Seffie took the two leather straps from him as he held them up to her.

"You stay close, Mose—don't you go no place!"

"I's right here where Jack can keep an eye on me—wiff his good eye, dat is. I jes' keep walkin' an' he'll keep follerin'."

They continued on another few steps.

"Dere, you see, Seffie—you's ridin' all alone. Keep da reins loose, don't pull 'em back or Jack'll get skittish. Jes' hold 'em loose an' let him walk."

Slowly Mose stood aside and let Jack continue on with Seffie on his back.

"Mose!" she called.

"I's right here. You's doin' jes' fine."

"How I git him ter turn!"

"Jes' real gently swing dem reins ter one side. Don't pull on 'em—keep 'em loose like I said, but jes' ease 'em against his neck to one side."

Seffie tried to do as he said and slowly Jack began to turn in a wide circle back to where Mose stood.

"He's doin' it, Mose!" Seffie cried. "He's doin' jes' like you said!"

"You's ridin' him an' now you's turnin' him. I tol' you you cud do it!—Now let's take him into da ribber."

He took hold of the reins in front again. "Come on,

Jack," he said, leading him back toward the water's edge.

"I don't think I kin do dat!" said Seffie.

"Shore you kin. Look how you's ridin'. We'll jes' get him down in da water an' den you kin slide right off."

"Oh, Mose, but—"

Already Jack's slowly clomping hooves had begun to splash into the edge of the river. With Mose in front slowly pulling him forward, he didn't hesitate but came straight in. Soon he was up to his knees, then the underside of his belly. Seffie's feet and the bottom of her dress were wet by then, but still Mose continued to lead Jack toward the middle of the river, himself submerged up to his waist.

"Mose, it's gettin' too deep!" cried Seffie.

"Jes' a little more . . . so's I kin git on—okay, now, Seffie, you kin slide off."

"It looks too deep!"

"No, look—I'm standin' right here an' it ain't even past my chest."

"But you's taller den me!"

"Jump, Seffie!"

Grimacing in fear, Seffie swung one leg over Jack's back, then closed her eyes and slid down into the slow-moving current with a cry.

"Mose, help me, I'm—"

But already Mose had her by the hand. He steadied her until her feet found the sandy bottom.

"Can you make it back to the shore, Seffie?" he said.

"I think so. I kin walk now," she said, steadying herself as she slowly inched her way into shallower water.

"Good, den I's gwine git back on Jack!—Come on, Jack!" cried Mose. "You an' me's gwine cross dis ol' ribber, an' wiff me on yo back!''

Seffie reached the shore and walked dripping out on the dry riverbank. She sighed deeply and sat down to watch as Mose half swam, half scampered onto Jack's back in the middle of the river, then rode him out into the deeper waters where the horse had to swim. She smiled as she watched Mose yelling with glee, as much for the satisfaction she felt for what she had managed to do herself as for the fun her friend was obviously having.

Another year passed. Mose began to take on the appearance of a strong teenage boy. Seffie grew a little stouter without adding enough height to compensate for it, and slowly her face became that of a girl poised at the edge of coming womanhood. Few took notice of the change for few took notice of her at all. After Grace died, she had become just one of the kitchen girls. She knew what to do with food, and for her white masters, that was all that mattered. She was not the kind of girl the master took notice of to try to get married off young. As long as she did what she was told and caused no trouble, life went on and no one noticed as she began to fill out in the places a woman does.

Still, at fifteen and twelve, Mose and Seffie remained best friends. By then Seffie was comfortable on a horse's back, and twice they had taken a long ride together on one-eyed Jack when they were both excused from work at the same time.

A Cup of Sugar
and Two Sweet Biscuits
6

T HE END OF THE SUMMER GRADUALLY CAME ON
and the trees began to turn color and the crops rip-
ened. An occasional fragrant nip could be felt in the air,
hinting that autumn was coming and that winter was waiting behind it.

Harvest was near. And with harvest would come feast-
ing and celebration and dancing and music. Even the
slaves, if they were lucky, might come in for their share of
the fun. They would never, of course, be invited to the big
house, or to its expansive gardens or even close enough to
look at the white folks' merrymaking. And the hired
orchestra would certainly not play any Negro music. But
slaves needed no orchestra to make music. Their mouths
and the feelings in their hearts, along with an occasional
fiddle, were all the instruments they needed.

But though their music could be made anytime and
anywhere, the news that the master and mistress were planning a gay evening of music and dancing and eating also

infected the community of slaves with anticipation of an evening of fun of their own. They would be given half a day off besides to prepare their own harvest feast.

For the week leading up to the harvest celebration, the wind steadily picked up. By week's end it was blowing a gale. But it was a warm wind, fragrant off the Gulf, and no rain seemed in sight. So no one minded too much. As the night of celebration drew near, the chief concern was that the outside lanterns be tied down securely.

The animals were fidgety from the wind, but they would be all safely inside their pens, corrals, stables, and barns by the time the guests began to arrive.

All the slave ladies not engaged at the big house were busy all afternoon talking gaily as they plucked chickens and shucked ear after ear of corn and cut up potatoes and okra and carrots and mixed up biscuits for dumplings. The men sat around on the porches with pipes and harmonicas and stories. For on a day like this even a slave, if he was of the right temperament, might think even in the midst of suffering, that life could be a good and precious thing. The slaves had each other, they had family, they had their dignity and self-respect, and no white master could take those away.

For most, that is. Family had already been taken away from a few.

Fifteen-year-old Mose usually slept in a cabin of single men. Seffie spent her nights on a pad in a corner of Mammy's small room off the kitchen of the big house.

"Hey, Mose, boy," called out a woman as she walked out onto the porch of one of the slave cabins, wiping her hands on her dirty apron.

"Yes'm," said Mose, running toward her from where he was playing with a group of younger slave boys.

"Run up ter da big house an' fetch me some sugar in dis," said the woman, handing him a cup. "Go to da back kitchen, you knows where I mean?"

"Yes'm—da small brown door."

"Dat's it. Don' let mistress or none er her folk see you. You jes' ax fo Mammy. We ain't ter be axin' fo nuthin', but Mammy'll gib it ter you—you tell her Mabel sent you ter fetch it."

Mose was off in a flash. As he approached the kitchen he stuffed the cup into his shirt in case one of the white ladies opened the door.

He knocked, and a minute later a plump black girl answered.

"Hi, Seffie," he said.

"Mose, whatchu doin' here?"

"I was sent ter ax Mammy fo somethin'."

"Fo what?"

"Some sugar," said Mose, pulling out the cup. "But none er da mistress's folk is ter know."

"Who dat at da door, Seffie, chil'?" came a voice from inside the kitchen. Seconds later a large black form filled the entryway.

"It's Mose, Mammy."

"I kin see dat well enuff."

"He wants some sugar."

"Keep yo voice down, chil'!" scolded Mammy, glancing behind her.

"Mabel sent me ter see you," said Mose.

Mammy glanced about again, then took the cup from his hand.

"Don't you say nuthin', Seffie," she said. "Now git back ter yo dough—you wait dere, Mose."

Seffie returned to the kitchen as Mammy closed the door.

Two or three minutes later it opened again.

"Dere's Mabel's sugar," said Mammy. "Now you skedaddle on back down dere afore anyone sees you."

"Yes'm," said Mose, taking the cup from her hand.

He turned and ran off as the door closed behind him.

"Mose . . . wait!" he heard a voice behind him.

He stopped and turned back. There was Seffie running toward him. She reached him and glanced back nervously. In her hand she clutched a cloth napkin.

"Here, Mose," she said. "I brung you dese. Dey's sweet biscuits."

Mose's eyes widened at the sight. He took the two biscuits in his free hand.

"Dey's still warm!"

"I jes' took 'em out ob da oven."

"Did you make 'em?"

"Dat I did."

Mose didn't even wait but bit off a third of the first one as they stood talking.

"Dat's good, Seffie! Whateber you makes is always da bes'!"

"I gots ter git back or Mammy'll box my ears."

She stuffed the empty napkin in her dress and ran off.

"Thanks, Seffie!" called Mose after her. "Dey's real good!"

He turned back toward the slave village and continued on, munching on his snack and in no hurry to deliver Mabel her cup of sugar. The best way not to have to share his unexpected treat was to make sure it was gone before he got back.

MINUET
7

THE EVENING CAME ON AND THE GUESTS BEGAN TO arrive from neighboring towns and plantations.

A lull came in the wind and a great calm descended. From far away in the slave village the faint music of a fiddle and clapping hands could be heard as darkness descended. In the gardens of the big house, however, the refined music of the small orchestra began to lure the ladies in their colorful dresses with strains of minuet and a selection of Mozart country dances.

Once dinner was past and all the dishes washed and dried and put away, Mammy told the girls who were helping her that they could go down to the village if they wanted, though by then it was after ten and the night starting to get a little chilly.

Seffie was already sleepy but she didn't want to miss out on anything. She followed the three or four other kitchen girls, all older than she was, through the night. Gradually the sounds of refined white music and culture faded behind them and the familiar sounds of slave voices

and laughter and fiddling and singing in rich Negro har-
mony grew louder and louder, until they were in the midst
of their own people again. A large bonfire was burning.

Seffie hung back and watched, terrified by the mere
sight of the fire in the center of the gathering. Mesmerized
and afraid of the fire at the same time, she was also capti-
vated by the music and dancing and laughter from the
community of slaves of which she was a part. They were a
people for whom happiness and celebration came easy even
in the midst of their poverty.

"Hi, Seffie, whatchu doin' here?" said a voice at the
girl's side. It was Mose.

"Mammy let us come when da dishes wuz all done,"
said Seffie. "But I's gettin' sleepy."

"Dem biscuits shore wuz good."

"I wuz gwine bring you anudder one. But dey wuz all
gone."

"Dat's all right. I had plenty ter eat anyway."

"You should see an' hear dem up at da big house. All
da ladies is wearin' pretty fancy dresses an' da dancin' an'
music is so fine." She brushed some flour from her plaid
dress with its two big pockets.

"Dere's dancin' down here too," said Mose.

"It's different up at da big house."

"What kind er dancin' dey doin'? Ain't dey dancin' like
dis here?" asked Mose, glancing toward the fire where fifteen or twenty men and women were stirring up the dust
with their high-stepping feet in rhythm to the fiddle and
the clapping of the onlookers.

"No, it ain't nuthin' like dat. Dey's all slow an'
graceful-like, an' dere ain't no stompin' or laughin'. Da

men dey reach up dere hands an' da ladies take dem all dainty-like wiff dere fingers, an' da only soun' 'cept da music you kin hear is dem wide fancy dresses swishin' as dey twirl roun' 'bout. It's a mighty fine sight."

"Let's go look—I want ter see it," said Mose. "Come, show me."

Already he had taken several steps away from the crowd gathered about the bonfire.

"You mean now?" said Seffie.

"Shore . . . why not? Come on, Seffie—let's go!"

They scampered off through the night toward the party in progress at the big house.

They slowed as they neared.

"Come on . . . aroun' here," said Mose, leading in a wide half circle behind the smokehouse, then creeping through the night toward the dancers on the lawn from the opposite side of the plantation house.

"But, Mose," said Seffie, "what ef dey sees us?"

"What dey gwine do?"

"Dey cud whip us."

"Dey won't do dat, not fo jes' watchin'."

Afraid to get closer, but even more afraid to be left alone in the dark, Seffie followed at Mose's side as he grabbed her hand and pulled her along.

In another several minutes they were crouched almost at the edge of the circle of light cast from twenty or more lanterns hanging around the garden where the orchestra was playing and the dancers were dancing. Intermingled light and shadows from the graceful movements of the minuet shot out in all directions, adding all the more to the mystery of the spectacle in the eyes of the two young black watchers.

"You wuz right, Seffie," whispered Mose. "Dat's mighty fine, ain't it? Dat ain't like no black folk kind er dancin', dat's fo sho'."

A sudden gust of wind blew across the garden, sending lanterns swinging and a few dresses up to ladies' knees with exclamations of alarm.

"Dere's dat blamed wind agin!" said Mose, looking up at the night sky.

They watched another few minutes in spellbound silence.

"You reckon we cud do dat, Seffie?" said Mose.

"What—like dey's doin'?"

"Yeah."

"I reckon so, effen we knew how."

"Den why don't we try it?"

"You mean . . . you an' me?"

"We kin do it—come on!"

He grabbed her hand and led her to a clear spot of ground in the darkness. The wind had begun to blow again like it had earlier in the day. A few more startled cries sounded and the whipping gusts sent a few ladies scurrying from the dancing lawn toward the house. But the orchestra kept on, and in the darkness, unseen by any other person, white or black, fifteen-year-old Mose and twelve-year-old Seffie stepped hand in hand toward each other and away, doing their best to keep time to the music and imitate the steps they had been watching.

Giggles brought a temporary end to the impromptu minuet, but almost as quickly they were at it again. Seffie had now captured the spirit of the adventure along with Mose. She stared at what remained of the dancers for a few seconds, watching their feet intently.

"I think I hab it now," she said eagerly. "Put yo feet dere, Mose, to da side . . . like dat."

As she spoke she took his hand in hers again.

"Dat's it," she said excitedly. "We's doin' it jes' like dem!"

They continued to dance in the night. Beneath Mose's dark hair and Seffie's kerchief, both of their brown faces beamed in fun when the occasional light from one of the lanterns happened to fall in their direction. Seffie would rehearse those steps in her mind for the rest of her life.

Storm and Fire
8

SEFFIE AND MOSE WERE HAVING SO MUCH FUN they hardly noticed the wind rising to such a fury that within another ten minutes the orchestra could no longer be heard and soon had to stop altogether. But in the darkness, the two black youths still danced forward and back, then to the right, then to the left.

"Dis is fun, Mose! Why don' black folks dance like dis?"

"I don't know, Seffie. Maybe dey don' know how."

Several great drops of rain suddenly splattered on their faces, bringing an end to their impromptu dance.

"Where dat rain come from!" said Mose, looking up again into the blackness.

A fierce blast of wind drowned out his voice.

The last of the dancers finally gave up and bolted for the house, with the orchestra on their heels. The drops of rain, swirling in every direction were now coming down rapidly.

"I's bes' be gittin' in da house," said Seffie. "It's late

an' Mammy's like ter skin me effen I's gone too long."

She started toward the house.

"You can't go dat way," said Mose. "Dey'll see you. Come wiff me. We gotta go back da way we come, den you go up ter da house by da kitchen. White folks don't want ter see no black folks in da middle er dere party."

He led her back out into the night and again around the smokehouse the way they had come.

"Hey, what's dat?" said Mose. "—look, dere's Robert." He pointed to a young white man in a suit.

"Who's he?"

"Dat no good son er da oberseer—he an' dat girl's goin' inter one ob da barns. Dey ain't up ter no good, dat's fo sho. Let's foller 'em!"

The young man with his arm around a teenaged girl in a fancy dress teetered on his feet. The girl giggled as he led her toward one of the smaller barns.

"Mose, I don't think we should. I gots ter git back afore Mammy gits riled."

"Aw, she won't neber know."

"She knows everythin'."

"But dey might be gwine—"

"I's gotter git back."

"Come on, Seffie."

He grabbed her hand again and pulled her toward the stables. By now the rain was coming down in earnest and the wind had risen to a gale. Men were running about from the big house, bringing in chairs, tying down carriages, running to the three or four outbuildings where the guests' horses were tied and were now neighing restlessly. At the same time, the women were taking down the lanterns blowing about before something caught on fire.

Several black men were running up from the slave village to help with the horses and carriages in the gale. Within minutes hurricane-force winds had blown the roof off one chicken coop, and other roofs seemed likely to follow. Animals and people alike were in a frenzy of pandemonium, animals squawking and baying and mooing and shrieking and people running every which way trying to take precautions against what was obviously going to be a destructive storm.

Nineteen-year-old Robert McCarty had been drinking so heavily throughout the evening that he was as near oblivion as was possible while remaining conscious and on his feet. The sixteen-year-old daughter of a neighboring plantation owner had snuck more mint juleps than either of her parents would have allowed. As the two disappeared into one of the smaller barns they could barely keep their knees from wobbling beneath them, and it was with some effort that Robert kept the lantern in his hand once they were under cover and out of the wind.

"Robert, be careful!" giggled the girl, stumbling inside as he closed the door behind them. "Uhh, I smell horses in here!"

"What did you expect?" laughed Robert in a near stupor. "They'll never look for us here."

He set the lantern down and looked about.

"But the horses don't take up the whole place. We'll find some nice dry straw."

"Robert!" exclaimed the girl, laughing again. "Keep your hands to yourself!"

"I didn't come in here to keep my hands to myself!"

"You *are* a naughty one!"

They had no idea that four black eyes were watching them through two cracks in the wall.

Suddenly a terrific blast of thunder exploded, sounding as if it was directly overhead. The three horses in their stalls screamed in terror. One reared on its hind legs and came crashing down, splitting the wall of its corral. Splintering wood flew about, knocking over the lantern where it sat. Instantly the dried straw beneath it was ablaze.

"Let's get out of here!" cried Robert.

He bolted for the door, in his stupor making no effort to put the fire out before it spread. The girl followed him out into the wind and rain, her dress blowing up into her face as they made for the house.

"Da horses!" cried Mose, leaping to his feet. "Seffie, you git back . . . git away!"

Within two or three minutes, shouts of "Fire!" were sounding both from the big house and the slave village.

Before the men could hope to stop it, the wind proved far stronger than the lashing rain and had whipped the barn into an inferno.

A great ripping sounded and a large portion of the roof tore back, caught in the wind briefly, sending sparks and flames high into the air, then collapsed back into the center of the building. Almost the same instant, a crack of wood turned all eyes toward the huge oak just in time to see one of its largest overspreading bows falling toward the roof of the sunroom of the big house. Glass from a dozen windows shattered as the roof collapsed under the weight of the massive branch.

Screams erupted from everywhere inside the house. For

a moment the fire was forgotten in the rush across the grass to see if anyone had been hurt. Further away, branches cracking like gunshot could be heard falling from trees everywhere. A few windows blew out from the sheer force of the wind. Boards from the main barn were falling dangerously to the ground everywhere, and shingles were blowing about as if they were bits of paper. Two or three slave cabins seemed about to lose their entire roofs.

By the time overseer McCarty ran back to the blaze, though only a couple of minutes had passed since the collapse of the sunroom roof, he knew there was nothing that could be done to save the barn. The wind-fanned flames had entirely engulfed it, and after the collapse of the roof the structure was mostly gone already. The storm was taking the flames and the sparks straight across the field toward the wood, so there was no danger to any other structure. The rain was coming down hard enough, in spite of the wind, that it would prevent any trees catching fire and would put the thing out on its own eventually. Might as well let it burn. Whether his thoughts would have been different had he known that his own drunken son was responsible, it would have been difficult to say.

Neither did McCarty know, as he stood there being pelted by wind and rain while the small barn was gradually reduced to cinders, that another set of eyes was watching the horrifying blaze from fifty feet away. Seffie stood as one in a trance, immobile, mute, eyes wide in terror for what she had witnessed, yet paralyzed and unable to cry out for help.

Still she stood an hour later, drenched to the bone, shivering, yet paralyzed in mute agony and unable to move a muscle. In the house, Mammy had grown worried when Seffie had not come back in. Braving the elements the moment the storm slackened a little, she went looking for her in the slave village. She came upon her standing alone in the night like a frozen statue.

"Seffie, chil'!" she exclaimed. "Whatchu doin' standin' dere? Dere's a storm on an' you's catch yo death. Come wiff me!"

She grabbed Seffie's hand and yanked her toward the house. Mammy was in truth relieved to find her safe yet annoyed anew at the inconvenience. She was about to begin upbraiding her all over again, but the shock of feeling her hand cold as ice stopped her. Then a tinge of genuine concern for the girl's health entered her mind. The moment she was inside, in spite of the pandemonium still everywhere from a houseful of guests having to make the best of spending the night in the midst of a hurricane, she managed to get some warm milk into her stomach and then got her to bed under six blankets.

A NEW DREAM
9

HOW SEFFIE MANAGED TO SLEEP THROUGH THE night is a wonder. She awoke weak, delirious, still chilled, and apparently unable to say a word.

She was conscious enough, however, to overhear the conversation between two of the older kitchen girls coming from the next room.

". . . hear 'bout da fire . . ."

". . . not much lef' da way I hear it . . . roof fell in on him, dat what massa says."

". . . wuz it?"

". . . don't know fo sho . . . burned up too bad . . . think hit's dat kid Mose."

". . . dat boy wiff no kin?"

"Dat's him."

"What wuz he doin' dere . . . middle ob a fire . . ."

"Who kin say . . . horses all got out . . ."

". . . roof musta fallen on him afore he cud git out hisse'f."

". . . shame . . . a nice boy . . ."

Seffie's eyes flooded with tears. She had known the truth last night, but somehow the shock and a night's sleep had temporarily erased the searing memory from her brain. Now it all came back, how she had stood . . . and stood . . . and stood . . . and done nothing to help.

She cried and cried in her silent agony, until she had cried herself to sleep on a pillow drenched in her own tears.

She awoke, hoped that she had dreamed the whole thing, remembered, cried again . . . and slept again.

Seffie remained in bed five days, gradually began to eat and drink, but did not speak for weeks. What good were words with her friend gone? What was there to talk about? Who was there to talk to? If life had held little interest for her before, it held no interest for her now.

The next months passed like a blur. She lost weight, but, with nothing to interest her now but her work in the kitchen, she eventually gained it back and continued to expand around the midsection. Within another two years Mammy had begun to value her skill and depended on her more than any of the other girls. And after a couple more years, by sixteen Seffie was responsible for most of the master's and mistress's meals, and they were more than appreciative for her gifts. She was a good worker but said little, for she had little to say. When the master began hinting that it was time she had a husband, then at last Seffie spoke up and declared that if he wanted to continue eating white biscuits, brown bread, apple and mince pie, assorted cakes, and all his other favorites with her special touch, then he had best forget such talk once and for all and let her decide for herself when and if she wanted to marry. She told him it was pretty easy to *accidentally* get too much salt in his food. She wasn't about to marry just to provide him more slaves to add to his tally. The master did not like being talked to with such determination by anybody, least of all one of his slaves. But she had him over a barrel. Nobody could cook like Seffie. He knew it. She knew it. And that was the end of any more such talk.

Deep inside, Seffie knew she would never marry. Ever since that tragic night, she had said to herself that she would never allow herself to have a friend again. What good came of loving? Only pain. She did not want to feel the pain that came from loving ever again. Mose had been her friend, her best friend, her only friend. She had loved him with the devotion of a young girl to a boy who watched out for her and took care of her and treated her with kindness.

Now he was gone. She would never love again. It hurt too much to love.

When and how the thought first entered her mind, Seffie could not have said. Perhaps it was that she felt no attachment to any person or place that she could truly call home. But along with the determination not to marry, Seffie began to hunger for freedom. She didn't know how slaves got to be free. But she knew some did. She knew blacks in the North weren't slaves. So why shouldn't she be free too?

If she had to, Seffie could speak her mind. But she didn't very often. She knew that most of the other slaves about the place, and all the whites, thought she wasn't quite all there. But as long as she was in the kitchen doing what she liked to do, she didn't much mind what people thought. As she got older she came to realize that it was a blessing in its own way to be taken for granted. She heard things she knew weren't meant for her ears, because people paid no attention to her and didn't stop talking when she was around.

That's how she first heard about the strange railroad.

At first she didn't know what they were talking about because there was no railroad anywhere around there. Gradually she realized they were talking about another kind of railroad, an invisible railroad, a railroad for people—colored people.

It was a railroad that took slaves to freedom!

She didn't know how it did it, but she knew that's what they were talking about. She overheard two of the men talking in quiet tones when she'd been sent by Mammy to dig some turnips from Mabel's garden. They were whispering and talking together about hitching a ride on the railroad.

". . . risky bizness . . . whites out lookin' fo you . . ."

". . . safe hidin' places . . ."

". . . effen a body kin fin' 'em . . . dem conducters ain't always dere . . ."

". . . chance you gotter take . . . freedom ain't cheap . . ."

Two weeks later, Rufus was gone. Everybody said he'd just disappeared. But among a few of the slaves there was a rumor that he'd bought himself a ticket on "dat ol' freedom railroad" and was on his way north.

Seffie didn't know how much the tickets cost. But she made up her mind to keep her ears open!

FLIGHT
10

PATIENCE IS NOT ONLY A CHRISTIAN VIRTUE, IT IS also an important part of courage. Being brave sometimes means waiting for the right time to act.

Eighteen-year-old cook and house slave Seffie Black would never have considered herself brave. She thought herself the worst coward that ever lived. Not a day, not a night, went by that she was not haunted by her inaction the night of the fire. She lived with the constant torment that Mose might still be alive had she run for help, or done *something* to try to save him.

But she had been terrified of fire since that night so long ago that had gotten her and Mose sold away from their families, never to see them again. The very sight of flames paralyzed her with images too terrible to think on.

So she had done nothing when he had run into the burning building after the horses, and would forever have to live with the memory.

Yet now as the thought of freedom stirred her heart, a new and strange kind of bravery awoke within her. She did not know it was bravery. But the seed, once planted, took root and grew. And she began to think what she would do when that railroad came again. Until then, she would wait.

In some strange and deep way, the thought of escaping to freedom became her dream to atone for her cowardice. In the only tests life had thrown at her, she had failed. Now maybe she could succeed in something important. It was something she had to do . . . for Mose. He had been a friend to her. She would one day be free as a way to honor that friendship, and his memory. She could never make up for what she had done or not done, but maybe some good might come out of it yet. The memory of Mose would give her strength to be brave.

In truth, Seffie had it better than many slaves because of her gift, her ability to make food taste good. The master and his wife treated her with respect. As Mammy began to slow down, more and more of the management of the kitchen fell to Seffie, though she was not yet even twenty. There was no more talk of marriage. The master knew he was lucky to have such a young woman as cook, and had no idea that he would not have her for much longer.

Seffie bided her time, listened, and waited. Patience and bravery grew side by side within her. Still she said little. A year went by, then two, then three. No one knew what Seffie was thinking or what opportunity she was patiently waiting for. She went about her duties, and, as much as a slave could be said to enjoy what she did, Seffie found satisfaction in making people happy by cooking delicious food for them to enjoy.

Occasionally strangers came and were hidden in the slave quarters, and then in a day or two were gone again.

They had no idea how closely Seffie was paying attention. But she missed nothing. She knew that such nighttime appearances by slaves on the run had to do with the railroad, and that all the strangers who appeared were moving in the same direction—north.

Another four or five years went by before her own chance arrived. By then she was a young woman in her midtwenties, large but strong, keen-eyed, intelligent, and more determined than ever to make good on her promise to herself and the memory of Mose.

Then came a night when there was a stirring in the slave village. Her years of patience were at last rewarded. She got wind of the news by overhearing whispers in the dark from across the room. Two sisters who also worked in the kitchen shared her sleeping quarters in the big house. One was the wife of a field worker. She had been out late with her husband, and now crept into bed in the darkness beside her sister. Both women assumed Seffie to be asleep.

"... two men, a mother, an' a chil' dis time ..." the one whispered.

"Laws almighty, where dey put 'em?"

"In da cabins ... overseer, he ain't been down dere in days."

"... how long?"

"Dey got here yesterday ... wuz plumb starvin', dey wuz. Dey's okay ter move on now."

"Where dey boun'?"

"Don' know ... Alabama, Carolinas maybe ... jes' norf, dat's all I know."

"... gone already?"

"... waitin' till da dark er da moon, till massa's ol'

houn' dogs is asleep. Den Uncle Fred'll take 'em ober da hill where dey'll meet somebody called a conductor, whatever dat is, who'll take 'em ter da nex' station.''

"Soun's fearsome ter me.''

"Hit don' go too good fo runaways dat git derselfs caught, dat's a fac'.''

Wide awake on her pad on the floor, Seffie strained to hear every word. Ten minutes later, when snoring from the bed told her that the two sisters were sound asleep, she rose quietly from the floor, hastily grabbed the few things she thought she would need, the few extra clothes she could carry. Then noiselessly she slipped from the room, passing through the kitchen for a few necessary foodstuffs, and then out of the house into the damp air. The night was black and cold. As predicted, the hounds were asleep, but one could never trust that, for a hound's nose never slept.

She glanced about to make sure of her bearings, then crept across the lawn and made for the slave village. She didn't know exactly what she was looking for, but she would wait near Uncle Fred's little shanty to see what might happen.

She sat down on the cold ground—patience and bravery now both rewarding themselves—and waited.

She had just begun to doze an hour and a half later when she heard movement. On the quietest of feet, Uncle Fred emerged into the night. Two men and a woman carrying a child followed. Not a single word was spoken. They made not a sound. A hound dog could have been asleep at their feet and remained still unless their scent betrayed them.

Seffie watched from her vantage point behind a tree

twenty feet away. Within seconds they had disappeared behind the cabin and were making their way with careful steps toward the woods opposite the cotton field.

She rose . . . and followed.

She kept far enough back that, in the moonless sky, even with the few backward glances Uncle Fred and his small troop took, they were unaware they were being pursued by the most unlikely of fugitives. They reached the woods, crossed through it with Uncle Fred leading the way in near total blackness, and came to a fork in the road. He took it to the right where it led steeply upward for a mile or two east, then down for another mile, until they came to a wooden platform at the river's edge.

Uncle Fred gathered his small band together, pulled out flints, and lit his lantern.

"Here's where I leab you," he said. "You'll meet yo conducter yonder on da udder side. Hit's mighty wide across dere. But dat cable'll git you 'cross effen you jes' keep haulin'.—Now, stan' away . . . I's gwine gib a signal 'cross dere. We don't want no bounty hunters waitin' fo you ober yonder."

He held up his lantern, then hid the light with his coat, and repeated the signal three times. Far across the way, a tiny light could be seen, then disappeared, then reappeared four times in succession.

"Dat's him, all right," said Uncle Fred. "Dat's yo conducter. He'll take you ter da nex' station, where you's be safe fo a coupla days. So git on dat dere skiff an' start pullin' yo'selves across. You ain't free yet, but you's one step closer, I reckon."

The two men and the woman with the child followed

the light of Uncle Fred's lantern toward the rickety make-shift barge. It did not look or feel safe, but this railroad was built on trust, and at this stage of their journey they did not ask questions.

. Suddenly a fifth passenger stepped out of the night and stepped aboard, tilting the barge precariously downward on one end for a moment or two.

"Seffie!" exclaimed Uncle Fred. "What'n tarnashun!"

"I follered you, Uncle Fred," said Seffie. "I'm goin' too."

"You can't go. I sent word ahead fo three passengers an' a chil'."

"Dey ain't gwine mind one more."

"You's mo like two mo, Seffie!"

"Dat may be. But I's goin', or else I's blabbin', an' none er you wants dat."

"It's too far. You cud neber keep up."

"Effen I don't keep up, den dey kin leab me behind. But I ain't goin' back. An' I reckon I kin keep up wiff dis chil'. An' I'm thinkin', missy," she added to the other young woman, "dat maybe I could be some help ter you wiff da young'un."

The nod and smile on the young mother's face said that she was only too glad to have another woman along.

"Laws almighty, Seffie," persisted Uncle Fred. "What's I gwine say?"

"You ain't gwine say nuthin', dat's what, 'cause as I understan' dis here railroad, no one knows nuthin' 'bout it anyway. So you jes' git back ter da plantashun an' me an' dese folks'll be jes' fine."

Still muttering to himself in disbelief, Uncle Fred

released the latch on the barge as the two men began to pull on the cable. The two women and child sat down in the middle as the barge began to ease out from the shore across the slow black current.

Within minutes Uncle Fred was on his way back to his bed with more secrets than he had expected to have to keep, while five runaway black slaves drifted in the night across the Pearl River into Mississippi.

"My name's Seffie," said Seffie when they were settled and on their way. "Dat ain't my whole name but dat what folk's been callin' me longer'n I kin remember. I ain't got much wiff me 'cause I couldn't carry but what my pockets would hold. But I got me a half dozen apples, some white biscuits, some dried oat crackers, a few hunks er cheese, an' a slab er smoked bacon, dat is ef anyone er y'all's hungry."

FUGITIVES
11

B Y THE TIME THEY REACHED THE OTHER SIDE OF
the river, the five runaways—or four, for the five-
year-old girl mostly slept in her mother's arms wrapped in
a small quilt—might have been friends for years. Nothing
can win a man's good graces faster than food, and cold
though they were, Seffie's provisions hit the spot.

The mother and one of the men were brother and sister.
The other man had joined them alone several days into
their journey. All were from New Orleans. The two sib-
lings had another sister in Georgia who had connections to
someone in South Carolina, they said, who had connections
to anywhere a runaway slave might want to go. If they
could make it to that station, they would be halfway to the
North!

But however high their hopes, the life of a runaway was
a treacherous one, filled with risks and danger on every
side, sometimes betrayal, and constant fear of nigger dogs
who could smell for miles and were known to have jaws
strong enough to tear a man's leg right off. At least so the

stories said. Slaves had been told such tales all their lives to keep them from running away. For those who ran anyway, the days and nights were therefore filled with more imagined terrors than were really there. Yet if they were caught, they might wind up dead or whipped until they wished to be dead, so the fear was real enough.

They all knew they were hunted, would not be difficult to spot, and with two women and a child would not be able to move as quickly as the two men might have liked.

Seffie's strange absence at the plantation was initially a mere curiosity. Nobody suspected the truth about their soft-spoken cook, nor would have guessed that she had been planning her escape for years.

Mr. Meisner was at first merely perturbed. By the second day, when his eggs were runny, his bacon limp, and his coffee bitter, he began to get worried, thinking that something had happened to her. By the third day, certain rumors of runaway activity in and around the area filtered vaguely into his mind, and he began to harbor suspicions. And on the fourth he issued a warrant for the arrest of one Seffie Black—even he did not know her real name, for he had not bought her until she was seven: —*house slave, mid-twenties, fat, soft-spoken.* He listed a two-hundred-dollar reward for her return, alive. It was a large bounty to offer for a single woman. He thought it best not to mention the fact that she was the best cook ever to serve himself or his family. Kitchen slaves of her caliber were very difficult to find. To broadcast the fact would insure that he never saw her again. The huge reward, however, to a perceptive bounty hunter, would tell the same story, and that in all likelihood she was worth even more.

Seffie never knew any of this. By the time she was officially listed as a runaway with a price on her head that in her mind would have been a fortune, she was three counties away.

She and her companions, led by their nightly conductors, crossed Stone County, then George County, and were soon moving steadily across Alabama on that mysterious mode of transit known to slaves seeking freedom as the Underground Railroad.

Two major river crossings stood ahead of them—the Tombigbee and the Alabama. After that their way would be mostly clear to Georgia.

Their path ahead into the unknown was marked with uncertainty and fear. Every day brought a new floor or stable or bed of straw or open field or woodsy hollow to sleep in. They usually didn't know the names of the dozens of people who led them from station to station. Mostly their guides were black, but a surprising number were white. They even slept in a few white houses along the way. Slavery was an institution with more enemies than the plantation owners of the South wanted black folks to know about.

Before many weeks were out, the five were all thinner and had blistered feet. Others joined them along the way, then left, the band of fugitives constantly changing. Seffie and the men helped the young mother carry her little girl when her small legs would no longer support her from exhaustion.

By day they slept, by night they walked . . . on and on in an endless and confused blur of fields and barns and lofts and cellars and streams and rivers, avoiding towns, listening for dogs barking in the distance, trusting strangers to keep them from danger. Cold and hunger and fatigue were with them all the way.

Many times Seffie wondered if she had made a mistake with her rash flight. But she could not have found her way back even if she'd wanted to. She had no choice but to continue on, though she had no idea where she was bound or what her future might hold. Yet occasionally she began to feel a tingle of satisfaction, even excitement. No matter what happened, she knew deep inside that she had *done* something, she had not just stayed in the same place for the rest of her life.

A great storm held them up between the two rivers. Waiting for the Alabama River to recede enough after the rains to make it safe to cross, they had to spend a month in the barn of a free black farmer. When time came for the crossing, the one man had left them to strike out straight north on his own, but they had been joined by three others—a father and his teenage son, and a woman in her thirties whose story, judging from her countenance, must have been a tragic one, though she never spoke a word about it.

They got across the Alabama safely in the farmer's boat—though it took two crossings to transport them all—and continued on. He led them himself for two hours more, then met another man several hours before daybreak who took them on while their host for a month returned to his farm.

An uneventful week went by.

They had lain dozing on and off most of the day under a bridge on the slope of the bank of the small river it crossed. Several wagons and riders on horseback had crossed above them throughout the day, but none had stopped. Any dog would have detected their presence in an instant. But they were by all appearances in the middle of nowhere and miles from any house or plantation.

"Dat's a mighty fine quilt you got fo yo young'un," said Seffie to her companion. "I been admirin' it da whole time an' I can't figger out what dat pattern is."

"Hab a closer look," said the young woman, taking the blanket from around her daughter's shoulders and handing it to Seffie. "Look at it *real* close an' see effen you don't see somethin'."

Seffie took it and held it up and looked it up and down, then shook her head.

"It's right nice, an' mighty colorful," she said, "but I can't make sense ob all dese lines an' squiggles er yarn an' thread. It ain't like no quilt I eber seen."

"It's a map."

"A map!" exclaimed Seffie. "What kind er map?"

"A map ter show us da way ter go effen we gits los'."

Seffie looked it over again.

"I reckon I kin see whatchu mean. But how you know where ter go from dis?"

"See—dem's ribbers, an' dere's towns . . . dere's da Alabama Ribber dat we come across las' week . . . an' dere's Souf Carolina where we's boun'."

"I see what you's sayin', but seems ter me dat wiff no conducters dat blanket wudn't do you no good nohow."

"I hope we don't hab ter fin' dat out. But dey gib it ter me jes' in case. I reckon we'd hab ter fin' some black folks ter tell us what it says an' which way ter go."

"What's dat dere?" asked Seffie, pointing to the tiny

little outline of a house embroidered into the fabric.

"Dat's where we's boun'. Dat's where da station mistress called Amaritta is who dey says knows more 'bout dis railroad den jes' about anyone. After dat we won't need dis ol' blanket no mo—least dat's what dey says."

"Who is da lady?"

"Jes' a slave woman dat helps folks meet up wiff other folks an' git norf."

"Why doesn't she go herse'f?"

"Don't know. I neber met her. Jes' heard 'bout her, dat's all."

As dusk began to fall, they wondered if they had mistaken their directions from the previous morning. Secretly Seffie wondered to herself if maybe they would have to try out the quilt-map sooner than they had thought.

Gradually the night came on.

Another hour passed. A quarter moon rose in the sky. All their stomachs were growling.

Suddenly a voice sounded so near that Seffie nearly jumped out of her skin. "Time ter git aboard," it said. "Come on—dis way."

How their new conductor for the night had come upon them so silently Seffie never knew. But they had learned by now not to ask questions but to trust. They climbed to their feet in the darkness and followed as he told why he'd been late—from having to keep out of the way of bounty hunters.

He led them up the bank and across the bridge. They followed the wide dirt road for ten or fifteen minutes. It wound through open country so that what little light the moon provided was enough to see where they were going.

They had just walked far enough to begin to warm up when suddenly the man stopped. He listened intently. Now they all heard it—the sound of galloping horses.

"Git off da road!" he cried. "Quick—foller me!"

He jumped down the road bank, then turned to wait, grabbed up the girl, and ran for a small wood some fifty yards away with the others hurrying after him.

As soon as they were surrounded by the cover of trees, he stopped, set the girl down, and fell to his stomach.

"Down, all ob you—git down and lay still."

Seconds later thundering hooves echoed in the distance across the wooden bridge under which they had passed the day, then grew louder and louder as they came toward them.

Watching the road from where they lay, four or five riders came into view and galloped past. They could just make out their silhouettes in the faint light of the moon.

Slowly the hoofbeats died away.

One of the men stood up and started walking back toward the road.

"Git back an' stay down!" whispered their guide. "We ain't goin' nowhere anytime soon."

"Why not?"

"Dem's bounty hunters, dat's why—git back, I tell you. Dey been troublin' me for a few munfs. Dey musta got word dat you wuz comin' dis way."

"But dey's gone now."

"Dey ain't gone. Dey sen' a few riders on ahead ter make a ruckus like dat, den one man'll foller on foot, hopin' da runaways'll do jes' what you wuz gwine do an' run out thinkin' dey's safe. He'll creep along behind on foot all quiet-like, an' when you's unsuspectin', suddenly dere he is comin' along da road wiff a gun, an' den he's got you an' you's in big trubble. So we's wait here a spell."

The man lay back down. They waited in silence.

Twenty minutes, then forty, went by.

As they continued to watch the road, slowly a lone figure came faintly into view, hardly visible except for his movement, walking quietly through the night. No one made a sound as slowly he passed. But they now realized their danger more than ever.

"Da others'll be waitin' fo him along da way yonder," said the conductor. "Then dey'll do da same thing agin fo anudder few miles, tryin' ter lure you out er hidin'. I doubt dey'd be doin' all dis effen dere wuzn't some good money on yo heads. One er you somebody important er somefin'?"

No one replied. Gradually they all shook their heads.

"Hit shore ain't me," said one of the men. "I's jes' a dirt poor slave dat's hoed cotton all my life an' ain't worf much dat I know ob."

"Well, I don't know, but dere dey is. So we's gwine hab ter be real careful da res' er dis night, an' hide you out fo a few days."

In another hour they finally crept from their hiding place and continued on. They did not return to the road but zigzagged through the fields and woodland on either side of it. Morning had nearly come when suddenly they heard a voice in front of them.

"Where you been?" said a woman. "I been worried sick when I heard dem horses!"

"Bounty hunters, Mama," said the man. "We had ter lay low a spell.—Dis here's my wife, folks. She's brung you some vittles. We'll wait here a spell while you hab somefin' ter eat.''

The news was welcome indeed to all the hungry, weary travelers.

''We bes' keep 'em wiff us a coupla days, Mama. Dem bounty hunters is too close fo comfort. When we git back, we gotta git word ter Isaac ter spread word along da line dat dis train's makin' a little stop fo repairs.''

Welcome Destination
12

P ROGRESS SLOWED WAY DOWN IN WINTER. WHOLE weeks went by in the same place when rain or cold delayed them. To travel in such conditions only invited sickness or chills or fever, and that did nobody any good. But spring came and gradually warmth returned and the train picked up speed along its invisible tracks.

Day and night again became a continuous blur of movement, change, fear, hope, hunger, and exhaustion.

Finally a night came when, a few hours before dawn, they were led into a cave that appeared to be an abandoned mine of some kind. At the far end shone a faint, flickering glow.

"Keep yo heads low so you don't whack dem on da roof," said the young man, who did not seem much older than a teenager but who had been leading them for several hours.

Gradually the cave widened until the roof overhead suddenly opened upward and they came to a fire burning brightly in the center of a dirt floor. Its smoke rose into the top of the cave and somehow found its way up and out through an invisible series of cracks to the outside.

Beside the fire sat a basket of provisions.

"Dere's food an' water," said the boy. "Ober dere's more wood an' blankets. Git some res' an' hab somefin' ter eat. You's safe here 'cause no white folks come up here ter da mountain. Someone'll come directly, but it may be two or three days. So don't eat dat food all at once. She'll be along when she kin git away wiffout bein' seen. She'll tell you what ter do."

He left the cave with Seffie wondering who the *she* was he was talking about.

They didn't have to wait three days, only a little more than a day and a half. They were just getting to the bottom of the food basket on the evening of their second day in the cozy little underground train station when they heard movement. Their heads turned to see a large black woman ducking low and approaching from the mouth of the cave.

"Somebody got somefin' fo me?" she said as she stopped and stood.

They all looked around at each other.

"Ef you be da woman I wuz sent ter see," said the young mother, "den maybe I does."

"Let me see what you got an' den I'll tell you ef I's da one you wuz sent ter see."

The young woman took the quilt from her daughter's shoulders and handed it to the black woman. A smile slowly spread over her face.

"I see da quilt er freedom made it back home agin!" she said. "Dat's what I wuz wantin' ter see, all right."

"Den is you da one dey call Amaritta?" asked the mother.

"Dat's me, all right." Looking around at the weary group sitting around the fire, she added, "So where's y'all boun'?"

WAYSTATION
13

T HE STATION MISTRESS CALLED AMARITTA WAS
housekeeper on the plantation of Master and Mistress Crawford in South Carolina. Neither of the Crawfords
had the faintest idea that an increasing number of runaway
slaves came and went under their very noses and that their
housekeeper helped direct many slaves on their way north.
People seemed to be coming and going and traveling in
every direction imaginable. They didn't even know that the
weathervane made of a horse's head on their barn had been
adopted by the railroad as a secret sign, and that houses
and barns all the way up to the North with the same design
were sought by fugitives as places of refuge.

Within three more days, two of the men of the group
were on their way to Ohio, a man and his wife headed for
Kentucky, where they would be met by a group traveling
to Indiana, and Seffie and the mother and brother and
daughter were left alone on the Crawford plantation. By
then they had been moved from the cave into the slave village where precautions were taken to keep them out of sight

from any of the white workers or slave children whose tongues might not be reliable.

Amaritta was making arrangements for the mother and her brother and daughter to join a train that would hopefully have their sister from Georgia onboard en route to eastern Ohio. Two days before they were to arrive she went to Seffie in the slave cabin where they were being kept.

"It's 'bout time you wuz decidin' where you's gwine be goin', honey chil'," she said. "You can't stay here much longer afore da master'll gits wind er somefin' he finds himself wonderin' 'bout."

"I got no place ter go," said Seffie. "I tol' you, I got no kin in da Norf dat I know 'bout. I jes' wanted to go norf to be free. I don't know what ter do."

"It ain't jes' gettin' you norf, hit's findin' a place fo you once you git dere. An' so—"

Amaritta was interrupted by two children—a girl of four or five and a boy a few years older—running into the cabin.

"Lucindy . . . Caleb," she exclaimed, "—what'n tarnashun . . . you skedaddle outta here!"

The little girl stopped at sight of the stranger, her eyes white and wide in the middle of her little black face.

"Who dat?" she asked.

"Hush yo mouf, Lucindy, chil'. It ain't nobody . . . now git!"

The two ran outside.

Amaritta shook her head. "Yep," she said, "we got's ter git you movin' along real soon. Dat scamp Caleb, he's a talker. Now dat he's seen you . . . yep, we gotta git you on anudder train mighty soon."

Within a week Seffie was on her way again, this time with two other women and one of their husbands. Their destination was southern New York State, where the man had a brother who had made good his own escape from the South three years earlier and now had a big house and small printing business where Seffie would be welcome. If they could put her to work, they would. If not, they would help her find something else.

By the time Seffie crossed into North Carolina, listening to her new traveling companions tell about what they had heard about life in the North, where everyone was free— whites and blacks alike—for the first time her hopes began to rise that she might really make it after all. The dream of freedom had been so vague and her journey from Louisiana so long. But now she was getting closer to the reality every day.

They moved slowly north for a month, passed from guide to guide in the night, traveling six to eight miles a day, and crossing into North Carolina, though they did not know it.

All seemed to be going well. But then a night came that changed Seffie's future forever.

As they went they had been vaguely aware of dogs barking in the distance for some time. This in itself was not so unusual, but on this night the sound was persistent and, they began to realize, growing gradually louder.

Their guide quickened their pace, pausing every few minutes to listen, muttering words of concern to himself, then urging them to hasten once again. No one else said a word. They sensed their danger.

For several hours they hurried through the night as

quickly and quietly as they were able, though the going was difficult. There were woods, streams, cultivated fields, a town or two to avoid, and uneven terrain most of the way. The strain and fatigue began to show, and gradually Seffie lagged behind.

"Come on . . . come on!" urged their conductor. "Hit ain't dat much further, but dem blamed dogs is still out dere! We gots ter move!"

He paused and listened again.

"My brother's waitin' jes' yonder at da ribber," he said. "He gots him a little oar boat. Hit's 'bout anudder mile. We git ter him an' we's safe. Da ribber moves along swif' fo a good spell an' dere ain't no bridges fo miles, an' by da time we's on da far bank, we's be miles from whoeber's been doggin' our steps all night."

"I don't know ef I kin make it anudder mile," groaned Seffie. "I's so tuckered I's about ter drop."

"You kin do it. We gots ter do it. Anudder half hour an' we'll be sittin' in dat boat floatin' along all da way ter yo nex' station."

Twenty minutes later they came to a clearing and had to cross a road. They paused and listened. It seemed safe.

"Dis way," said their guide, leading onto the road as the others did their best to keep up. Seffie's legs felt made of lead and she could hardly pick up her feet as she shuffled along. The endless journey over the past year had taken off a few excess pounds but had not exactly trimmed her down. She was still a very large young woman, and the effort of this night's flight had nearly taxed her to the limit of her physical endurance.

"Come on . . . dis way!" urged their guide yet again.

But Seffie could tell she was falling further and further behind.

Suddenly the sound of riders could be heard galloping toward them.

"Off da road . . . into da trees!" shouted the guide. "Hit's jes' a short run ter da boat. We kin make it!"

He and the other three were into the woods and sprinting for the river within seconds.

Seffie struggled along the road to keep up. Behind her the pounding of hooves grew louder.

Just as she left the road where she had seen the others disappear, she heard a shout behind her.

"There's one of them!"

A gunshot exploded in the night. In terror Seffie screamed and broke into what for her was an all-out run into the trees. She could only hope she was going the same direction her comrades had taken. But she could hardly lift her feet off the ground as her lungs gasped for air.

Behind her, two or three horses galloped up and stopped. Their riders quickly dismounted. Booted feet ran off the road, spreading out as they listened for movement.

"This way—they're over here!" came a shout.

Another gunshot echoed.

"Stop, all of you!" cried a white man's voice. "You can't get away. We've got you now!"

But Seffie hardly heard the words. Her dress was nearly drenched and sweat was falling from her face in great drops as she struggled on.

She came out of the woods. There was the river. A hundred yards ahead the others were already climbing into the boat.

"Run, Seffie . . . come on—you kin make it!" came a shout, followed by yells of frantic encouragement.

But the terrain was badly uneven and the slope down to the river steep. Rocks and small boulders of varying size were scattered up and down the riverbank and the footing was treacherous.

Cries from the river were now suddenly mingled with shouts and running footsteps from behind. Another shout sounded into the air.

In panic Seffie tried to increase her speed. All at once her foot stumbled on a huge rock nearly knee height. She tumbled over it, twisted her ankle as she hit the ground, and rolled several feet down the embankment.

She cried out in pain and struggled to stand. But she could not.

Seconds later, two men ran past. One paused to glance down at her where she lay, then hurried on.

"Stop, the rest of you niggers!" he yelled, "or we'll shoot the lot of you."

But Seffie's comrades had seen her fall and knew they could do nothing for her now. Capture was a risk they all took, and the capture of five slaves and the discovery of the local railroad line was not worth trying to help a single individual against angry pursuers with guns.

They understood. Seffie understood.

The small boat glided out into the current. By the time their pursuers reached the water's edge, it was just faintly visible going around a bend thirty yards away.

Several curses and a volley of gunshots followed. But within seconds the boat with its passengers was out of sight.

The two walked back the way they had come. They paused where Seffie lay groaning in pain.

"Well, it's not a complete loss," said one of the men. "We got this one at least."

"Doesn't look like much to me. What should we do with her?"

"Take her back and see what the boss says."

Seffie felt rude hands grab her and yank her to her feet.

Her ankle exploded in pain. She began to faint as she felt them pulling her along and yelling at her to walk. She felt her knees wobble, and they grabbed at her to keep her upright.

Finally everything went black.

New Surroundings
14

S EFFIE AWOKE CONSCIOUS OF NOTHING BUT A terrific pain in her right ankle.

It was still dark. She lay on her back on the ground and was nearly freezing to death.

Coming to herself and remembering what had happened, she was filled with panic. She had to catch up with the others!

She rolled over on her side and struggled to get up. Her whole body shouted out in pain from her fall. The moment she tried to stand she realized it was no use. Something was badly wrong. She knew she wouldn't be able to walk a step.

She lay back down and tried to think what to do. She didn't even know where she was. She had either walked or been moved from where she had fallen. She could remember nothing. And where were the men who had been chasing them?

She did not have time to think about it long.

The sounds of a wagon clattering along the road intruded into her thoughts, then gradually grew louder. She realized she was lying on the side of the road they had crossed earlier. Frantically she tried to rise again. When she couldn't, she tried to crawl into the undergrowth to the side of the road.

But it was no use. The horses pulling the wagon galloped up and the driver pulled them to a stop almost beside her.

"There she is," he called. Two men jumped down from behind.

"Wait for me," said the driver, joining them. "It'll take all three of us to lift her—she's a big one."

Seffie struggled momentarily as she felt hands grabbing at her legs and shoulders and arms, but a slap in the face stopped her. They lifted her up and rolled her into the wagon bed as if she had been a sack of potatoes, then jumped back up themselves. Moments later the horses began to move, got turned around, then the wagon lurched into motion and went bounding along the road. The jostling about on the wagon's wooden bed, without benefit of straw or any other cushioning, was almost more painful to her bruised legs and hips and shoulders than she could bear.

Before they reached their destination, she had fainted again.

Again she awoke, still in pain, now with even less idea where she was. She lay in semidarkness, but it was obviously morning. She heard cows and chickens not far away. She opened her eyes but did not move so as not to draw attention to herself. The rafters above her, the slanted shafts of light coming from the walls, and the smell of the place told her she was in a barn of some kind, still lying in the back of the wagon. Three men were talking nearby.

"... think she's hurt ... moaned when we tried to move her ..."

"... couldn't stand up ... ankle or foot ..."

"She was with the runaways we heard about. What'll we do with her?"

"Put her down in Hazel's cabin. She'll look after her."

"... ought to look at her ... see how badly she's hurt ..."

"... notify the marshal?"

"No need for that ... see if anything develops ... if there's a fugitive warrant on her ..."

"... can't be worth much ... big thing like her."

"If not, she's no good to us ..."

"... what use could she be?"

"... get a few dollars for her in Charlotte."

"All right, then ... couple of the boys to help you get her down ... into a cart ... haul her down to Wayne and Hazel's till we decide what to do with her."

Seffie pretended to be asleep when several men came a few minutes later to get her out of the wagon. But a cry of pain when her lower leg bumped the floor gave her away, and only made the men treat her even rougher. She did not know it, but her ankle had swollen to twice its normal size and she would not be able to walk on it normally again for months.

By the time they reached their destination and deposited her on the floor of what she took for one of the slave cabins, the pain had again become excruciating.

"Soun's ter me dat you's hurtin' mighty fearsome," said a woman's voice.

"Yes'm," moaned Seffie with tears in her eyes.

"What's yo name, chil'?"

"Seffie."

"Where you come from?"

"Don't know exactly . . . Louisiana, I think, but I been travelin' a long time."

"How you git here?"

"On da railroad."

"Da freedom railroad!"

"I reckon so—dat's what dey sometimes called it."

"You's a runaway?"

"Yes'm."

"Laws almighty—you's lucky you's still alive. Da way dey tell it, dey kill runaways when dey fin' 'em."

"Dey wuz shootin' las' night," said Seffie.

"Who wuz?"

"Da white men dat got me. Dey wuz shootin' at da others. But dey got away downribber in a boat. But I fell an' cudn't keep up. So dey got me an' brung me here."

"Laws, Laws," muttered the woman, shaking her head. "Dem hired hands er da master—dey's bad'ns all right. You's lucky dey didn't shoot you jes' fo da fun ob it. We's gotter take care er you, chil'. But one thing's fo sho'—you ain't gettin' back on dat railroad no time soon."

"What's gwine happen ter me?" asked Seffie.

"Can't say, chil'. Dey might sen' you back, or dey might sell you, or dey might kill you, or dey might keep you."

Seffie shuddered at the prospects.

"In da meantime, we's better hab a look at dat foot ter see what's ter be done."

SWEET BISCUITS AND
WHAT BECAME OF THEM
15

S EFFIE SPENT THE NEXT SEVERAL DAYS INSIDE THE one-room shanty of the old woman and her husband, called Wayne Jukes. Once she was able to get a good look at the wrinkled face of her nursemaid, Seffie thought she must be more than eighty years old. In fact, Hazel was only sixty-nine. But those years had taught her more than most people learn in three lifetimes, which was one of the reasons the master told his men to put the injured runaway in her charge.

Hazel sent for nettles and mud. When her husband and the men came in from the fields for lunch, she told Wayne what wood she would need for a splint, how long and how thick. He and their son Hank, a childless man in his late thirties who had lost his wife to pneumonia several winters earlier, set about preparations at once. When Seffie's foot had been thoroughly cooled and the swelling somewhat reduced, Hazel herself, with Hank's help, set and bound the splints in place, from Seffie's foot up to just below the

knee, with tight wraps of clean cloth. A huge man's old
boot was slit apart so that both the bottom of the splint and
her foot would fit into it. They bound her foot to the boot
with more strips, enabling her, with the aid of crutches, to
get around on it. Within a week the pain was considerably
reduced and Seffie was able to slowly move about with rel-
ative ease. Neither the master nor his workers had come
down to ask about her or give any instructions concerning
her.

Hank, who shared the little cabin with his mother and
father, was attentive and kind to the invalid. Out of respect
for Seffie's condition and privacy, during her convalescence
he moved into the slave house where most of the other
single men stayed.

Seffie could do nothing but stay every day in the cabin
with Hazel, but before two weeks were out had begun to
make herself useful with meals. She and the old woman
gradually began to laugh and talk together like old friends.
Seffie still did not know what would become of her. But
there was no question of moving on or getting back on
board the railroad anytime soon. That was the one thing
she could not do. If she was going anyplace now, it would
take a *real* railroad to get her there. But there was no actual
railroad line within miles of this place, and she hadn't a
penny to her name. And she had no idea how to reconnect
with the underground and invisible railroad that had
brought her here. Hazel did not seem to know anything
about it like the woman called Amaritta had.

What would happen when her ankle was completely
healed, she didn't know.

In the meantime she tried to help with the cooking as

much as she could. Gradually she took over more and more of the cooking duties for the cabin's small family, enabling Hazel, who was past field-working age, to spend more of her own time with the washing or cooking for the single men or helping out with the other women's young children.

Finally the day came they had all been expecting. The master appeared walking toward the slave village. Everyone knew he was coming about the newcomer. He didn't usually come to their living quarters with good news. Usually his presence meant that somebody was about to get sold. Most expected him to take her away.

He went straight to Wayne and Hazel's little one-room house, then walked inside like he owned the place, which he did. Hazel and Seffie were occupied near the wood cook stove. Wayne sat seated at the one table in the room with a plate of warm biscuits in front of him.

The three all stopped and turned their heads at the sound of feet coming up their steps and through the open door. The master nodded an expressionless greeting, then glanced toward Seffie's leg. Wayne stood up.

"Looks like you're getting around all right now," he said.

"Yes, suh," said Seffie, staring at him in fear for what was about to happen.

"You fix up her leg, Hazel?"

"Yes, suh . . . me an' Wayne an' Hank."

"Looks like a fine job."

The master pulled out one of the rickety chairs and nodded to Wayne to sit down.

"What's your name, girl?" he asked.

"Seffie, suh."

"Where you from?"

"Don't know exactly, suh . . . Louisiana, I think."

"You're a long way from home."

"Yes, suh."

"You ran away?"

"I reckon so, suh."

"Why'd you run away? Did your master mistreat you?"

"Not too bad, suh."

"Why then?"

"I didn't hab no kin dere. I reckon I wanted ter be free, suh."

The master nodded his head, then scratched his chin thoughtfully. Whether unconsciously drawn by the smell, or whether he was actually hungry, he slowly reached out and took one of the biscuits from the plate. The silence continued another several seconds.

"What do you think I should do with you, girl?" he asked as he bit off a corner of it.

"Don't know, suh," replied Seffie.

"It's wrong to run away, you know—it's breaking the law."

"Yes, suh."

"I could send you back. They would probably whip you. They might even kill you."

Seffie's eyes widened. She began to tremble.

"Or I might take you into Charlotte and sell you.—You ever been married?"

"No, suh."

"You want to be?" asked the master, chewing off another third of the biscuit.

"No, suh."

"Why not?"

"Don't know, suh."

"I thought all girls wanted to be married."

Seffie stood staring but said nothing.

"Hazel and Wayne here, they got a boy who needs another wife. You met Hank?"

"Yes, suh."

"He's a nice boy."

"Yes, suh."

"Most slave owners want their coloreds to make lots of babies."

"Yes, suh."

Suddenly he paused. An odd look spread over his face, as if he had just thought of something. He glanced down at the biscuit in his hand, slowly took another bite, and began to munch on it.

He stopped.

"Who made this?" he said, gesturing toward the two women with what was left of the piece of biscuit between his fingers. "You make this, Hazel?"

"No, suh. She did. She been helpin' me wiff da cookin'."

The master popped the remaining bite in his mouth, again nodding with thoughtful expression.

"Has she now . . . hmm, that's mighty interesting."

He rose, grabbed another biscuit from the plate on the table, and turned toward the door.

"Get her bathed, Hazel," he said, "then bring her up to the big house with her things by the middle of the afternoon."

"She don't got no things, Master McSimmons. She

come wiff nuthin' but what she had on."

"Oh . . . right, of course. Well, get her bathed regardless, and then bring her along. Put her in a clean dress if you can find one to fit her. If not, we'll get her something up there."

He walked out of the cabin, leaving the three black slaves staring after him.

MORE BISCUITS AND
A NEW JOB
16

WHETHER SEFFIE WAS BEING TESTED IN THE
mistress's kitchen later that day, or whether both
master and mistress had become bored, if not outright dis-
satisfied, with their present cook's offerings, she was immediately put to work that same afternoon.

"I want you to," began the mistress the moment she
appeared, "—what is your name again?"

"Seffie, missus," replied Seffie, intimidated by being in
the big house around people she had never seen before and
still having no idea why she had been summoned.

"That sounds like a nickname."

"Yes'm."

"I do not call my kitchen and house slaves by nick-
names. What is your given name?"

"Josepha, missus . . . Josepha Black."

"Very well, Josepha—I want you to make a batch of
those biscuits my husband was raving about for our supper
this evening."

"Yes'm," said Seffie, so overjoyed with relief by the request that she almost broke into a smile.

"Can you bake a pie?"

"Yes'm."

"What kind?"

"Anythin' dat you got fruit fo, missus."

"Good. Then along with the biscuits, make two apple pies—we should have plenty of apples—and we will see how you get along with that."

"Yes'm."

It took Mrs. McSimmons no longer than it had her husband, after tasting Seffie's biscuits that evening, to realize that the runaway with the broken ankle had been a cook somewhere before. The apple pies after supper, eggs and bacon and grits for the following morning's breakfast along with the first truly delicious cup of coffee the master had tasted in months, fresh bread and a pot of beans with ham for dinner, and within twenty-four hours Seffie's move to the big house was settled.

She was provided new clothes, a place to sleep with the other house slaves, and in the weeks that followed, as her ankle gradually healed and gained strength, was given more and more duties about the place. Within a year the former cook had been sold and Seffie was in charge of the McSimmons kitchen. There was no more talk of marrying her off, or of making much of an attempt to learn where she might have come from. Louisiana was a long way from North Carolina, reasoned McSimmons. He would never be able to learn anything about her anyway, so why not make the best of it and give her a better home than she would probably have most other places? He would have to keep an eye on her, of course, to make sure the freedom bug didn't bite again. But that shouldn't be too difficult.

As for Seffie, she was so happy just to be back in the familiar environment of a kitchen, especially where her efforts seemed to be appreciated, that the thought of running away again scarcely occurred to her. The long journey on the Underground Railroad, though she came to look back on it with a certain fondness as the great adventure of her life, had been more taxing than she thought she could ever endure again. Being captured and so badly hurt sobered her about the reality of the danger. She realized how lucky she had been to make it this far.

And the fact was, she was happier in a kitchen than anywhere. Even if she made it to the North, where would she go, what would she do? Maybe she didn't need to be free. Working in the kitchen of the big house wasn't so bad. Maybe it was all someone like her ought to expect.

Three years went by. Seffie, who now went by her given name, Josepha, turned thirty and was mostly content with her lot in life. Master and Mrs. McSimmons' two sons grew into rambunctious youngsters with more energy than was good for them. They gave every appearance of becoming typical sons of the new South, with disgust for the race of blacks, which their parents, though slave owners, attempted to treat with at least some measure of courtesy. By the time the older boy, his father's namesake, was six, he spoke to his father's slaves with a contempt and rudeness that made some of the older slaves shudder to think what it would be like if he ever took over the plantation.

A new slave girl arrived at the McSimmons plantation.

She was uncommonly pretty and refined. No one knew where she had come from and she kept to herself. She was downcast and did not look altogether well. She seemed out of place and unaccustomed to the hard work. It was not until later that the other slaves learned she had never been a slave before, that she was an educated free black born in the North, who had secretly been sold without realizing what was happening to her. She found herself trapped, not even exactly sure where she was, with no way to escape.

Not many weeks passed since her arrival before some of the women recognized another cause for her weakness and downcast spirits. Her midsection was growing and it was not from eating too much. She was obviously pregnant and had probably been forced to leave someone she was in love with. She never uttered a word about her past, and no one ever learned the circumstances of her being so strangely sold or of the man she had been forced to leave with only his child growing within her as a reminder of the love they had shared.

She was brought to the big house two months after her arrival when her condition had become obvious. The mistress expressed surprise, though her husband seemed to take the news as if it was expected.

Josepha recognized the look on the girl's face. She had no doubt worn a similar look when she had first arrived as a runaway—an expression of aloneness, uncertainty, and fear. Her heart went out to the girl, who was probably nine or ten years younger than she was. She knew what it was like to be torn away from those you loved and suddenly to find yourself among strangers. She herself had been seven—not so long ago that she would have forgotten.

She had vowed to herself long ago that she would not allow herself to have another friend, to be close to anyone again. What good came of loving? Only pain. Ever since being torn from her mama, and then Grace dying, and then her loss of Mose, she had protected herself from the pain that came of loving. It hurt too much to love. She determined never to open her heart again.

But this young girl carrying an unborn child *needed* a friend.

Maybe she needed *her*. Maybe it wasn't her own pain she should be thinking of now. She was older and had gotten over her pain. But this poor thing was in the midst of her loss right now. One look on her face said that she was suffering the loss of a friend too, a man, her love, the father of her child. She herself would never have a man to love, Josepha thought. It was too late for that. She was not the kind of woman a man looked at. The time for loving a man had passed her by. But she could still be a friend to this lost young girl in need.

"Whatchu want me ter do wiff her, missus?" asked Hazel.

"Whatever you people do with young pregnant women," replied Mrs. McSimmons. "Take care of her until the child is born. She looks too weak to get much work out of.—What do you want to do with her, William?" she said, turning to her husband.

"You're right, she looks too frail to put to work. We'll get our value out of her later. I'm not worried about that."

"Should we keep her up here?"

"No, we don't need any more coloreds in the house just now. They're already overrunning the place. Keep her with the single women where she's been. But she doesn't need to go out into the fields. Have her help with the cooking and washing and with the children till her time comes."

Hazel and the new girl turned to leave the house. Josepha caught her eyes and smiled. The girl returned it with a feeble smile of her own.

Later that day Josepha left the big house with a basket of fresh bread and walked down to the slave village. She went first to the cabin that had been her temporary home after her own arrival. Hazel and her new young ward sat inside at the table together.

"Josepha, darlin', whatchu doin' here?" said Hazel, greeting her warmly.

"I brung some fresh bread. I thought maybe our new frien' here might like some."

She walked to the table and set the basket down, then took a chair with the other two women.

"I's Josepha," she said, smiling again at the newcomer. "Sometimes it seems like I been here all my life, but I ain't been here so long dat I don't recollect what it wuz like comin' here an' bein' all alone. Hazel here took care ob me an' I know she will you too, ain't dat right, Hazel?"

"Dat's right," nodded the old woman, whose skin was even more wrinkled than when Josepha had first made her acquaintance.

"But effen you eber need somethin' an' Hazel ain't dere, you jes' come up ter da big house an' ask fo Josepha."

"Thank you," smiled the girl. "You're very kind."

"Now you eat some er dis bread while it's still warm, 'cause we gotta keep you strong 'cause by da look ob it, you's gwine be bringin' somebody new into dis worl'. So we gots ter keep you bof strong, ain't dat right, Hazel?"

Hazel nodded.

Before another hour had passed, the two young women, though separated by ten years in age, and though their arrivals were separated by five or six years, had already discovered many things they had in common—one of which, though neither let the other find out, was that they could talk white man's talk if they had wanted to—and were on their way to becoming fast friends.

New Life

17

MONTHS PASSED. THE TIME DREW NEAR.

As a warm August evening grew late, and dusk gave way to night, a knock came on the door of the big house. There stood a slave boy of six or seven.

"I wuz sent ter fetch Josepha," he said. "Hazel says dat she needs ter come quick. Hazel says ter tell her dat hit's time."

Josepha was hurrying down to the slave village within two minutes.

She found Hazel and five or six of the women in the single women's house where the birthing was already under way. A cry of pain sounded just as she walked in.

"Is Josepha here yet!" came a moan.

"She's here, chil'. She jes' came in."

Josepha walked into the cabin dimly lit with a half dozen candles.

"Hey dere, how's you feelin', Lemuela?"

"Not so good. It hurts, Josepha!" whispered the girl.

"I reckon dat's all right. Hit always does, da way I hear it."

Josepha sat down beside the bed, where some of the women were sponging the expectant mother's face and forehead. Hazel and the older women were busy with hot rags and towels to soothe and warm and dull the pain as Lemuela's child struggled to enter the world of men.

But the birth was slow and difficult. The labor continued for hours. The exhaustion was clearly evident on the poor girl's face. Most of those in attendance had been through it themselves, but this was taking longer than any of theirs. Some of the women began to fear for the mother's life.

Lemuela herself must have been thinking the same thing. With sweat pouring off her forehead and dripping down her cheeks, she motioned with a weary hand for Josepha.

Josepha came. Lemuela pulled her ear down close to her mouth.

"Tell them all to go away," she whispered, "—just for a minute . . . all but you . . . I want you to stay."

Wondering what it was all about, Josepha rose from the bedside and conveyed the request. Bewildered, Hazel and the others retreated just outside the door.

"I'm afraid, Josepha," said the girl. "Promise me, if something happens to me—"

"Ain't nothing going to happen to you, dearie—" began Josepha.

"But if it does," interrupted Lemuela, "promise me that you'll look after my little girl."

"I will."

"I know it's a girl . . . I can tell . . . promise me you'll take good care of her."

"I will, sweetie, of course I will."

"Hazel's old, and she's a dear, but she's too old to take care of a baby."

"You can rest easy . . . we'll all look after you and your child."

"But if I die—"

"Oh, sweetie, you're—"

"Please . . . make sure she has a good life—as good a life as a slave can have."

"I'll do my best. And maybe she won't always be a slave."

Hardly hearing the prophetic statement, Lemuela smiled and laid her head back down on the pillow, at peace for the moment, whatever should happen. Gradually the other women returned.

An hour later a little girl was born. The minute she appeared Josepha suspected the reason for Lemuela's silence—the father of her daughter was surely white.

But though Lemuela's life was never really in any danger and she fully recovered, Josepha never forgot her promise. As the girl grew, Josepha's secret devotion to the daughter grew equal to her devotion to the mother.

Much to Hazel's joy, the new mother became Lemuela Jukes two years later when she became the wife of Wayne and Hazel's son. She gave the old couple four grandchildren before Hazel died of influenza one particularly bad winter. The growing family continued to live in the cabin with Grandpapa Wayne, though as the years went by, being field slaves, Lemuela's children did not see as much of Josepha in the big house as she might have wished.

Josepha continued to work in the McSimmons kitchen. As she had foreseen, the younger sons of the plantation owner grew to become wild, with a mean streak not to be found in the father.

A day came in the mid 1850s when Josepha heard a knock on the front door. Both master and mistress were out. She went to answer it. A tall, thin black man she had never seen before stood on the porch.

"Mornin' ter you, ma'am," he said, smiling and tipping his hat.

Josepha stood staring. She had never been called *ma'am* in her life!

"I's new ter dis area," he said, "an' I's lookin' fo work."

In the distance Josepha saw the master and his thirteen-year-old son walking toward the barn.

"Mister McSimmons, suh," she called, descending the steps past her visitor. "Dis man says he's lookin' fo work."

Master McSimmons turned and approached.

"What do you mean looking for work?" said the McSimmons boy. "He's just a nigger like you. We don't pay niggers to work. We tell them what to do and they do it."

"Shut up, William," said the father. "You're not as smart as you think you are.—What are you, a freedman?" he asked, walking toward the house where the black man still stood.

"Yes, suh," he answered.

"You from the North?"

"No, suh. I's from down Mississippi way. I earned my freedom, suh."

"I see. Well, I'm sorry but I've got all the help I need."

"I's good wiff horses, suh."

McSimmons nodded and scratched his chin for a moment.

"Hmm . . . all right," he said, "—tell you what . . . let me think on it a spell. Then you come back and see me in a week or so. I'm not promising anything, mind you. I'm just saying come back and see me just in case."

"Yes, suh. I'll do dat, suh."

The master and his son turned away and continued on toward the barn. Josepha stood staring after them. The moment they were out of sight she turned and motioned for their visitor to follow. She led him around the house toward the side entrance to the kitchen, where she walked in, gesturing for him to follow. He did so.

"Sit down ober dere at da table," she said as she immediately began gathering a plate and putting things on it. "By da looks ob it, you could use somefin' ter eat."

The man chuckled. "Hit's true," he said. "I been travelin' a long time. Sometimes hit's a mighty long time between meals."

"Well then, you eat as much as you kin," said Josepha, setting a plate of sliced bread in front of him. Butter, cheese, milk, and a generous slice of apple pie followed.

"Dis is mighty kind er you."

"I knows what it's like ter be on da move an' be hungry."

"How's dat?" he asked as he spread a slice of bread with butter.

Briefly Josepha told him her story. Before long the two were talking and laughing like old friends. After twenty or thirty minutes, Josepha's ears perked up. "Dat's da mistress's voice. You bes' be gettin' on, I reckon."

"I's much obliged ter you," said the black man rising from the table. "By da way, I's Henry Patterson."

"An' I's Josepha Black."

"Pleased ter make yo acquaintance. I reckon I's be seein' you agin when I come back ter see ef yo master's got work fo me."

"He won't. Dat jes' his way er gittin' rid ob folks. He figgers nobody'll wait aroun' a week. But tell you what— you say you's good wiff horses?"

"Dat I is."

"Den you go ter da nex' town—hit's called Greens Crossin'. Dere's a coupla white men dere dat dey says is more den usually kind ter coloreds. One ob dem's a man called Mister Watson at da mill, an' da other's at da livery . . . I forgot his name. But maybe one er dem's got work. Can't say fo sho."

"I'm obliged ter you, Miz Black."

"Good day ter you, Mister Patterson."

TERROR
18

JOSEPHA DIDN'T SEE THE FREEDMAN AGAIN THAT next week. Whether he had taken her advice and what might have been the result, she did not know.

When another new black face appeared at the McSimmons plantation, young William McSimmons showed a much different reaction. By then twenty-two years old and home from the war convalescing from a leg wound and subsequent infection, he lost no time turning the charm toward an unusually pretty new young house slave. He was good-looking enough to turn her head at the same time.

Josepha knew it was trouble from the beginning. She tried to befriend the new girl. Josepha knew what it was like to be alone in the world. But at the age of seventeen, the dim-witted girl was not ready to grow and change, and Josepha feared what the result would be. She did what she could for the foolish girl, but she could not prevent her sneaking out at night.

Mistress McSimmons had died, struck down by a rare form of malaria, and the master was allowing his eldest son more and more leeway about the place than was good for him. The loss of his wife had been hard on Mr. Mc-Simmons, and most of his slaves felt a sympathy for him. He had also lost one of his sons to the war. They were especially concerned that his grief might cause him to turn over the affairs of the plantation to the son who was his namesake when and if the war with the North ever ended.

As it turned out, their fears were not completely unfounded. The younger McSimmons had been seeing the daughter of a wealthy plantation owner from Charlotte, who had named his daughter after the fair city. At about the same time as his tryst with the new slave girl named Emma, the announcement was made of William and Charlotte's engagement.

The moment she laid eyes on the future Mrs. Mc-Simmons, Josepha knew that the new mistress would have no soft spot in her heart for slaves.

When the young McSimmons heir led his betrothed into the kitchen one day on the way to the parlor, where a sumptuous tea had been spread, she paused and glanced around at the assembled black staff.

"Can these darkies cook?" she asked, disdain dripping from her voice.

"As well as any, I suppose," laughed her husband-to-be.

"Well, I can see right now that there will have to be some changes around here—clean aprons for one thing, and everyone with matching dresses. It looks like a hodgepodge. I take pride in my kitchen. And that stack of pans over there—why haven't they been cleaned?"

The slave women and girls glanced around at one

another, too intimidated by the woman's forcefulness to speak.

"We's been gettin' da bakin' done, miss," said Josepha at last. "Den we's wash up."

"Well, I don't like an unsightly kitchen," she snapped back, taking the opportunity to send her eyes up and down Josepha's large frame. "I also don't like the idea of a slave eating us out of house and home. You'll have to find somewhere else to spend your time when I entertain. I can't have someone of your size serving my guests."

"Yes'm," mumbled Josepha, duly humiliated by the lady's tongue.

As the master's son and his bride-to-be continued into the parlor, Josepha realized that hard times lay ahead for herself and the rest of the McSimmons slaves.

But before the wedding came a day no one who lived through it would ever forget.

The war was over, and roving bands of angry Southern soldiers were all around in the weeks following the surrender of the South.

Josepha was in the kitchen with the rest of the house slaves working on preparations for the day's dinner when they all heard what sounded like a dozen horses thundering toward the plantation in the distance. Josepha paused and listened. A grave expression came over her face.

The master had gone into town for the morning and none of the other men were at the house. She shuddered momentarily at the sound, realizing that something wasn't right.

Explosions of gunfire followed a few seconds later.

Then Josepha really knew that something was wrong.

Shouts and more gunfire had stilled everyone else in the kitchen. The commotion was coming from the direction of the slave village. They continued to listen with dread.

"Come wiff me!" shouted Josepha, leading the others to the cellar door and pulling it open.

"Inter da cellar, all ob you!" she cried. "I don't know what's goin' on, but it ain't good. Git goin'—down dem stairs!"

The girls and women scurried down through the black hole, even more terrified now to hear the fear in Josepha's voice.

Josepha glanced back into the kitchen where one girl still stood.

"Emma, you fool chil', git ober here!" she cried. "Else we'll jes' leab you dere all alone. Git ober here!"

By now Emma was six or seven months along with young William's child, and because she was still skinny as a rail, her pregnancy was easily noticeable. At last she came and began awkwardly inching down the narrow stairs, crying and babbling incoherently.

Finally Josepha followed. The stairs creaked under her weight. She hoped the stairs did not collapse beneath her. She pulled the door shut behind them, hoping nobody would think to look down here. They were left in total darkness, a few whimpering, the newcomer Emma talking to herself.

They stayed there the better part of an hour in complete blackness and silence until Josepha judged that whatever had been going on must be done with. She was almost afraid to go up and look, but she knew she had to.

She rose to her feet, felt for the steps, made her way back up them till she felt the door. She pushed it open.

Light flooded the cellar. She poked her head out, then stepped slowly out into the room and walked into the kitchen, listening intently.

A deathly silence was everywhere.

Almost on tiptoe, Josepha crept toward the back door. Fearfully she opened it. Outside, the quiet stretched in all directions from the house. An eerie silence. Again Josepha shuddered. Everything looked normal. But the occasional bark of a dog or bellow of a cow or cackle of a chicken in the distance sounded strangely off-key. There were no human noises to go with them—no singing, no shouts and laughter of children, no calls to plough horses.

Something was dreadfully wrong. She could *feel* it.

"Kin we come out now?" came a voice from inside the house behind her.

Startled in the midst of the silence, Josepha turned back inside. There was Emma's frightened face peeking out from the cellar door. It wouldn't be Emma's last time hiding in a dark cellar.

Josepha hurried toward her.

"Come on out," she said, giving the pregnant girl her hand. "You kin come out, all ob you. But we's stayin' inside an' ain't goin' out anywhere till we find out what happened."

"Why, Josepha—what does you think happened?" asked Emma.

"I don't know, chil'. I jes' got me a bad feelin', dat's all. So we's stayin' right here."

It was William McSimmons, the father, who later that day was the first to discover the horror and devastation that had resulted from what eventually came to be called the Massacre of Shenandoah County by a roving band of soldiers called Bilsby's Marauders.

With the Confederacy failed, though many of them didn't know it yet, his slaves were now free men and women. The former life of the Southern plantation was changed forever.

Whether it was those changes or something else, the awful sight hit William McSimmons hard.

As he stood surveying the scene of desolation and death, the realization came over him that even though he had opposed the idea of it all along, his own blacks would never be able to enjoy the freedom they had yearned for so long. He was sad, not for himself, but for them—that they would not live to know freedom.

As William McSimmons stood staring in stomach-wrenching disbelief at the slave village of his plantation, and at the dead bodies strewn about, tears slowly filled his eyes, and he wept for the loss of his people. For the first time in his life, he realized how much he cared for them despite the color of their skin, even, perhaps, in some measure, *loved* them. What kind of animals would do such a thing!

He did not even notice at first the crude, hasty burial of the Jukes family among all the other slaves, nor stop to think what it signified—that *someone* must either have come upon the horrifying scene before him, or else survived it.

His son and fiancée were not so equally moved.

William McSimmons the younger, in fact, lamented the fact that the scatterbrained house slave he had gotten pregnant was not among those killed. He would have to devise some other means to get rid of her. One way or another she would have to be gone before he brought his new bride to the plantation.

It was no secret on the plantation who the father of the unborn child was. And when Emma suddenly disappeared two months later, no one doubted that young William McSimmons was behind it.

Everyone assumed she was dead.

Unexpected Reunion
19

JOSEPHA GRIEVED FOR ALL THE FRIENDS SHE HAD lost in the massacre. How strange it was to think back to her first days here, when she had been the newcomer. Now suddenly she had been with the McSimmons longer than anyone who was left.

Mostly she grieved for dear Lemuela, who was one of the main reasons she had stayed and never again tried to escape to the North. Now Lemuela and her family were dead, gone to join her husband, Hank, who had died a few years before. They were now free. But it didn't seem to matter anymore. What was freedom with no friends to enjoy it with?

Freedom had come too late for her. And once again those she loved had been torn from her.

Josepha never stopped to puzzle over the fact that only six mounded graves marked the resting places of what everyone assumed to be the remains of Lemuela and her children, and her father-in-law Wayne, since their bodies were the only ones not accounted for. Josepha did not wonder why there wasn't a seventh grave, nor imagine for a moment that the oldest daughter whom Josepha had helped into the world might still be alive. Neither did she know that the time would come to remember the promise of that night, though not as Josepha expected.

Several months went by.

The McSimmons plantation, as well as others in the area that had been attacked and brutalized, slowly recovered, though life would never be the same again. A few workers were hired, both white and black, to keep the work of the plantation going. Those house blacks who had not been killed were given their freedom. Two or three left. Josepha chose to stay and began receiving a meager wage for her work. How long she could tolerate it, however, under the rule of the new Mistress McSimmons, she didn't know. The new mistress was the kind of woman who made her presence felt, and with no wife to administer the affairs of the house and its staff, her father-in-law was not inclined to prevent her treating the blacks however she saw fit. Kindness toward blacks was not an element of her personal creed.

Then came a day when Josepha received the shock of her life.

She was on her way to the well when she saw a girl of what looked like fifteen or sixteen crouching behind the well-house, apparently hiding. Wondering who she might be, Josepha slowed and continued on.

Suddenly she recognized her. It was Lemuela's own daughter!

"Mayme!" Josepha exclaimed. "What'n tarnashun . . . dat really you!"

"It's me, Josepha," said the girl, turning and smiling almost sheepishly.

"We thought you wuz dead wif da others . . . how in tarnashun . . . but where you been all dis time, chil'!"

"I ran away," she said.

"Come in da house!" she said, standing back and running a scrutinizing eye up and down the girl's frame. "You always wuz a scrawny one, but wherever yo been, dey ain't been givin' you enuff food. You needs some vittles in yo tummy."

"I can't stay, Josepha," said Mayme.

"Whatchu mean . . . you ain't fixin' ter run off agin?"

"I can't come back here, Josepha," she said. "I've got another place that's home to me now that my kin's gone."

"You set yo min' at ease, chil'," she said. "Jes come wiff me. I'll take care ob you, chil'. Why, I wuz dere when you wuz borned—"

She paused a moment, an odd expression passing briefly across her face as she looked the girl over.

"—What I's sayin is dat you's always been a mite special ter me. 'Sides, no white man ain't gwine tell you what ter do no mo, nohow."

"Why, what do you mean?" asked Mayme.

"Ain't you heard . . . ain't no mo slaves. We all been done set free."

"Free," she said, not understanding what Josepha meant.

"Dat's right—you's free now, chil'. Dere's somefin' called a 'mancerpashun proklermashun what's done made it against da law ter own slaves. Some feller named Lincoln done it. You's a free black girl. Da white man can't do nuthin' ter hurt you no mo."

"But what about the war?" asked Mayme.

"Dat's all over, Mayme, chil'. Dat's what dey was fightin' 'bout, near as I kin tell. Da Norf won an' da Souf had ter set us coloreds free. Leastways, somefin' like dat's what der master done tol' me."

Josepha put her great big arm around Mayme and led her up the steps into the house.

In another minute a plate of bread and cheese was on the table.

"Whatchu gwine do now, chil'?" Josepha said. "Da master'd likely keep you on like he done me."

"You mean, stay here like before?" asked Mayme.

"Dat's what I mean. But not like no slave. You'd git paid fer yo work now. You could stay here in da house wiff me, an' be a house girl an' work wiff me."

"What do you mean, get paid?"

"Jes' like I say. Dey gots ter pay us now, since we ain't slaves. I's be gittin' five cents er day ter stay an' work fer Master McSimmons. I don' know what's ter become er me wiff dis new mistress what don' seem ter like me none. But fer now I gots me my same room ter sleep in, an' you can see wif yo own eyes dat I ain't sufferin' from not havin' enuff ter eat."

"And . . . and you *want* to stay here?" said Mayme.

"Where would a fat ol' black woman go, chil'? I reckon I'm free, but I gots noplace else t' go. I been here so long it seems dat I been here all my life, so I figure dis'll be my home fer what years I got lef'."

"I don't think I could do that, Josepha. And so I reckon I oughta be going."

Mayme stood up from the table.

"Whatchu gwine do den, effen you don' plan ter stay here?" Josepha asked.

"Like I said, I've got another place that's home now."

Josepha turned and trundled into another room and disappeared for a minute. When she came back she was holding something in her hand. It was a piece of white cloth. She took some more of the bread and cheese and wrapped it inside the cloth, and handed it to Mayme.

"Don' open it till yo gone," she said. "Dis is jes' from me ter you. I know it won' make up fer losin' yo mama, but maybe it'll help some."

Then she took Mayme in her arms and held her for a long time. Josepha had never stopped to think about it before, but this girl she was holding was closer to a daughter of her own than anyone in the world.

Slowly they both stepped back.

"Thank you, Josepha," said Mayme. "It was real good to see you."

"An' God bless you, chil'," said Josepha, big tears starting to drip down her face. "Now dat I knows yer alive, I ain't gonna be able ter keep from thinkin' 'bout you. Anytime you want, you come back an' see Josepha, you hear?"

Mayme smiled. "I may do that," she said. "I reckon you'll see me again."

They walked back outside together. Mayme walked slowly down the steps from the porch, then away from the house. She glanced back one more time. Josepha was standing there sniffling and wiping her eyes with the back of one hand, her other hand half raised.

All of a sudden from around the side of the house the old master came walking straight toward them.

He slowed as he saw the girl, then stopped.

Mayme froze.

There used to be a saying among the slaves that all coloreds looked alike to a white man's eyes. And one look at Mr. McSimmons' face said that he was confused seeing the girl walking away from the house. He knew she didn't belong there. But at the same time, the way his eyes and forehead wrinkled slightly said that he recognized her, even though he didn't quite know why.

Then slowly a light came over his face.

"I see you came back," he said. "You're old Hank and Lemuela Jukes' kid, ain't you?"

Mayme nodded.

"You didn't get killed?"

"No, sir."

"Where you been all this time?"

"Over yonder."

"Well, don't matter now, I guess," he said. "I reckon what you do's your own business. You ain't mine no more. Well . . . talk to Josepha—she'll put you to work."

Then he kept going the way he'd been walking, and disappeared around the other side of the house.

Josepha looked at Mayme from the porch, like maybe she thought now she'd change her mind. But Mayme just waved again, then kept going.

A PROMISE FULFILLED
20

*T*hat was the first time I saw Josepha after my family had been killed and I'd gone to Rosewood to live with Katie and eventually my father, Templeton Daniels.

I hadn't realized all that Josepha was thinking and feeling inside on that day when I went back to my old home—about the promise she'd made to my mother Lemuela the night I was born. No wonder she'd cried when she saw me that day—thinking I was dead, and then seeing me like that, reminding herself of my mama and remembering her promise to take care of me.

Josepha and I were bound closer to each other than either of us had ever realized—or at least more than I had realized. She had no family left that she knew about. My mother was gone. But she was the most like kin to me that I had besides Papa and Katie, of course. And I suppose, though I hadn't really thought of it until I knew her whole story, that

I was something like kin to her too.

In one of those funny ways that life has of turning things and circumstances upside down in ways you don't expect, as it turned out, though Josepha had promised my mama to take care of me, when a little more than a year and a half later she found herself in a situation she didn't know how to get out of with her new mistress, she came to me—well, to Katie and me both—for help. In a manner of speaking we were the ones who had the chance to take care of her.

≈ ※ ≈

Rumors had begun to spread around the area, mostly thanks to a busybody named Mrs. Hammond at the general store in Greens Crossing, that made everyone at the McSimmons plantation realize that maybe they'd been wrong all this time about Emma being dead.

When young William McSimmons' new wife caught wind of what was being said, that a colored baby from a white father was being hid somewhere with a house full of urchins, she hit the roof.

She had known about Emma, though had tried to forget. She thought that her troubles from her husband's promiscuity were behind her. She went into a rage at the news.

She took her anger out on the nearest and most convenient person she could, whom she still suspected of knowing more about the affair than she let on. That person happened to be the McSimmons' cook, Josepha.

The tirade so caught Josepha off guard at first that she hardly knew its cause. She had heard the rumors about the half-black baby too, and of course *did* know more than she was telling. But why Mistress McSimmons would direct such venom toward her, she didn't understand.

"No need ter git riled at me," Josepha said in an irritable voice. "I don' know nuthin'. Why wud I know what you's talkin' 'bout?"

"You fat old sow!" the lady shrieked. "I'll teach you to talk back to your betters! Maybe the sting of the whip will put some respect into you, and loosen that lying tongue of yours!"

Three quick strides took her to the wall where her husband's riding whip hung. She grabbed it and turned on Josepha.

Josepha had not felt the lash in years and certainly never expected to feel it again now that she was a free woman.

Three or four sharp blows to her arms, shoulders, and back were sufficient to rouse her indignation.

She put up her hand, trying to ward off the blows and grab at the whip.

"How dare you raise your hand against me!" cried Mrs. McSimmons, preparing to begin a new volley more violent than the first. But suddenly Josepha stepped toward her, fire in her eyes, and latched onto the lady's wrist with fingers as strong as a vise. Her hand stopped the whip in midair and shocked her mistress into a fuming silence.

"I don' hab ter take dis no mo!" said Josepha in a huff. "You may be white an' I may be black, you may be thin an' I may be fat like you say. But I's a person ob God's makin jes' like you, an' you ain't got no right ter—"

"How *dare* you talk to me in such a tone!" cried Mrs. McSimmons in a white wrath, struggling with all her might to free her arm from Josepha's hold.

"An' how dare you whip me like I wuz one ob yer barn dogs!" retorted Josepha, continuing to hold the mistress's wrist fast, for Josepha was easily the stronger of the two by at least double. "I's a free woman, I ain't yo slave. I can come an' go when I like an' I ain't gotter put up wiff no whippin jes' cuz you married a low-down man what can't keep his trousers on. Lemuela's girl, she'll gib me work, so I think I'll jes' be movin' on. Effen she can't pay me, she ain't likely ter let me starve neither an' it'll be a sight better'n puttin' up wiff da evil mischief ob a lady like you. So I'll thank you ter gib me da week's pay I gots comin' ter me an'—"

"You swine!" seethed the woman through clenched teeth. "You'll get not a cent if you desert me without notice!"

"Well, den . . . no matter. I's leavin' anyway," said Josepha.

Still holding the lady's wrist with one hand, she now reached up with her other and twisted the whip away from her, then released her and walked to the door and threw it out into the dirt. She then turned, went to her room trembling but with head high, and packed her few belongings and put them in a pillow slip. Three minutes later she was walking out the same door for good, leaving Mistress McSimmons in stunned and broken silence behind her. Feeling brave and strangely proud of herself, she walked away with her head held high. If she didn't exactly have a smile on her face, she had one in her heart.

Josepha had no more idea where Lemuela's daughter lived than did Mrs. McSimmons. But she had not forgotten Henry Patterson, and knew from an occasional delivery he had made through the years to the McSimmons plantation that he had followed her advice and had been working at the livery at Greens Crossing ever since their first meeting. He was more likely than anyone she could think of to have caught wind of where a black girl calling herself *Mayme* might have gotten to.

Three hours after Josepha's unceremonious departure from the only home she had known for more than twenty years, Henry looked up from his work and saw the large black woman ambling wearily in his direction. He set down his pitchfork and waited.

"You be Henry, effen I'm not mistaken," she said, puffing from her long walk.

"Dat I is," said Henry.

"I'm Josepha," said Josepha, "from da McSimmons place."

"I knows who you is," chuckled Henry. "You don't think I forgot our first meetin'. Why I owe you dis job er mine. But whatchu doin' so far from home, an' on what looks ter be sech tired feet?"

"Ain't my home no mo," said Josepha. "I's a free woman, so I done lef'. I ain't gotter take dat kin' er treatment no mo from nobody. An' now I'm lookin' fer Miz Mayme, an' I'm hopin' you might be familiar 'nuff wiff her ter be able ter direc' me ter where I kin fin' her."

Henry chuckled again. "I reckon I kin do dat, all right," he said. "Why I might jes' take you dere myse'f, effen you ain't in too much a hurry. Hit's a longer walk den I think you wants ter make, an' effen you kin wait till I'm dun here, I'll fetch you dere in dat nice buckboard ober dere dat I's repairin' fer Mr. Thurmond. I reckon hit's 'bout ready fer me ter take ter him, an' Rosewood's right on da way. I don' think he'll min' a passenger ridin' 'long wiff me."

Just as the sun was going down that evening, the sound of a horse and wagon approached the Clairborne plantation known as Rosewood.

Henry reined in as Mayme ran out of the house toward the buckboard. It took a little while for Josepha to get down to the ground, even with Henry's help. One look at her face said that she was exhausted.

"Mayme, chil'!" she said, taking Lemuela's girl in her arms. When the two stepped back a minute later, Mayme saw that Josepha was crying.

"What is it, Josepha?" said Mayme.

"I lef', Mayme," she said. "I dun lef' da McSimmons. Dat young mistress, she's a bad woman, an' I finally jes' lef'. I didn't know where ter go 'cept ter you."

"Oh, Josepha . . . I'm sorry," said Mayme, embracing her again.

"Does you think yer mistress'll hab room fer an' ol' black woman somewheres?"

Just then a white girl a year or two younger than Mayme ran out of the house.

"We've always got room," said Mayme, "—especially for you! Don't we, Katie?"

"Of course!" exclaimed the white girl. "How wonderful. I'll hurry back in and start preparing one of the rooms immediately."

"What dat she say?" said Josepha in surprise as she watched the girl go. "She be da mistress? She can't be fixin' no room fer me!"

"Things are different here, Josepha," Mayme laughed. "There's no black or white, no mistress or slaves. We're not even hired coloreds because there's no money either. I'm sorry, but Katie won't be able to pay you any more than she does me. But we're a family and we've got enough to eat. We've learned that being together and being a family is all we need, and is the most important thing of all. I reckon that's a sight better than money. We're happy to have you."

"Den let's go an' help Miz Katie wiff dat gettin' ready. I still don' like the idea ob her white han's waitin' on me nohow."

⸲ ❋ ⸱

And that's how Josepha came to be at Rosewood, where I'd gone myself after the massacre, and was now part of the Rosewood family.

We've been together ever since.

It still made me sad to think of my mama. But after I knew Josepha's story, whenever I thought of her, I imagined that it made her happy where she was in heaven that Josepha and me were together.

⸲ ❋ ⸱

THE NEW HOUSE
21

I'LL HAVE ANOTHER CUP OF THAT COFFEE OF YOURS, Josepha," said Mayme's father, Templeton Daniels, where he and his brother, Mayme's and Katie's Uncle Ward, sat at Rosewood's kitchen table.

His voice brought Josepha out of her reminiscences.

"Shore, 'nuff, Mister Daniels," she said in a soft voice.

Josepha smiled, wiped at her eyes, and walked to the stove where the pot of coffee stood steaming.

He looked over at her. "Are you all right, Josepha?" he asked. "From that look on your face, I'd think you were . . . well, I don't know what I'd think."

"Dat's all I wuz doin', Mr. Templeton—jes' thinking'," said Josepha, "—thinkin' 'bout some times long ago an' how da good Lord brung me here."

"Why don't you tell us about it?"

"Maybe I will . . . maybe I will at dat one day. But I don't reckon dat day's jes' yet."

She poured him another cup of coffee and then went about with dinner preparations, while the two Daniels brothers continued their conversation at the table.

"So what I was thinking, Ward," said Templeton, "is that we need to be thinking of the future. Micah and Emma are gone, and it's not going to be long before Mayme and Jeremiah are going to figure they've waited long enough. We've got to get to work on a place for them, so it's ready when the time comes."

"What did you have in mind," asked Ward, "building a place?"

"We could. But it seems it would be simpler and quicker, not to mention cheaper, to add on to one of the places we've already got. There's that slave cabin that sits away from the others. It's run down and the roof leaks, but it's sound. With a new roof . . . maybe add on another room, put in a nice kitchen, running water, new windows, we could turn it into a right fine little house. There's room for a garden. We could build a small barn to go with it."

"You think that'd be easier than starting with a new place?"

"Seems like it to me. I don't much like the idea of my little girl having to live in a slave cabin again. And not that I wouldn't like them to have a big brand new place one day, like we talked about before, out past the barn. But this seems like the easiest to make a start with. Then after they begin having a family, we can make plans for something larger. We'll ask Henry. But either way, we could pay him to work on it when he's not at the livery and to watch over the thing as we go. He knows how to do most anything. I never built a house before. Seems like we ought to start out with something we can handle."

"I haven't either. That's a good idea. Henry'll know what to do."

☙ ❁ ❧

Just then I walked into the kitchen. Papa and Uncle Ward immediately stopped talking.

"What were you two talking about?" I asked.

"Nothing, little girl," said Papa with a grin.

"Papa!" I said, "I'm twenty years old. When are you going to stop calling me a little girl?"

"When you learn to mind your own business!" he said with a mischievous wink.

I went about what I was doing, but I always knew from that look on his face when he'd been talking about me and suspected that was the reason for it this time too.

He was right about Jeremiah and me. Jeremiah was Henry's son and he'd asked me to marry him and I'd said yes. But we were waiting until it was a little safer. A lot of things had happened recently that showed how dangerous things were after the war. Some folks in the community weren't any too pleased with what had been going on at Rosewood, with whites and blacks mixing together. There'd been threats and they'd tried to kill Jeremiah and had killed Emma's boy William. So the danger was real enough and that's why we were waiting.

But Papa and Uncle Ward didn't wait. They spoke to Henry about starting to work on one of the cabins like they'd talked about. And after making plans and deciding what to do, they got to work on it.

⋐ ✳ ⋑

One day after lunch a couple of weeks later, when Josepha had just finished washing up, she heard hammering in the direction of what used to be the slave village. She stepped to the kitchen door and peered out. All she could see was the outline of a man on a roof against the light of the sun. Slowly and with some huffing and puffing she crossed the yard and walked down to the cabins.

"Henry Patterson, whatchu doin' up dere?" she said, reaching the spot and glancing up, shielding her eyes from the sun.

"I's tearin' off dis ol' rotten roof," replied Henry. "Didn't dey tell you?"

"Dey don't tell me nuthin' roun' here."

Henry laughed. "You know more ob what's goin' on roun' here den you let on."

"Whatchu know 'bout dat?"

"I gots me two eyes," he said with a grin. "I kin see fo myself. You like ter pretend dat you don't know what you knows well enuff."

"Well, I swan!" exclaimed Josepha in a huff.

Henry chuckled at her seeming outrage.

"You know's I's right," he said.

"I don't know no such thing! An' you still ain't answered my question—whatchu doin' up dere?"

"An' I done tol' you dat I's tearin' off dis ol' roof."

"But *why's* what I want ter know."

"'Cause we's gwine build on to dis place an' make a right fine little house outta it."

"What fo?"

"Fo Jeremiah an' Mayme is what I figger, though Mister Templeton didn't say so in so many words. An' you can't tell me you din't know all 'bout it."

"Well . . . maybe I did, but maybe I jes' wanted ter see fo mysel'," said Josepha. She turned and walked back toward the house.

Henry watched her go, still grinning to himself, then returned to his work.

Forty minutes later he glanced up to see Josepha walking toward him again. This time she was carrying something.

She came close to the cabin and set down a basket covered with a red-checkered cloth.

"Dere's you some bread an' coffee ef you gits hungry," she said up to him, then turned and made her way back again.

Henry watched her go, smiling to himself. He kept working for another five or ten minutes, then climbed down the ladder to investigate. What he found under the cloth was enough food and drink for three men!

He whistled lightly under his breath.

"My, oh my!" he said, chuckling. "Dat's some kind er feast fo an ol' colored boy! What did I do ter deserve dis?"

But it was just about the time of day when a man's stomach begins talking to him. So Henry sat down without any more questions. After all, he thought to himself, he knew what pride Josepha took in what came out of her kitchen.

He didn't want to hurt her feelings!

EXTRA HELPER
22

The weather remained warm and Henry's work on the cabin continued every day he had off from the livery, which turned out to be oftener than he might have thought. Henry hadn't exactly said it directly, but he had the feeling that his boss was being pressured to get rid of him because he was colored.

Papa and Uncle Ward weren't saying why they were fixing up the cabin. I know they didn't want Jeremiah and me to feel funny or to rush into getting married before we were ready. But after what Papa had said when I'd asked what they were talking about, and from the expression on his face, I suspected the reason. Jeremiah and I talked about it sometimes, what it would be like after we were married. But something kept making us both feel like the time still wasn't quite right. It was like we were waiting for something . . . but we didn't know what.

Henry always ate lunch with everyone else when he was working at Rosewood. But after that first day,

Josepha lost no opportunity to take coffee or lemonade and bread or cake or biscuits down to him. Sometimes she went two or three times, and gradually stayed longer and longer. When dinner and supper came, Henry never had any appetite left after all the snacks through the day!

⇀ ❅ ↼

"Josepha," Henry called down one morning when she appeared with the basket that he'd begun to expect almost like clockwork, "I's mighty glad ter see you. Set dat basket down an' gib me a hand wif dat board."

Josepha did as Henry had asked, then looked up to where he sat straddling the open beams of the roof.

"What you want me ter do?" she asked.

"Grab dat plank dere, dat's leanin' against da wall. See ef you kin scoot it up off da groun' enuff fo me ter git hold ob it."

Josepha walked over, took hold of the board as low down as she could stoop, and tried to lift it.

"It's heavy!"

"I ain't surprised," said Henry. "Ef you kin jes' git it up two or three feet off da groun' . . ."

She strained with the board a little harder.

"Dat's it!" cried Henry.

He leaned toward the top end as Josepha inched it a little higher off the ground.

"I almost got it!" he called down. "Jes' a hair more . . ."

Henry reached and managed to grasp the end.

"Now . . . one mo shove on yer end wiff me pullin'—"
The plank slid up another several feet.

"Dat's good—I got it!" cried Henry.

Josepha let go and stood back. At last Henry was able to swing the board up and leverage it enough to slide it the rest of the way toward him. In another minute he had it up on the roof and in place.

"Dat wuz good . . . thanks, Josepha!" he called down. "You saved me havin' ter go down an' back up dat ladder."

"Well, now you kin come down anyways an' hab some er dis bread an' lemonade I brung."

"Maybe I'll do dat all right . . . jes' let me git a coupler nails in dis board ter hold it down."

Three minutes later Henry scrambled to the ground. He sat on the cabin steps where Josepha had set out the things she had brought almost like a picnic.

"Why dis looks right fine!" said Henry.

Josepha handed him a tall glass of lemonade.

Henry downed nearly half the contents in a single gulp, then wiped the sweat from his forehead with the back of his hand.

"Dat hits da spot!" he said with a satisfied sigh. "I didn't know how thirsty I wuz."

"You really think dat dis house be fo Mayme an' Jeremiah?" asked Josepha.

"Like I said, I don't know fo sho, but dat's what I's thinkin'."

"How you know how ter do dis, build a house an' put on a roof an' walls?" said Josepha as she poured out another glass of lemonade, and then gave Henry a sandwich.

Henry laughed. "A man picks up things as he goes along—mostly by watchin' I reckon. How you know how ter cook?"

"I reckon you's right—I just picked it up. I always liked everythin' 'bout food—fixin' it . . . an' eatin' it," she added with a laugh, patting her belly. "An' it always seemed like da kitchen wuz da livliest place in da house. Even when I wuz jes' a girl I liked bein' in da kitchen. But den by an' by I reckon I sort ob discovered dat I had a knack wiff food—least dat's what da white men said when dey ate my food, an' by an' by I figgered da kitchen wuz my way er stayin' outta da fields."

"You gots a way wiff food, all right!" said Henry. "An' maybe it's somethin' like dat fo a man. A boy sees growed men doin' things an' makin' things, an' ter him it's like da kitchen wuz fo you, an' a boy wants ter be aroun' men who's doin' an' makin' an' fixin' an' buildin'. An' when you's a slave you git told ter do things an' you figger out how ter do dem. One time I wuz tol' ter take some water ter a man puttin' a roof on one ob da slave cabins where I lived on da Mississippi. I muster been five or six. I watched him a spell an' pretty soon I wuz up on a ladder handin' him tools an' nails an' watchin' what he wuz doin'. Dat's how you learn anythin', I reckon—watchin', den tryin' it fo yo'self."

"But you seem ter know how ter do most anythin'," said Josepha.

"After I left Mississippi, lookin' fo Jeremiah an' his mama, I done lots er jobs. Whatever I cud do so I cud eat, I done it. So I reckon I learned ter do a heap a things."

"How'd you git separated from dem? Wuz dat when you got yo freedom?"

Henry smiled sadly. "Dey wuz sent away just before. So when I got da chance ter be free, I took it an' went lookin' for dem."

"You always live down dere in Mississippi?"

A faraway look came into Henry's eye.

"Yep, I always did," he said slowly and with a faint smile. "My papa wuz a big strong man, muscular wiff big shoulders. He had nuthin' ob my build. His father had come from France as a free black man hired ter a Frenchman—dat wuz before France sol' Louisiana an' all up da Mississippi ter dis country like dey dun."

"So wuz yo people all free?"

"My papa wuz free like his father," said Henry. "My papa worked on da ribber, I think he might eben er had his own boat—a small boat, jes' a one-man steamer. He took freight up an' down between New Orleans an' Memphis. I don't know effen it wuz his own boat er not."

"An' yo mama?"

"My mama wuz a slave girl in Mississippi on a farm where da ribber ran alongside it. An' when my papa wuz dere, dat's where he'd stay. The owner ob da boat or, ef it wuz my papa's boat, da man he had bought it from, it wuz his brother's farm, so papa'd stay dere though he wuzn't one er der slaves. Dat be where he met my mama an' dey wuz married an' I wuz born. Since chilluns foller dere mother, I wuz a slave too. Dat wuz papa's home whenever he wuzn't on da ribber. He always wuz gwine git enuff saved ter buy our freedom. But den dere wuz an explosion ob da steam boiler, an' his boat went down an' wuz los', an' papa along wiff it."

"How old wuz you?" asked Josepha.

" 'Bout eleben. But I always loved da ribber cuz it reminded me ob my daddy. I wuz baptized in dat ol' Mississippi too."

"How old wuz you den?"

"I reckon I wuz nine er ten."

"Dat's mighty young ter git saved."

"I didn't say dat's when I got saved, I said dat's when I wuz baptized."

"I don't rightly unnerstan' what you's gettin' at," said Josepha.

"Jes' dat gettin' baptized ain't necessarily da same as gettin' saved. Gettin' baptized happens only once—or I reckon fo mos' folks it happens only once. But I always figgered learnin' to walk wiff da Master wuz a mite mo complicated den what can jes' happen in a few seconds. Always seemed mo like a lifetime thing ter me."

"You sometimes got a mighty peculiar way er sayin' things, Henry Patterson!" said Josepha.

"I been tol' dat a time er two!" laughed Henry

Josepha thought a minute.

"Maybe dat's true all right," she said. "Dat wuz good when dat Rev. Smithers, or whatever his name wuz, wuz here an' wuz baptizin' folks an' all. I'm glad for dem, but I reckon what's going on here at Rosewood's more like what Jesus had in mind den all dat."

"Yep," said Henry, a smile spreading over his face, "it's mo 'bout what kind er person you is inside den all dat hands in da air an' singin' an' yellin'. None er dat makes you a better person when you walk away from da river an' da preachin's done."

"I reckon you's right 'bout dat," said Josepha.

"You 'member how da preachers used ter come roun' an' all the black folks'd go an' he'd git 'em all worked up an' then ask who wanted ter git saved?"

Josepha laughed. "I 'member all right. An' everybody'd call out, *Amen, brother.*"

"I never did any ob dat," said Henry. "I figgered bein' saved wuz somethin' a mite longer lastin' den dat. It's one thing to pray and say *Amen,* it's anudder to start walkin' and livin' like Jesus. Dat's a fearsome thing—a lifetime thing. I reckon I'm still workin' my way tards bein' who da Lord wants me to be."

"What you mean, who da Lord wants you to be?" asked Josepha. "You's a Christian, ain't you?"

"I reckon I's a Christian, all right," said Henry. "'Cause I believe, an' dat's a fact. But I ain't altogether rid er my sin quite yet. The Lord's got a heap er work lef' ter do in me. So let's jes' say dat me an' da Lord's workin' on it."

Josepha shook her head. "I don't know ef I hab any idea what you mean. You make it soun' like you's *half* saved or somethin'. What ef you die—you gotta go ter da one place er da other. So a body's either gotter be saved or he ain't saved—don't seem like dere's no in between 'bout it."

"Well, sometimes I wonder effen it might be a mite mo' complicated den dat," said Henry. "What about dose folks dat are on dere way tards Him but aren't quite dere yet? Don' you eber hab a hard time believin' dat God's gwine send 'em ter hell jes' 'cause dey didn't git quite enuff time ter come ter believin' in Him?"

"I don't know. All I want ter know is when did you believe in da Lord Jesus?"

"That's a mite easier ter answer," replied Henry. "I always believed. My mama was a good woman an' she taught me 'bout God an' obeyin' Jesus from afore I kin remember. But den I got older an' I reckon I got a mite ornery 'bout my belief."

"What dat supposed ter mean?"

"Jes' dat I din't know when ter keep my mouf shut 'bout it. Faith is mostly a private thing, it seems ter me, but sometimes it takes a while ter learn dat. I wuz a mite outspoken. I riled white folks, an' I don' know dat dere wuz any cause ter do dat."

"How you rile 'em?"

"I always tried ter obey da gospels. Dat's what my mama taught me. So when da Lord said ter call no man *Master*, I wudn't call no white man Master dis or Master dat, but only *Mister*. Dat made 'em mad."

"Dat don't soun' wrong ter me. But I neber saw da point er rilin' a white man."

"Maybe you's right," nodded Henry. "But a man's gotter stan' up fo what he believes come what may. But den maybe I cud er still obeyed wiffout bein' proud spirited 'bout it."

"*You* wuz proud spirited? Why you ain't got a proud bone in yo body, Henry Patterson."

"Don't be too sure er dat, Josepha. My pa was proud er bein' free, an' my mama wuz real proud ob bein' married ter a free man. I figger da kind er pride dey had wuz da good kind. But den maybe it came down ter me an' I turned it into da bad kind. I know lots 'bout pride cuz it's been a companion er mine fo many a year, an' I knows it when I sees it. We all's got a heap er pride, an' we all's gotter learn how ter deal wiff it da only way it kin be dealt wiff."

"An' what's dat."

"Ter kill it. An' I ask you, which is worse—ter call anudder man *Master*, or ter be proud an' ter look down on somebody else in yo heart? Seems ter me da pride's da worse ob da two."

"I neber thought 'bout all dat," said Josepha. "Seems like dat's carryin' religion a mite far ter me. Whoeber said we wuz supposed ter be perfect?"

"You askin' da question?" said Henry.

"I reckon I is."

"Den I'll answer it—da Lord himself said we wuz ter be perfect."

"But nobody kin do what *He* says. He's different."

"He's different, all right, but we gots ter try ter do what He says. Dere ain't nuthin' else we's supposed ter be doin' in dis life but learnin' how ter do what He says."

Josepha shook her head. "Still seems ter me dat dat's carryin' it a mite far."

"Ef we don't carry it all da way, den what good is what we believe? Seems like we gotter carry it all da way, or else it don't mean much."

"Most folks don't do dat."

"Yer right," said Henry. "Most folks don't."

It was quiet a minute. Henry swallowed the last of the lemonade in his glass, then stood.

"I reckon it's time I wuz gettin' back ter work," he said.

"Thanks fo da sandwich an' lemonade."

He climbed back up the ladder.

"What 'bout you?" Henry asked as he went back to the board they had hoisted up. "Why did you want to get free?"

"I don't know," she answered. "Dere jes' came a day when I heard 'bout dat unnergroun' railroad, an' I figgered, why shouldn't I git on board an' find some freedom fo myself jes' like other coloreds wuz doin'? So I did. I didn't git ter da Norf, but I got dis far."

Henry pounded a few nails but then paused again, asked another question or two, and then sat back and listened with interest as Josepha told him of the adventure of her travels, and how she had ended up at the McSimmons plantation.

"Dat's some story, all right," said Henry when she had finished. "I heard 'bout dat railroad, but I ain't never met anybody dat actually did it. Muster taken some courage soun's ter me."

"I neber thought dat I had no courage," said Josepha. "I jes' wanted ter go, so I went."

"Well, I's mighty glad you did, 'cause we's all glad you wound up here."

Catching Supper
23

T HE ROOF WAS FINISHED IN A COUPLE OF WEEKS,
then Henry moved down to begin working on the
new walls inside the cabin.

When Josepha next came to the cabin with her basket,
Henry had just walked outside and was wiping his face. It
was a hot day without a breath of wind.

"How do, Josepha," he said.

"I brung you somethin' ter eat."

"I see dat, but you know what I wuz jes' thinkin'? I wuz
thinkin' 'bout dat ribber an' dis hot sun. An' den I got ter
thinkin' how good some fresh fish would taste tonight,
cooked up da way you does. How 'bout you an' me go catch
us some fish!"

"I ain't no fisherwoman!" laughed Josepha.

"Who says?"

"I says."

"Well, den you kin jes' come an' keep me company.
We'll take dat basket an' set it down an' enjoy whatever's

inside it wiff our feet in da ribber an' a line out catchin' us tonight's supper!''

Without waiting for her to say anything further, Henry hurried to his cabin and returned a few minutes later with two poles, a little bag of tackle, and a big grin on his face.

"Come on, Josepha," he said, "I'll show you da bes' fishin' hole fo miles.''

They reached the river. Henry stopped, set down his things, stooped down and took off his boots and socks, then ran down the slight slope to the river till his feet were wet.

"Ah, dat's what I wanted ter feel!''

"Dis ain't da fishin' hole you meant?'' said Josepha.

"No, I jes' wanted ter git my feet in dis water! Come on—set dat basket down an' come git a little wet. Come on!''

Josepha hesitated only a moment, then set down the basket, took off her boots, and ambled down the bank. Soon she and Henry were laughing and kicking water at each other like two children, their trousers and dress getting wet.

"Won't we scare da fish?'' said Josepha.

"Nah, we's plenty downribber from where we's goin'. Dey won't git no hint we's aroun' till we yank 'em up outta da water. Come on, let's git our things an' head upribber. It's only 'bout a quarter mile is all.''

Josepha was quiet as they walked upriver, carrying their shoes and staying close to the bank. Her mind went back to the last time she had played in a river with a friend. That time it wasn't fishing but riding a horse. Suddenly she felt tears in her eyes. She still missed Mose and his happy smile. Being with Henry brought out memories that she had tried to keep hidden and tucked away.

By the time they reached the fishing hole ten or twelve minutes later, Josepha was puffing from the walk and both were perspiring freely.

"It's too hot fo dis!" she sighed. "I need ter git in dat water again."

"We'll go down ter da edge ob da ribber dis time," said Henry, "nice an' slow so we don't stir up da water. We'll git a coupla hooks out in dat deep green pond yonder an' den see what you got in dis basket er yours."

They sat down at the water's edge, feet in the cool water.

Josepha sighed with satisfied relief. Such physical activity and the long walk were not her favorite pastimes. Henry busied himself getting the two poles and bait ready. Several minutes later he tossed their two lines out into the middle where the current was slow and wound around a large rock, where the shade and deep hole he knew from experience usually drew the fish on a hot day like this.

"Now you git us somethin' ter eat," he said, "den I'll hand you dis pole."

"What I want wiff a pole?" said Josepha.

"You's gwine catch a fish er two, dat's what!" laughed Henry.

"I reckon I kin try, but I ain't neber caught no fish before."

"Jes' hold it still an' watch fer da line."

"Watch fo what?"

"Ter feel da fish, or maybe seein' a little jiggle er da line."

"Den what?"

"Don't git too anxious at da first little nibbles. But when some ol' fish takes da bait hard, an' you feel a tug, dat's when you yank back an' snags him wiff da hook."

❦ ✳ ❦

When I went out to start taking the laundry off the line in the middle of the afternoon, I realized I hadn't seen Josepha in two or three hours. Katie was on the porch reading a letter that had come from Rob Paxton that day. Uncle Ward had just returned from town with it a little while before.

"What does Rob have to say?" I asked.

"He's wondering whether to move or not," answered Katie. "His boss, Sheriff Heyes, is going to Pennsylvania and has asked Rob to go with him."

"Is he going to?"

"Probably. I think he needed to write it all down, to talk it over with someone."

"Not just someone," I said with a smile. "Someone special."

Katie smiled back. "I suppose so," she said softly. Then an odd look came over her face.

"What is it?" I asked.

"I don't know, it's just . . . this is such an interesting letter. I've never heard Rob talk this way before. I'm seeing a different side of him . . . no, not different—deeper maybe."

"In what way?"

"His faith in God, I guess you'd say. He says he's not trying to decide what he wants to do, but is try-

ing to find out what God wants him to do. I guess it struck me because of what he does—being a deputy. I mean, how many men who wear guns on their belts talk about doing what God wants them to do? Don't you think it's unusual?"

"Hmm . . . I see what you mean."

"I think maybe there is more to Rob Paxton than meets the eye."

"He still thinks you're special," I said, smiling again.

Katie smiled back, then turned again to the letter.

"I haven't seen Josepha since lunch," I said. "Do you know where she went?"

"No, I haven't seen her either," answered Katie, looking up. "Is she taking a nap?"

"No, she's not in the house anywhere."

"She didn't go into town with one of the men, did she?"

"I'm sure she'd have told us."

"Didn't I see her packing up a basket to take down to Henry?" said Katie.

"That's right, now that you mention it. But that was hours ago."

"I've heard nothing from down there. Usually you can hear Henry banging or singing or sawing away. It is awfully quiet now that I think about it."

Katie looked at me, then slowly a smile spread across her lips.

"Hmm . . ." she said, "that is interesting—our cook and handyman running off together!"

"Katie!" I laughed. "I can't imagine it's anything like that!"

"They've been spending a lot of time together. Haven't you noticed . . . and Josepha humming to herself when she's busy making up those baskets to take to Henry?"

"Sure, I've noticed. I think it's sweet."

"I do too. I think it's wonderful. All I was saying is that . . . well, maybe . . ."

Before we had the chance to speculate further on the mystery, in the distance we heard voices. There was no mistaking whose they were.

And they were singing!

Jimmy crack corn, an' I don' care.
Jimmy crack corn, an' I don' care.
Jimmy crack corn, an' I don' care . . .
da master's gone away!

Josepha's loud high soprano was unmistakable, and with Henry's low bass mingled with it, they made quite a duet.

When they came into sight, neither Katie nor I could believe our eyes. They were both barefoot, carrying their boots and the picnic basket. Josepha had two fishing poles slung over her shoulder. And Henry, trouser legs rolled up halfway to his knees, was carrying eight or ten fish strung together.

They looked like a couple of kids. From the expressions on their faces as they laughed and sang, it was obvious they were having the time of their lives.

Jimmy crack corn, an' I don' care.
Jimmy crack corn, an' I don' care.
Jimmy crack corn, an' I don' care . . .
da master's gone away!

"Our master ain't gone away," laughed Henry. "We's da ones dat's gone away an' he don't know where ter find us!"

Josepha howled like it was the funniest thing she had ever heard in her life.

"Dat's 'cause we's free," she said, "an' we don't call nobody master no more!"

"You got dat right!"

Katie and I watched them coming with our mouths hanging open.

"Where have you two been!" exclaimed Katie as they walked slowly up to the house.

"Fishin'," said Josepha. "Henry took me fishin' on da ribber. Look—we caught our supper!"

"Josepha snagged half ob 'em herself, didn't you, girl!" said Henry with obvious pride.

"I did at dat," she said. "I didn't think I cud, but dis ol' Mississippi boy showed me how . . . and I did."

So we had fresh fish that evening and were in a happy and festive mood. The fun and singing and laughter of Henry and Josepha coming back from the river seemed to last all day and infected the rest of us too. Josepha was so proud of herself. She couldn't wait to get back out to the river to try it again.

After supper when most of the things were cleaned up and Uncle Ward was sitting in his favorite chair lighting his pipe and Papa sat down with the newspaper, Henry got up to leave.

"Sit down a spell, Henry," said Papa. "No sense running off."

"Dere's a few things I didn't git done on da cabin today."

"Played hooky, eh!" winked Papa. "Come on—the work will keep. We're in no hurry with that cabin. Besides, you caught us our supper, and mighty good it was."

By then Katie had wandered in and sat down at the piano and was trying to pick out "Jimmy Crack Corn," gradually adding chords and bass to the melody.

"Why'd you think er dat!" laughed Henry.

"From hearing you and Josepha singing it today," said Katie.

"What's this?" asked Papa.

"They were singing it," said Katie. "It sounded good too."

Already Josepha's voice could be heard from the other room and she came in singing and pretty soon we had all joined in. Katie went on from that to "Old Dan Tucker," then to "Buffalo Gals," and then from folk song to folk song as we all sang and laughed and clapped while she played.

As often happened, after several clapping songs, everyone slowly quieted, and Katie soon went into softer music. She could completely set the tone and atmosphere in the whole house just by the kind of music she played. This time everybody got kind of thoughtful as she played. Before long she was playing the minuet dance that she loved so much. But everyone just sat peacefully listening.

At last to everyone's surprise, Henry stood up and walked over to Josepha. He reached down his hand. She took it and stood up.

Then daintily—amazing, I thought, because she was pretty big—she began taking the tiniest little steps on her toes, perfectly in time with the music. We sat watching in complete amazement. Henry didn't know what to do, he just kind of shuffled back and forth. But it was obvious Josepha had done it before. She had a faraway smile on her face and Katie kept playing and playing, not wanting to spoil the moment.

Finally Josepha seemed to realize that every eye on the house was on her, and got embarrassed and stopped.

"You've done that before!" I exclaimed.

"Only once," she said, "an' only fo a few minutes."

"Tell us about it."

"It wuz a stormy night," Josepha began, sitting back down in her chair, "an' all the white folks wuz havin' a dance an' celebration in da big house an' da garden. A slave boy an' me were watchin' from da dark on da other side ob da garden, an' dat wuz da music dat wuz playing, an' we tried it a little."

All of a sudden a sob escaped her throat. The

rest of us were quiet and we waited.

That was the first time we learned about Mose and that, although she didn't tell us just then, it was also the night he had died in a fire and that she was still haunted by it.

Josepha was quiet after telling us how she and Mose had danced the minuet. It was obvious there was more to the story. But then Henry broke the spell.

"Tell da others," he said, "what you wuz tellin' me 'bout yo travels on dat secret colored railroad, an' how you excaped an' woun' up here."

"Yes, Josepha, do . . . please," said Katie.

Josepha took a deep breath and glanced briefly at Henry with a look of gratitude for changing the subject.

Before long, Josepha was her lively old self again, telling us story after story and keeping us all laughing till nearly midnight.

⤙ ❋ ⤚

Rob's Letter
24

K ATIE SAT DOWN THE NEXT DAY TO READ THE
letter from Rob again.

Dear Katie, she read. *I hope you don't mind if I write
this letter to you to help me sort out my thoughts. A decision
has been placed before me, and I'm not sure what I should
do. My boss, Sheriff Heyes, whom you met when you and
your uncle were in Ellicott City, has been offered a job in
Hanover, a town in Lancaster County, Pennsylvania. A
good friend of his, Mr. Evans, who has owned a large farm
and property near there for years, and also operates the
telegraph office, informed him of it. The current assistant
sheriff for York County in Hanover is retiring before the
end of his term, and they have offered the position to Sheriff Heyes.*

*The decision I am facing is that John Heyes has asked
me to go with him as his deputy. It is not such a great distance, only thirty or forty miles. I spent some time in Pennsylvania when I served in the Union Army. But the fact
that it is in Pennsylvania, when I have been a Maryland
native and resident most of my life, makes it seem a larger*

decision than it probably really is. It would be farther from my family in Baltimore, and I would not have the opportunity to see them quite as often. That is, I think, an important aspect of the decision. Because along with this, my older sister Rachel is engaged to be married in a few months. I don't remember if I have told you or not, but I am a twin. My twin sister is no longer living. She went to be with God when we were seventeen—a very difficult and tragic farewell for all of us in the family. Her death—and the circumstances surrounding it—was the major turning point in my life, both spiritually and in the choice of my present vocation. I hope one day I shall have the opportunity to tell you about it in detail.

Now with Rachel's upcoming marriage, it will mean that my parents will be alone for the first time, and I feel a responsibility to be as near them as I can. They are in good health, and my father has never in my hearing spoken of retirement. But they are in their fifties, and as their only son, and with Rachel marrying, I need to be attentive to the passage of the years and my duty toward them. So a potential move farther from them is something I must weigh seriously.

My chief concern, of course, is what God wants me to do. I would appreciate your prayers that I would be able to discern His will in this matter. Early in my life, before my sister's death, I planned to follow in my father's footsteps into the ministry. The decision not to pursue the ministry was precipitated by a crisis in my life that actually deepened my faith, not lessened it. I know it may sound strange to say that a deepening of my faith led me away from the ministry, but that is how the circumstances worked out in my life. Now that I am a deputy sheriff instead of a pastor does not mean I am any less a Christian, or any less obligated to *find out what God wants me to do above what I might want to do myself. Dad's wisdom has always guided my growth and my perspective in spiritual things. His common sense in seeking God's will has always been an example to me, and now I am attempting, once again, to find out what God's will is for me through the principles my father always taught our family.*

Well, I do not want to bore you with my dilemma, but I did want to ask for your prayers and, if you have any, your thoughts on the matter. Even if you do not have any pearls of wisdom for me, it is always a pleasure to hear from you. Your life down there at Rosewood, even if occasionally dangerous, from some of the things you have told me, always sounds so much more interesting than mine and I never tire of hearing about it. But we all have to do our best to live faithfully where the Lord places us, and therefore I am very grateful for the opportunities He gives me to do His work wherever I am.

> *I am,*
> *Yours faithfully,*
> *Rob Paxton*

Katie set down the letter and did as Rob asked. She prayed that God would show him what he was supposed to do.

A Scare
25

One Sunday Jeremiah and I went for a ride through the woods on the road west toward Mr. Thurston's. It was a pretty hot day, and the two horses were wet with salt and sweat when we got back to Rosewood. We were hot and sweaty too.

We washed the horses down and scrubbed and brushed them with several buckets of water. Then, like always seemed to happen on a hot day around the pump, we got to playing and splashing in the water ourselves, pumping it out and dousing each other with water as fast as we could pump it.

Pretty soon Katie had come along and was getting in on the fun and the three of us were running all over the place, laughing and yelling at each other. It wasn't quite as out of control and silly as the water fights used to be with Emma and William. Emma could get mighty wild! But it got wild enough that Josepha came out and stood on the porch watching, with her dish towel in hand, wondering what had got into us.

Jeremiah had the easiest time of it since he could easily outrun Katie and me, especially after our dresses got soaked and heavy and clingy. But it felt so good!

Frantic to escape Jeremiah as he came after me with a bucket half full of water, I ran laughing and giggling toward the cabin Henry had been working on.

"Henry . . . Henry!" I cried, running inside full of the spirit of play. But Henry wasn't there.

I ran through the house and out the back door just as I heard Jeremiah pounding up the front steps. Laughing and giving myself away, I dashed around the back side of the house between the wall of a new room Henry had added and a woodpile of boards and wood scraps. I was so caught up in the chase that I never saw the tail of a snake sticking out from beneath the wood where it had crawled to find shade. Startled from the sudden noise and my kicking the edge of the board and disturbing him, it quickly reacted.

I screamed in pain as it struck, and I fell to the ground as I ran. My leg was almost numb.

Jeremiah was beside me in an instant. He picked up the nearest board and clubbed the snake to death with a fury I'd never seen. Then he stooped down, picked me up, and ran for the house, yelling for Papa and everyone else that I'd been bit by a copperhead.

By the time we reached the house I was already feeling faint. I heard voices and shouts and was aware of people hurrying up, but everything was a confusion in my brain. I didn't know whether I was afraid or not. Jeremiah laid me down on the porch, and it's a good thing I didn't see what was about to happen because it would have scared me to death, but the next instant Uncle Ward pulled out his long sharp knife and sliced a huge gash in my leg and then sucked at the blood as hard as he could, spitting it out on the ground.

"Laws almighty!" I heard Josepha exclaim, "dat blood's all yeller!"

"That's not blood, Josepha," said my papa. "That's venom.—Kathleen, Jeremiah . . . run for ice. See if there's any left in the icehouse. Bring it all! We've got to cool that leg down."

I was hardly aware of the pain because my leg was numb. Uncle Ward sucked at the wound several more times, then cut it again, even deeper, and did the same thing just like before.

"Templeton, start pumping water into the big washtub!" he yelled. "I'll do what I can here, then we've got to get her into cold water to try to keep it from spreading through her body. I saw it in California. Sometimes it works. And keep the dogs away!"

That was all I heard.

The next thing I knew I was in my own bed upstairs. I woke up all dreamy-like, sort of coming only half awake. All I could feel in my leg was a cold numbness. And heaviness. It was so heavy I couldn't move it if I'd tried. I was cold all over even though I was in bed. I heard myself groan and someone came hurrying over. I think it was Katie. She bent down over me and said some words and kissed me, but I didn't know what she said, or even if it was her. Then I moaned some more and the light faded and I fell asleep again.

I awoke to pitch black. My first thought was that I was dead. Then I heard a few crickets and the bark of a dog in the distance, and I knew it was night. I was no longer cold. I felt an itching. I tried to scratch at my leg but felt nothing.

Again consciousness faded.

Voices and movement disturbed me.

Again it was light but I could see nothing clearly. All was a blur. I tried to say something, but no sound came from my mouth.

People were talking . . . strange voices.

". . . have to wait and see," said a man I did not seem to know. "It's . . . get her to drink . . . got to have water . . ."

"How long before . . . know?" said another man's voice.

"Can't . . . see how . . . lose the leg . . . better than dying."

Somebody started to cry.

Again I fell asleep.

When I awoke the next time, instead of cold I was on fire—my leg, my whole body. I couldn't imagine what I was doing in this bed with blankets heaped up over me!

I tried to say something but again all that came out was a moan.

Voices . . . someone came to the bedside . . . whoever it was put a cup to my lips and lifted me enough so that I could drink. The water felt good. I was so hot all over!

"Drink . . . drink as much as you can, Mayme," said the voice.

But I felt half the water dribble down my face and neck. I lay back down, so hot I couldn't stand it. A cool wet cloth went over my face and forehead. It felt good.

I awoke in a thin light of what seemed to be dusk.

I wasn't quite so hot. Two people were in the room sitting beside my bed. I recognized their voices.

". . . layin' dere like dat reminds me er da day she wuz born," said a woman's voice.

"You were there?" said a man.

" 'Course I wuz—her mama hadn't been dere long an' she wuz feared somethin' wuz gwine happen ter her. She knew her little baby wuz gwine be a girl. She tol' me so."

I could hear them clearly. But I couldn't move or say anything. I knew they were talking about me.

"What was she like?" asked the man.

"She wuz uncommonly pretty, an' refined too. We didn't know where she'd come from, an' she kept to herself. You could tell she wuz sad. I figgered it had to do wiff leavin' a man. I knew what it wuz like ter be alone, an' tried ter be her frien'."

"Did she . . . did she ever say anything about . . . you know, what she'd left behind?"

"She thought 'bout it—I could tell from the look on her face dat she never stopped lovin' da man. But she didn't talk none 'bout it."

"Tell me about the day of the birth," said the man.

"Dat wuz da day she asked me to promise . . ."

They continued to talk, but I was drifting away again and could hardly hear them.

After a while it got real quiet. I felt a hand on my body. I almost thought I heard what might have been someone crying. But then the blurry light faded again and I heard nothing more.

When my brain came to itself the next time, I was dreaming. Though I couldn't tell the difference between dreaming and lying awake. Everything was a dream.

My mama was talking to me this time. I didn't know if I was a little girl, or if it was now, or if she was talking to me before I was born or from heaven.

"Someday we'll all be together again," she was saying. "Then you'll know your papa and what a fine man he was. We'll get our Tear Drop back then, and we'll all be together. But we may have to wait a little while 'cause we don't know where he's gone. . . ."

I saw my mama's face, smiling and laughing. I

tried to cry, but I couldn't make a sound. But my heart wanted to cry for love of her. But now it was my mama crying in my dream. And seeing her cry made me so sad it overwhelmed me in grief, but I still couldn't cry, though I wanted to because the whole world seemed so sad that it must have made even God want to cry.

Slowly my mama's laughing, crying, sad face faded.

Maybe God was crying, I thought. And then I felt that someone was nearby my bed. I tried to open my eyes, but all I could see was a head lying against my arm and long blond hair, and whoever it was was crying and praying. I don't know if I was dreaming or if it was real.

"Oh, God," I heard her say, "please don't let her die."

And then she wept. I didn't know if I was dreaming, or maybe I was dying. Was this what dying felt like . . . like a dream, where people and images came and went but where you couldn't make a sound, couldn't even cry when you wanted to for the sadness of it all.

Then I heard rain . . . hard rain pouring down on the roof somewhere above me. God was crying, just like I thought. Everybody was crying. The whole world was sad because there was pain and aloneness and grief everywhere.

I felt the sadness in my dream-heart. But I couldn't cry.

Was God crying because He couldn't answer the

prayer, because He couldn't keep me alive? Was I drifting somewhere between the worlds of life and death, between God's world and this world of people and beds and tears and prayers and sadness?

Still the teardrops fell from heaven, still the sky poured down its sorrow out of God's eyes . . . and still God wept because the world was sad and even He couldn't wake me up.

Another awaking came.

Was it a day later . . . an hour later? Had a night passed, or a whole day?

I opened my eyes. A beam of sunlight reflecting off the wall opposite the window was too bright and quickly I shut my eyes. The dreamy haziness was gone. I was aware of actual light and dark and shadows and shapes.

I moaned, then was surprised to hear my own voice.

". . . thirsty . . . water . . ."

"Mayme!" Katie shrieked. Steps ran across the room. The next instant I was smothered in kisses. "Are . . . are you . . . are you really there, Mayme?" she asked.

"What?" I tried to say, but my voice came out as a dry croak. "What . . . what do . . . you mean?"

"Oh, you are awake! Let me get you some water!"

She dashed across the room and returned and sat down beside me on the bed. She lifted and propped me up, then held the glass to my mouth.

"Drink, Mayme . . . drink as much as you can.

You need lots of water."

My throat hurt to swallow, but I did as she said and managed to get almost the whole glass down.

"Have you been there all night?" I asked. "I thought I heard . . . wasn't Josepha sitting there too . . . was it raining?"

"We've all been sitting with you, Mayme," said Katie. "Sitting and praying and trying to get you to drink in your sleep. The doctor said you needed water, but we could hardly get you to drink a drop. You were too delirious, and yes, there was a big rainstorm one night."

"The doctor was here during the night too?"

"During the night . . . he's been here three times."

"How long have I been asleep?"

"Mayme, you've been lying in bed nine days."

"Nine days!"

"We thought you were going to die. Oh, Mayme, I was so frightened!"

The others downstairs must have heard our voices because I now heard footsteps running up the stairs. Within seconds everybody poured into the room—Papa, Jeremiah, Uncle Ward, Henry, and finally a few seconds later, puffing from the hurried climb, Josepha.

"Hey, little girl!" said Papa. "Welcome back to the world. We thought we were going to lose you!"

⤳ ❅ ⤲

RECOVERY
26

I *didn't exactly bound out of bed that same day.*
The more awake I got the more I realized how weak
and dehydrated I was—that's what the doctor called
it, that I hadn't had enough water. Katie and Jere-
miah didn't leave me alone all day, and Katie didn't
leave me alone all night either but slept in the room
on the floor next to me. And they sat with me most
of the next day too, just like my two ministering
angels.

They poured what seemed like gallons of water
and tea down my throat. Josepha had a new batch
of broth or soup for them to give me every few hours
it seemed.

Somebody had ridden in for the doctor and he
came and looked at my leg.

"Can she keep it, Doc!" laughed my papa, but I
glanced at the others and could tell that they didn't
think it was something to laugh about. Neither did
the doctor.

"It looks like it," he said. "But that was a close
one. The ice probably saved not only her leg, it may
have saved her life too."

The next day Josepha herself came up with yet
another bowl of soup with lots of vegetables in it. I
sat up in bed and took it from her.

"Thank you, Josepha," I said as I sipped at it
with the spoon. She turned to go.

"Josepha," I said, "I had something like a dream
of you and somebody else talking about me, or
maybe about my mama. Were you really up here like
that?"

"Dat wuz me an' your papa," she said. "We wuz
sittin' here wiff you an' I wuz tellin' him 'bout when
yor mama came ter da McSimmons' an' den about
da day you wuz born."

"Tell me about it again," I said.

Josepha sat down. "Well, you see," she began,
"I'd been at da McSimmons place a coupla years
when yer mama came. I remembered what it wuz
like ter feel alone an' afraid, an' I saw on her face
dat she'd had ter leave someone she loved. I could
see da pain, an' so I tried ter make it as easy on her
as I cud, an' dat's how we became friends."

"What was the promise?" I asked.

"Well, when da night came when it wuz yo
mama's time, dey sent fer me at da big house, an' I
went down ter where she wuz in da village wiff da
older women an' a few ob da single colored women.

"'Is Josepha here yet!' wuz da first words I heard
when I walked in. Dat wuz yo mama an' she wuz

already in pain. I hurried ter da bed and asked how she wuz feelin'.

"She said, 'Not so good,' an' I cud tell she was hurtin' somethin' fierce. I sat down beside the bed where some ob da others wuz sponging off her face an' forehead. Hazel an' da other women wuz busy wiff hot rags an' towels.

"Da birth wuz slow an' difficult. Yo mama wuz exhausted an' we wuz worried 'bout whether she'd live through it. Yo mama must hab been thinkin' da same thing. With sweat pourin' off her forehead an' dripping down her cheeks, she motioned ter me ter come closer. So I did.

"She pulled my ear down close ter her mouf.

"'Tell them all to go away,' she whispered, '—just for a minute . . . all but you . . . I want you to stay.'

"I didn't know what it wuz all about, but I got up an' told Hazel what she'd said. Den da other women left da cabin for a minute.

"'I'm afraid, Josepha,' said yo mama. 'Promise me, if something happens to me—'

"I tried to tell her nuthin' was gwine happen to her. But she said, 'If it does, promise me that you'll look after my little girl.'

"Of course I said I wud.

"'I know it's a girl,' she said. 'I can tell . . . promise me you'll take good care of her.'

"'You can rest easy, sweetie,' I said. 'We'll all look after you and yer child.'

"'Please . . . if I die, make sure she has a good life—as good a life as a slave can have.'

"'I'll do my best,' I tol' her. I remember I even said, 'And maybe she won't always be a slave.' Though I'm not sure I really believed sech a thing back den.

"Den I asked her, 'Ef you know she's gwine be a girl, what do you want ter call her?'

" 'Mary Ann,' said yo mama. 'She'll be Mary Ann.'"

By then I was in tears as I listened.

"It wuz 'bout an hour later dat you wuz born. An' though yo mama's life was never really in any danger and she fully recovered, I never forgot my promise.

"Den yo mother married Hazel's boy a couple years later, an' dat's why you an' yo whole family wuz called Jukes. I didn't see as much ob you all or Lemuela as I wanted, since I wuz in da big house. But yo mama an' I wuz always special friends."

I lay in my bed peacefully after Josepha left. Gradually so many thoughts about my past were fitting into place.

⟡ ✳ ⟡

A BOOKCASE
27

ONE AFTERNOON WHEN WARD AND TEMPLETON were out in the fields and Mayme was ironing, Josepha slipped out of the house and headed for the cabins.

Henry was outside sanding boards. She paused in the shade of the old oak and watched him for a minute or two. When she had caught her breath, she walked the rest of the way.

"Afternoon, Henry. Whatchu workin' on?"

"Just a coupler planks fo inside da kitchen," he said, nodding back toward the house that was slowly taking shape.

She walked closer, looked at the board, and ran her palm across it.

"Mighty smooth," she said. "Seems almost too nice for da kitchen. What's it fo?"

"A work counter."

"Yep, den it needs ter be nice an' smooth. Dis'll be right nice. Nice hard oak too so's it won't git all knicked up. But you know, seein' dat board puts another idea in my head."

"What's dat?" asked Henry.

"Dat unless I's mistaken, Mayme'd like a bookshelf in dat house too. A nice big bookshelf full er lots an' lots er books."

"Hmm . . . dat's a good idea, all right. Mayme read lots er books?"

"She an' Miz Katie's always got dere heads in some book or nuther, least it seems dat way ter me. Not dat Mayme's got too many books er her own, but I reckon she will someday."

"Well, den, maybe I'll jest pick up a few more planks in town, narrower den dese, an' see what I kin do. Yes, sir'ee . . . dat's a good idea, all right. You read, Josepha?"

"I kin read all right, I reckon, but I always kept it to myself when I wuz at da McSimmons'."

Henry chuckled.

"You's right, some white folks, dey don't like coloreds knowin' how ter do *too* much. Like readin'."

"Or thinkin' at all . . . dey don't want you ter know how ter hold a single idea in yo head."

This time Henry laughed outright.

"You know how ter read, Henry?" asked Josepha.

"Yep, I do. Not real good, but enuff ter git by. But my ol' master, Mister Clarkson, he hated me fo it. Dey hate what dey call an uppity nigger an' I reckon dat's what I wuz. I wuz a little uppity an' it got me an' Jeremiah an' his mother into trouble. After dat I kept what little readin' I done ter myself."

"You ever read dat *Uncle Tom's Cabin?*"

"Nope, jes' heard plenty 'bout it."

"Nuthin' but trash," said Josepha. "Bein' a slave weren't no picnic, we all know dat, but dat lady didn't know nuthin' 'bout how it really wuz. It sho wuzn't as bad as she tol' it."

"Some folks might not agree wiff you on dat."

She shrugged. "I reckon I din't have it as bad as some."

"Well, Josepha. Now dat you's free," said Henry, "ef you wuz gwine hab a house er yo own someday, an' you had a bookshelf, what kind er books would you put in it?"

"Well, I reckon dere'd hab ter be dat *Pilgrim's Progress*. I ain't never had a copy er my own, but I's seen real pretty ones an' heard it read ter me when I wuz young an' learnin' ter read wiff Miz Grace. An' dere'd have ter be a Bible, wouldn't dere? An' it'd be pretty special ter hab a book ob poems ob my very own. I'd like ter be able ter read more poems sometime. What 'bout you?"

"I don't know . . . neber thought er havin' books er my own. Men don't keep books—dat's mo somefin' for women."

"Nonsense, Henry Patterson—where'd you git a fool notion like dat? Books is fo anybody dat kin read."

Henry chuckled at Josepha's pretended outrage.

"I reckon you's right. I's trying ter teach Jeremiah ter read. Being aroun' Micah got him interested in learnin', an' I reckon I's usin' a book fer dat."

"What book?"

"One er dem *McGuffy Readers* I borrowed from Miz Kathleen."

Henry continued to sand the plank as Josepha stood watching.

"You ever used ter dream 'bout havin' a house er yo own?" Henry asked after a minute.

"What . . . me?" said Josepha.

"Yeah."

"A house . . . ob my own? I wuz a slave, what would I be thinkin' 'bout such things like dat for?"

"I mean after you wuz free."

"How cud I? I wuz too old an' didn't hab a penny ter my name."

"Maybe you's right—din't you eber think 'bout marryin'?"

"Don't reckon I ever did," replied Josepha. "Who'd marry da likes er me? One er my masters tried ter git me married an' I tol' him not ter think ob it ef he wanted my cakes an' breads ter turn out da way he liked."

"Why did you tell him dat?"

Josepha thought a few seconds.

"To tell you da truf, I ain't altogether sure," she said. "At da time I didn't figger I wanted nobody else. Maybe I'd been hurt too many times. Maybe I figgered I cud take care ob myself an' dat wuz fine wiff me."

She paused and a distant look came into her eyes.

"To tell you da truf, Henry," she said again, "I don't know why I said it. But den a woman gits ter my age, when it's too late fo all dat, an' den suddenly she finds herself a free woman, an' I reckon it's natural she'd sometimes wonder ef she made a mistake."

Josepha's voice quivered momentarily. She paused and glanced away. A quick hand against her eyes was the only betrayal of the lone tear that had risen and was quickly brushed away. She drew in a deep breath.

"But den dere ain't no goin' back in life, is dere?" she said.

She looked up at Henry. His hand lay still on the board and he was listening intently.

"Uh . . . uh, no," he said, "dat's da truf—dere ain't no goin' back."

"So what 'bout you," said Josepha. "You wouldn't hab asked a question like dat unless you'd had such notions. So how wuz it dat you thought 'bout havin' yo own house? Dat muster been when you wuz married."

"No, not den," said Henry. "We wuz slaves den too, an' freedom wuz too far off er thing ter see back in dose days. But den when I got my freedom, an' den when Mister Lincoln freed all ob us, dat's when I began ter dream ob findin' Jeremiah's mama an' maybe, jes' maybe gittin' enuff money saved ter hab a house er my own. My own papa dreamed 'bout it, but den I thought dat maybe I cud do it. Really do it. I reckon dat's every man's dream. But den when I foun' out she wuz dead . . . it didn't seem ter matter much no more after dat."

Again it was quiet. Henry looked down at the board beneath his hand and slowly began sanding again, though his thoughts were far away.

"I's sorry 'bout yo wife, Henry," said Josepha after a while. "Must be mighty hard ter love someone an' lose 'em like dat."

Henry nodded. "But like you say, dere's no goin' back. All we kin do is look ahead. Life only goes one direction, don't it—dat's forward."

Josepha took in his words thoughtfully, then turned and began making her way back to the house. Henry watched her go in silence. They were both full of many thoughts, but for the present neither had anything more to say.

That night Josepha lay awake thinking.

Talking with Henry over the last few weeks, gradually telling him her story, and especially today's talk, sent Josepha's mind back to the past more than it had in years.

Would Mose ever really have loved her . . . as a woman? Or had it only been a friendship of childhood and youth?

She would never know. The years had quickly slipped by, and now . . .

She shook from her mind thoughts of what might have been. Choices were made for her, and then she had made her choices through the years too. It was too late for all that, too late to turn back, too late for regrets. Her life was what it was. No more, no less. Just like she had said to Henry, there was no going back.

Henry also lay reflecting on his talk with Josepha. But whereas Josepha was thinking about what had *never* been and what was too late for her to know, Henry was thinking about what had been and what he *had* known. He thought of his papa and mama, but especially about Jeremiah's mother, Lacina. Not a day went by that he did not think of her. He had lost his life's only love and had never expected to love another.

But these last few weeks he had found himself genuine enjoying the company of a woman his own age again. Everyone else was wonderful to him. Templeton and Ward had become good friends. But there was something different about laughing and talking and sharing with a woman of your own kind, your own background, who had been through some of the same kinds of things and was at the same stage on life's journey. It wasn't the kind of friendship you could have with another man, or that a black man could have with a white man.

He hoped Lacina didn't mind. He was sure she would understand.

Henry continued to lay awake thinking about the day recently past. He had not expected it, not suspected how slowly and invisibly a quiet affection for the dear lady had snuck up on him.

He smiled to himself as he thought of her. She was different than Lacina. They were as different as two ladies could be. But he wouldn't want them to be the same.

Was it too late, he wondered—too late for the kinds of strange sensations he felt stirring within him for the first time in more than twenty years?

Or was it ever too late for love?

Talk About the Past
28

*O*ne day I was in my room. I'd been spending a lot of time upstairs since the snake bite. I seemed to get tired easily and usually had to lay down for a nap on most days.

I heard Henry's hammer in the distance. I looked out the window and there was Josepha on her way down to see him. I kept watching. She got there and Henry stopped hammering. Pretty soon I could hear faint laughter. It was so nice to see Josepha laugh.

I turned and began to go downstairs. Voices from below stopped me.

It was Katie and her two uncles talking.

I didn't want to intrude, so I sat down on the stairs and listened. I didn't feel too much like I was eavesdropping, since they were my kin too.

⤿ ❊ ⤾

". . . doing in California, Uncle Ward?" Katie had just asked.

"Trying to find gold, little girl—what else?"

"And you did too!" laughed Katie. "But why did you go to California in the first place? Was it only for the gold?"

It was silent a moment.

"I don't know. I was always sort of like the black sheep of the family," said Ward after a bit.

"I thought that honor was reserved for me!" laughed Templeton.

"Maybe we both were," said Uncle Ward. "The two girls—your mama and Nelda—did what they were told and we two boys were always in trouble for something. Boy, Pa could black our bottoms with his belt and with that paddle of his."

"That thing stung like the devil!" said Templeton.

"But God bless him," said Ward, "he knew right from wrong and was determined to get the difference through our thick skulls. But you were smooth. You could talk your way out of anything."

"Not with Pa!" laughed Templeton. "He always saw through me."

"Yeah, but with everyone else."

"Did it bother you?" asked Templeton.

Ward seemed to think a minute.

"I don't reckon I ever thought about it much," he said. "I don't think I blamed you about it. That's just the way you were. I knew you meant me no harm. But it did rile me sometimes that everyone else—everyone but Pa, that is—couldn't see past it like I could and that things fell on me instead."

Templeton chuckled a little sadly.

"I am sorry about that, Ward," he said. "I was just a conniving little kid who didn't know any better. I suppose I learned early that I could fast-talk my way through most things with a smile or two, and I never stopped to think about what might be happening to you."

He paused.

"Who am I trying to kid?" he went on. "I did know better. I knew it was wrong. But when you're young you don't see that wrong really is wrong."

"Yeah, well . . . that was a long time ago. No hard feelings. You were my brother and best friend. Life was always fun with you, but by the time we were sixteen, eighteen, something like that, I figured I'd be better off maybe keeping my distance from you. Maybe I just wanted to be my own man, I don't know. I reckon I'd felt a mite overshadowed by you and maybe I needed to know who Ward Daniels was all by himself."

"So what did you do, Uncle Ward?" asked Katie.

"I left home and bounced around on what jobs I could get for a few years—"

He stopped. "It was hard on Ma and Pa, wasn't it?" he asked, turning to his brother.

"Your leaving . . . yeah, it was," replied Templeton. "Ma cried and cried after you left. Pa was just quiet. Back then I always used to think those silent spells of his meant that he was mad. I hated it when he got quiet. Later I realized that he was just hurting inside. He carried his love deep. That was Pa."

"He cared about us more than we ever knew."

"Yep, you're right about that. But we were just boys. We couldn't see it until it was too late and he was gone."

"Where did you go, Uncle Ward?" asked Katie.

"I bounced around from here to there—St. Louis, Chicago, Memphis. If you went west, you could always find work of some kind—pounding nails, digging ditches. The country was spreading west and there was plenty to do. Of course, back in those days St. Louis was a western frontier town. Things have changed since then! I just worked enough to keep traveling about. I saw a lot of country, but now I regret I didn't keep in closer touch. I never wrote home—they never had any idea where I was. By the time I finally went back, Pa was gone."

He sighed and the room got real quiet.

"I miss him, you know, Templeton," said Ward at length. "We thought he was pretty hard on us, but he really wasn't. He just wanted us to learn to keep our mouths shut and show respect. He was a good man. Actually, he was a good friend to us when we were growing up. Remember how we used to laugh and play with him? But . . . after I left I never saw him again. I never knew what we had till it was too late. By then Ma was older and I'd hurt her so much by the way I just left without a word that we could never really patch it up. I'm not saying she didn't forgive me. Knowing Ma, I'm sure she did. But I had hurt her too deep. She had the two girls, and it was like we split into two families—the girls and the boys. You ever think of that, Templeton?"

"Can't say I did. But now that you say it like that, it's kind of how it was, all right."

"Then the news of the gold hit and I was on my way within a week. That was just the kind of adventure I'd been looking for! Remember how I talked you into going with me, Templeton?"

Templeton laughed. "How could I forget? I thought I would never forgive you during those months on the trail! Indians, sun, rain, draught, snakes . . . weeks and weeks in the saddle! I wasn't cut out for that kind of thing. It wasn't my idea of a good life. But once we got to California . . . San Francisco was something in those days, wasn't it, Ward?"

"A wide-open raucous place!" laughed Ward. "I wonder what it's like now. Maybe we ought to go back sometime, Templeton. We could take the train now."

"I don't know, brother Ward. Don't you think we're getting a little old for such adventures?"

"Probably. But I'd still like to see the place again."

"What did you do?" asked Katie.

"Same thing as thousands of other men were doing— we wandered around up in the gold country looking for a place to stake a claim that wasn't already taken."

"Did you find one?"

"We bounced around some, working the rivers and streams. There was gold too, but it was hard work. We worked a short while in a little place called Miracle Springs—remember that old prospector who helped us get started . . . what was his name?"

"Jones, wasn't it?"

"That's it—Alkali Jones! What a character. But he did right by us and I started doing pretty well."

"And Drum Hollister and Parish's Mine and Freight— there were some good folks in that town."

"What about you, Uncle Templeton?" asked Katie.

"The work was too hard for me!" laughed Templeton. "I couldn't get as excited as Ward did about a few little flakes of gold in the bottom of a pan. So I went to Sacramento, and that's when I discovered I had a knack for cards. I think I made almost as much at poker as Ward did in the gold fields."

"I'm sure you made a lot more than I did," said Ward. "But you also lost as much as you won."

"Is that true, Uncle Templeton?"

"I'm afraid that's the way poker is. Your Uncle Ward was a steady worker, I was a flighty poker player. I played honest and I don't think I ever once cheated in my life. But I sometimes played reckless. So when all was said and done, he had stashed away a couple thousand dollars of dust and nuggets, and I had maybe a hundred to my name."

"And then you came back east?"

"I came back first," said Templeton. "There was some trouble brewing and that's when Ward and I parted ways."

"What kind of trouble?"

"There was always trouble in the gold fields, Kathleen," sighed Ward. "Money doesn't usually attract the best crowd. The lure of wealth is sometimes stronger on men who aren't altogether honest inside. I don't know why that is. Seems puzzling now that I think of it. But it's the way it is. The more dishonest a man, the more he'll go chasing after money, and do whatever it takes to get it. So there were all kinds of bad men out there—and they fought and lied and cheated for that gold, because there was lots of gold in those days. And they killed for it too."

He drew in a deep breath.

"I got involved in a ruckus with two or three men who were trying to rustle claims where I was working. They figured no one would stand up to them because several of us were working alone on the Yuba River north of Nevada City. They came one night and were going to run out an old man whose claim was next to mine. The gunshots woke me up. I grabbed my rifle and hurried outside. I snuck to the man's little cabin just in time to see them shoot him in the head as he was pleading for his life. All for a claim probably worth less than five hundred dollars. I went berserk and starting firing through the window, and when I came to myself, one of the men was dead and the others riding away yelling that they'd get me no matter how long it took. I'd run them off before they found my neighbor's gold.

"I could hardly believe what I'd done. I was in shock as I stood with my rifle in my hand in his cabin over two dead bodies. I'd learned to be a crack shot and now I regretted it. I knew they'd be back. One of them was a man named Bilsby, who already had a reputation as a killer. He wasn't much older than a kid back then, but he was a bad one."

"Bilsby!" said Katie. The very word still sent a chill up her spine.

"I threw the rifle from my hands," Ward went on, "vowing I'd never pick up a gun again as long as I lived. I knew Bilsby'd come after me. So that same night I cleared out. I buried Mac—an old Irishman—gathered up his gold and took it with me, along with some letters I found in his place, hoping I'd be able to find an address and send the money to whatever kin he had. Then I cleared out all my own belongings, and my gold, and by morning I was miles away.

"I never looked back. I made my way back east and that's when I went to your mama, Kathleen, and gave her the gold. After that it was just a matter of staying ahead of Bilsby and his gang. It wasn't as if I had that much gold to make it worth following me all those years. I think he was more bent on revenge than anything."

"I think he thought you had more than you did," said Templeton. "I can't imagine he'd have kept on our trail for a few hundred dollars. But I don't suppose we'll ever know now."

"Not likely," sighed Ward.

There was a long silence.

"What about you, Uncle Templeton?" asked Katie. "Didn't you come back from California sooner than Uncle Ward?"

"Yeah, I did. I won enough money to book passage back east on a steamer. It was a lot easier than riding two thousand miles on the back of a horse."

"What did you do then?"

"After discovering that I was pretty good with cards, that's mostly what I did. I moved around, played from city to city, most of the big hotels, spent some time up and down the Mississippi. I suppose I thought it was a good life, but looking back now it seems pretty empty. I don't know what I was thinking."

MRS. HAMMOND
29

*T*he work on the remodeling of the cabin had been
going on now for several months. Henry still went
into town to the livery three, four, sometimes five
days a week. He didn't seem to relish going to town
like he used to, except that most of the time he and
Jeremiah rode in together, which they both liked.

Things were different in Greens Crossing by that
time. It wasn't comfortable being black, and I know
both Henry and Jeremiah felt it. I reckon it had
never been comfortable being black in a white man's
world. But it was worse now. The looks that came
our way were mean and frightening. Josepha hardly
ever went to town, and I only went when I was with
Katie or Papa or Uncle Ward. Jeremiah had to watch
himself especially close because it seemed that
young white no-goods wanted nothing more than to
beat up a strong young black man. Jeremiah never
went anywhere with me or Katie, knowing that
would rile anyone who saw him. Any trouble he got

into with Deke Steeves or any other of the rowdy white boys could bring danger to us all, and he knew it.

But someone had to go into town at least once a week to get our mail and a few supplies. And Papa and Uncle Ward liked to keep up on what was going on and so we always got a newspaper too.

Katie and I went into the store one day while Papa was talking to Mr. Watson at the mill about something. Mrs. Hammond was alone behind her counter. She glanced up as we walked in and a strange look came over her face. A brief little smile crossed her lips. It was the first thing like that I'd ever seen from her. Maybe she smiled when Katie came into the store alone, but never when I was around.

"Hello, young ladies," she said. Her voice was quieter than usual, like she wasn't feeling well.

"Hi, Mrs. Hammond," said Katie. "We're here for our mail and a newspaper and a few things."

Mrs. Hammond pulled out our mail from underneath and set it on the counter.

"Looks like you have a letter from up north . . . Pennsylvania," she said.

Katie picked up the letter and glanced at it.

"It's from my aunt Nelda—my mother's sister," she said. "My uncles' sister too."

"Ah . . . your aunt—you're Northerners, then?"

"My mother and uncles came from Pennsylvania," said Katie. "I suppose the only reason we're down here in North Carolina is because my mother married my father and moved down here with him."

"Your mother was a fine woman—strong and a hard worker, and was always nice to folks."

Mrs. Hammond paused, and again that strange expression came over her face.

"I remember the day she first came into the store," she said. "She couldn't have been much older than you are now, Kathleen. Her voice sounded so strange to me—so Northern. But I got used to it. She had that darkie girl of hers with her—"

She glanced momentarily at me.

"They always came in together," she went on to Katie, "—just like the two of you. I don't even think I ever knew the girl's name."

"Lemuela," I said.

"Ah . . . hmm . . ." She nodded. "They were always together, just like you. When you walked in just now I was reminded of them, especially of your mama, Kathleen. You look more like her every day."

Again she glanced at me with an inquisitive expression.

Just then Mrs. Hammond's hand went to her face and she turned pale. She groped for the stool behind the counter and sat down.

"Mrs. Hammond, what is it?" asked Katie in alarm. "Are you ill?"

Mrs. Hammond tried to force a smile.

"I haven't been feeling too well," she said.

"Have you seen the doctor?"

"No, I don't have time. I have to keep the store open."

"But if you are sick—"

"I will be all right. I can't . . . you know, close the store. If people—"

She paused and looked away. Her voice sounded different than it ever had before.

"What is it, Mrs. Hammond?" asked Katie.

"If people . . . you know, if I was closed they would start going to the store in Oakwood—"

"They would understand. Everybody gets sick once in a while."

"I can't take any chances. No one in town likes me, you know that, Kathleen. No one would care . . . and I can't say I would blame them.—No," she added, drawing in a deep breath of resolve and standing up again, "I must keep the store open. I will be fine. Now, what else was it you needed, Kathleen?"

Katie and I exchanged brief looks, but said nothing. Within moments Mrs. Hammond was her same usual gruff self. When another customer came in a minute later, no one would have been able to tell she was the least bit different.

All the way home Katie and I couldn't stop thinking about her. To feel sorry for Mrs. Hammond was the last thing I'd ever expected to feel. But I did. I know Katie did too. It wasn't just that she seemed sick, she seemed sad too, in a way neither of us had ever noticed before.

But even then I didn't know what Katie was thinking.

As soon as we got home we walked into the

house. Josepha and Henry were sitting at the table talking together.

"Josepha," said Katie, "would you cook up a batch of your chicken broth this afternoon?"

"Sure, Miz Katie," replied Josepha. "You got a hankering for chicken soup?"

"No, but Mrs. Hammond in town isn't feeling well. I thought it would be a neighborly thing to do to take her some. She's having a hard enough time keeping the store open without having to worry about cooking for herself."

"You want to take my broth to Mrs. Hammond?"

"Why not?"

"Cuz she'd likely throw it out!"

"Well, I want to try anyway. I'm going into town again tomorrow morning. Nobody has to go with me if they don't want to, but I'm going regardless and I want to take her some soup."

"Well, I'll make you da broff," said Josepha, "as a favor to you. But I still ain't gonna be doing dat lady no favors. Not after da way I seen her treat colored folk."

Katie and I glanced at each other, but Katie said nothing more.

The next morning bright and early Katie and I set off again for Greens Crossing.

We got to town well after the time when Mrs. Hammond's store should have been open—it was probably eight-thirty or nine o'clock. But the front door of the shop was locked and there was no sign of life inside.

"We'll go around back," said Katie.

The back door into where Mrs. Hammond lived up the stairs above the shop was unlocked.

Katie knocked, then opened it a crack and called inside.

"Mrs. Hammond . . . Mrs. Hammond, it's me— Kathleen Clairborne."

But there was no sign of life here either.

"Mrs. Hammond," Katie called again. "Mrs. Hammond . . . it's Katie Clairborne."

Still there was no reply. Katie opened the door wider and crept inside. Timidly I followed. I wouldn't have dared to do anything like this without Katie. She was a lot braver than me. And she was white, which made a difference too.

Neither of us had ever been inside Mrs. Hammond's house before, but Katie went straight for the stairs and tiptoed up them. It was so quiet, I couldn't help being a little afraid. But I followed, carrying the pot of soup.

We reached the top. The door was ajar.

"Mrs. Hammond," said Katie, walking into her sitting room. "Mrs. Hammond, it's Kathleen Clairborne."

Still there was no sign of her.

"Mrs. Hammond . . ."

A faint moan sounded from a room to our right.

Katie hurried toward it. I waited.

Katie disappeared inside the bedroom. I heard another moan, then sounds of recognition.

"Mayme!" Katie called out, "she's on the floor.—

Oh, Mrs. Hammond, what is the matter!"

"I'm not well . . . I couldn't get up."

"We're here now, Mrs. Hammond. We'll take care of you. We brought you some chicken broth, didn't we, Mayme.—Mayme, come in and help me get her into bed!"

Mrs. Hammond glanced up at me from where she lay, and I thought I saw the hint of a smile.

We got on both sides of her and were able to get her back into bed.

"That's so good of you girls," she said. "I don't deserve such kindness. I'm just a grumpy old—"

"Don't talk like that, Mrs. Hammond," interrupted Katie. "This is what friends and neighbors are for. Mayme, why don't you see if you can get a fire started in the cook stove and then get that soup warming.—Mrs. Hammond, what else can we do for you?"

"The store . . . what time is it?"

"I think it's close to nine o'clock."

"Oh, my goodness . . . I have to open the shop."

She struggled to sit up in bed, but her face was pale and she was obviously weak.

"You just lie still and rest, Mrs. Hammond," said Katie. "You tell me what to do and I'll go downstairs and open the store. Mayme will heat up the soup. I'll come up if I have any questions."

"That's so good of you, Kathleen. I don't . . . let me see . . . all right . . . the key to the door is hanging on a nail behind the counter. The mail is behind the counter. If people want to buy something, just write down their names and what it is and tell them I will give them a bill later. I don't think anyone will mind."

"No one will mind, Mrs. Hammond. If I have questions, I'll come up or call for Mayme. You just rest and if you're not feeling better soon, we'll send for the doctor."

Katie left the bedroom and went downstairs, leaving me alone with Mrs. Hammond. I went into her kitchen to make a fire. There were no coals left, which I'd figured from how cold it was. But with Mrs. Hammond's supplies and some old newspapers, I had a fire going before long and the pot of soup on top of the cook stove. Then I made a fire in the woodstove in her sitting room. Just as I had a few sticks of kindling burning, Katie came back up the stairs.

"How is she doing?" she asked.

"I don't know," I answered. "I just got the fires started."

Katie went into the bedroom. Mrs. Hammond was sitting up trying to take off her nightclothes.

"Would you like me to help you get dressed?" Katie asked.

"Yes, thank you dear," she said. "I'm sorry to be such a bother."

"You are not a bother, Mrs. Hammond," said Katie, getting her dress from where it lay draped over the chest of drawers from the night before. "Everyone needs a little help sometimes."

Together they got the dress over her head.

"Mr. Thurston was in. He said you were going to fill an order for him."

"Oh, yes . . . I'd . . . I'd forgotten to finish it."

"Just tell me what to do."

"Is he waiting?"

"No, he had some other errands. He said he would come back when he was done with them. He said to give you his regards and he hopes you will be feeling better."

Katie buttoned the last of Mrs. Hammond's buttons and then helped her lie back down.

"That is very kind of him. He is a good man." Mrs. Hammond sighed like she was already too tired out to keep talking.

"What should I do about his order?" asked Katie.

"I had started gathering it together. There is a small pile of things to the left of the counter."

"Yes, I saw it."

"His list is with it . . . I think. If you want to, Kathleen . . . you can try to find the things. If you can't find something, come ask me."

Katie pulled the blanket back up over her and turned to go. Mrs. Hammond reached out and took Katie's hand.

"Thank you, Kathleen," she said, smiling again. "This means more to me than I can tell you."

Katie smiled back, then returned downstairs to the shop.

I was a little timid about being left alone with Mrs. Hammond, especially knowing how she felt about blacks. So I stayed in the other room, tending the fires and stirring the soup until steam finally began to rise from the pot.

When I thought the soup was ready, I looked around and found a ladle, a bowl, and a spoon. I ladled two scoops into the bowl, then walked toward the bedroom and poked my head inside.

"Mrs. Hammond?" I said nervously.

She was still in bed just like Katie had left her. She glanced toward me.

"Hello . . . uh, Mayme, isn't it?"

"Yes, ma'am.—Would you like some of the broth Josepha made for you? I think it's hot enough."

"It smells so good," she sighed. "I've been lying here for the last five minutes thinking of nothing else."

I walked forward and stood beside the bed.

"It's all right," she said. "You can sit down."

I sat down on the edge of the bed next to her, still holding the bowl and spoon.

"Do you, uh . . . shall I set this on the night-stand?" I asked.

"I don't think I could get up to eat it just now."

"Would you, uh . . . like me to help you?"

"That would be nice—it smells so good!"

I set the bowl on the nightstand.

"Just help me sit up," she said.

Gingerly I reached my arm around her shoulders and eased her up from the bed. I couldn't believe I was doing this! And sitting on Mrs. Hammond's bed! But she didn't seem to mind.

"Here . . . prop those pillows behind my back . . .

that's it . . . oh, that's better. Thank you! Now spoon me some of that nice broth. I don't want to hold the bowl . . . I'm afraid I might drop it."

I took the bowl again, and even more gingerly took out a spoonful and set it to her lips. She took it and swallowed it, closing her eyes and sighing.

"That is delicious!" she said. "I didn't realize how hungry I was. I didn't eat anything last night because I went straight to bed."

I gave her a second spoonful, then a third, and before long the bowl was empty.

As I was pulling the spoon back from her mouth, Mrs. Hammond reached up with her hand that had been lying on the blanket. Gently she stretched out two fingers and touched the back of my hand. The look on her face was almost one of curiosity.

"Your skin is brown," she said.

"I'm a Negro," I said.

"Yes," she smiled. "I know. I've never touched colored skin before. It feels the same as white skin."

Her words reminded me of my first days at Rosewood. "It was funny for me when I first touched Katie's skin," I said.

"When was that?" she asked.

"When I went to Rosewood after my family and hers were killed."

"The two of you so remind me of Katie's mother and her colored friend. What did you say her name was?"

"Lemuela."

Mrs. Hammond nodded. "They were such good

friends, just like you and Kathleen. I never had a friend like that."

"I've never had a friend like Katie," I said.

"It's strange," said Mrs. Hammond. "I know Kathleen bears a resemblance to her mother. But you—and I know what they say about whites thinking all coloreds look alike, but I don't really think that—but what I was going to say is that—and I didn't see her that many times, but if my memory isn't playing tricks on me, it seems that you look a little like Rosalind's slave."

"She was my mother," I said. "She wasn't a slave. She was from the North. She was free."

Mrs. Hammond gasped in astonishment.

"You don't say!"

I nodded. "Katie's father sold her to Mr. McSimmons . . . the older Mr. McSimmons, when he found out that my mother was carrying me."

"Well, I never!"

"And your father . . ."

"My father is Templeton Daniels," I said. "Katie and I are cousins."

"Well, I . . . that does explain a great deal."

I went on to tell her the rest of the story.

Mrs. Hammond was quiet a long time after I finished telling her about Katie's and my families. I didn't know what she might be thinking.

"I didn't know all that," she said finally. "It must have been very hard on you and Kathleen."

"I reckon it was," I said. "But we grew close through it and weathered it. God's been mighty good to us to bring us a new family. I might not have met my father otherwise."

"Templeton Daniels is really your father?"

"Yes, ma'am."

"He seems a nice man."

"He is, ma'am."

"I'm afraid I haven't been as gracious to him as I ought to have been," she said a little sadly. "But he always treats me kindly in return.—Is Mayme your real name?"

"My full name is Mary Ann," I said.

"Oh . . . Mary Ann—that is a nice name. Do you think I could have a little more of that soup, Mary Ann? I'm feeling better already."

"Yes, ma'am, I'll get you some more."

I started to get up, and like she had done with Katie, she took hold of my arm. I paused and glanced down at her where she lay. She was looking at my brown arm, with her white fingers around it. Then she looked up at me, smiled, and released my arm. I stood up and walked back into the other room.

⤜ ❋ ⤏

SHOPKEEPER KATIE
30

*W*hen we got back to Rosewood that evening, Papa and Uncle Ward and Josepha were all worried about us, since we had been gone all day. Jeremiah rode up behind us on his way home from Mr. Watson's, surprised to see us too. We rode the rest of the way together.

"Where have you two been!" asked Papa as we clattered up in the buggy, Jeremiah on his horse beside us. "I was just about to go out looking for you."

"We went to Mrs. Hammond's," said Katie.

"I know that . . . but all day?"

"She was on the floor when we got there and was too weak to get up. So I ran her store for the day while Mayme took care of her upstairs."

"What!" laughed Papa, looking at me. "You took care . . . of Mrs. Hammond!"

"It was great fun!" said Katie as we got down. "I

was surprised how nearly everyone who came into the shop knew who I was. Most of the people were real nice."

"And she let you nursemaid her?" said Papa to me.

"She was as nice as she could be," I said. "I was surprised too. Later I went for the doctor to ask him to call on her. She seemed appreciative of our help, didn't she, Katie?"

"I would never have believed it."

"Sounds like you won her over, all right. Is she feeling better?"

"Yes, but she's still pale. The doctor said she needs to rest for a few days and drink as much as she can—and finish up Josepha's chicken soup. We're going back in tomorrow to help with the store again. Now that I know what to do, I'll enjoy it even more!"

"My niece, the shopkeeper!" laughed Papa. "—What about you, Mary Ann?"

"I'll go into town too," I answered. "But I'm not sure Greens Crossing, or Mrs. Hammond either for that matter, is ready for a colored shopkeeper. Not that I wouldn't like to try to help. Katie had the time of her life. She didn't stop talking about it all the way home."

Katie laughed and we went inside and repeated the whole story to Josepha, Uncle Ward, and Henry, who were already at the table as Josepha was just finishing up supper preparations. Jeremiah had had a good day too at the mill and we were all in pretty good spirits.

"Josepha," said Katie as we sat around the table eating, "I'm sorry to ask so late in the day, but you wouldn't mind making up another pot of soup for Mrs. Hammond this evening, would you? She enjoyed that broth so much. She said to tell you thank you."

Josepha nodded but said nothing. She didn't seem in as good spirits as the rest of us.

"What's on your mind, Josepha?" said Uncle Ward. "Did something happen today that's got this supper turning sour in your mouth? You look like you're about ready to start grumping at us."

"It ain't dat," she said. "I just ain't fond er da notion er sweatin' over da cook stove fo da likes er dat lady."

"But she's sick," said Katie. "She needs our help."

"That's what neighbors are for," said Papa.

"But we ain't her neighbors."

"We're neighbors to everybody," said Katie, "at least everybody we want to be a neighbor to. And maybe her own neighbors aren't being as neighborly as they ought to be."

"Well, she ain't my neighbor, an' she ain't never treated me neighborly, nohow."

"We all know that Mrs. Hammond hasn't been in the habit of treating anyone too neighborly!" laughed Papa. "But people can change."

"I don't know dat she can," muttered Josepha.

"What are you talking about!" laughed Papa.

"Look at me . . . Kathleen can tell you, when I used to come around visiting here I stole her mama's money from the cookie jar."

"It was a coffee can, Uncle Templeton," smiled Katie.

"Well, there you are—from the coffee can! But gradually I changed and Kathleen forgave me, and here I am."

"We've all changed," I said. "I can hardly imagine how different I am now than when I came to Rosewood."

"We've all grown," added Katie. "That's what growth is, isn't it?—learning to change and live with people, and maybe forgive them too."

"All I know is dat dat lady ain't never been nuthin' but ornery an' mean ter me an' Miz Mayme, so why should I or any ob us be nice ter her?"

"Maybe because she's trying to change, like Kathleen says," said Uncle Ward.

"Den let her change an' den maybe I'll see."

"But, Josepha," said Katie, "maybe people have to change together. What if she needs our help to grow?"

"How you figger dat?"

"Well, maybe we've got to match a little spark of growth in someone else with a little spark of growth in ourselves to keep the spark in them alive. I don't think that explains it very well, but it's something like what I'm feeling. Maybe it's something inside us that makes the other person want to grow more, and then again we have to respond by changing some more too, and pretty soon two people are growing closer together because both were willing to change a little bit at a time. All growth comes a little bit at a time, doesn't it, Uncle Templeton? Everybody's got to be willing to do their share, or they don't grow and change, and instead get stale inside."

"I think you've explained it about as well as anyone could, Kathleen," said Papa. "Mary Ann and I had a struggle getting used to each other at first, didn't we, little girl?" he added, turning to me. "We changed together, just like you say."

"Well, you an' Mayme's gone visitin' her," said Josepha, "an' I done made da broff, an' I'll do like you say an' make some mo soup tonight."

"But maybe Mrs. Hammond needs more from you than that," said Katie.

"Like what? What cud she need from me? I hardly know da lady, 'ceptin' a time or two when I wuz in her store an' she looked at me wiff her nose in da air like I wuz somethin' dat come in on da bottom ob somebody's boot."

"She might need something from you that no one else in the whole world can give her," persisted Katie.

"An' what cud dat be?"

"She might need your forgiveness, Josepha," said Katie. "No one else can give her that—nobody but you. And maybe that's what she needs so that she can keep growing inside—forgiveness . . . from all of us. If she's trying to change, and we forgive her and grow and change ourselves, then she'll be able to keep growing all the more."

We all sat quietly thinking about what Katie had said. I think we were as amazed at the wisdom she had as at anything she had actually said, although that was amazing in itself. She had really grown into a lady who understood life and people. Her mother would sure be proud of her! The look on Henry's face was almost like he had known that wisdom was there all along. But when he glanced at Josepha, the look on his face changed. I could tell he was concerned about the things she had said.

We went into Greens Crossing again the next morning about the same time, with another batch of soup and a loaf of fresh bread and butter. Katie had put a notice on the door of Mrs. Hammond's store the day before, saying that the shop wouldn't open until nine so that we would be sure to be there on time. And she told Mrs. Hammond to stay in bed until we got there. The doctor had said she needed to get at least two good days of rest before going back to work.

We arrived and went upstairs. She greeted us almost like old friends. The change because of what had happened the day before was amazing. It was like seeing what Katie had said at supper the night before coming true right before our eyes.

Mrs. Hammond was much better. We could tell that from one look at her. But she stayed in bed like Katie had said and let us take care of her like the day before. Katie helped her get dressed and I got the fires going again in her two stoves and made her something to eat while Katie went downstairs to open the shop. I swept the floors and emptied the chamber pot and brought clean water for her washbasin. Mrs. Hammond had her strength back enough to hold the bowl of soup herself this time, so I didn't feed her. But she still wanted me to sit on the bedside with her. She talked to me like we'd been friends for years. My being colored never came up again. I think she had already started not to notice the color of my skin.

"The week's mail delivery should arrive today, Kathleen," she said when Katie came back up after about an hour. "I will have to sign for it. Bring up the paper when the delivery man comes."

Katie went back downstairs, and Mrs. Hammond and I talked some more as she ate what was left of what I had brought her. The mail delivery came. Katie brought up the paper for Mrs. Hammond to sign.

"You can take the mail out of the bag, Kathleen," said Mrs. Hammond, "and sort it alphabetically by names. Then if anyone comes in and asks for their mail, you can find it easily."

Katie nodded and returned downstairs.

"You and Kathleen are good friends, aren't you?" said Mrs. Hammond. "I don't think I've hardly ever seen you when you weren't together."

"The best of friends," I said. "We both say that we couldn't have survived after the war without each other."

"No one knew you two were alone out there,"

said Mrs. Hammond. "Everyone thought Rosalind was still alive."

I smiled. "We had to work hard to make it seem like everything was normal," I said. "It was Katie's idea. She thought if people found out, they would send us both away. Actually, I thought so too. We were both afraid for our own reasons. She was worried about her uncle. I was afraid of being beaten or sold or killed."

"I had my suspicions that something funny was going on, but—"

Mrs. Hammond paused briefly.

"Well, that's not entirely true," she said. "I suppose I was suspicious of everything and everybody. I haven't been a very nice person sometimes. But," she laughed sheepishly, almost like a little girl, "at first you fooled me too! Then after it came out, I tried to pretend that I'd known all along . . . but I really hadn't."

I laughed and Mrs. Hammond laughed again along with me. I'd never heard her laugh before. Imagine—me sitting on the side of Mrs. Hammond's bed serving her food, and us laughing together!

"I always try to make people think I know more than I do," she added. "It's one of my worst faults. I know I shouldn't, but I've been doing it so long— trying to make myself look good in other people's eyes, that pretty soon it was second nature. But I don't think I ever really fooled anyone."

"It's hard to make yourself look good in other people's eyes if you're black," I said. "Everyone looks down on you—whites, I mean, not other blacks."

Mrs. Hammond seemed to take in what I said thoughtfully, as though the idea of what it was like to be black had never occurred to her.

"Were you a slave, Mayme?" she asked.

"Yes, ma'am. At the McSimmons plantation."

"Oh yes, of course. Was it . . . was it pretty terrible?"

"I was young," I said. "It was far worse for the older ones. But still, I was whipped four times and hung once. I would have died if Katie and Jeremiah and Emma hadn't rescued me."

"That's awful."

"That's what they did to slaves, Mrs. Hammond."

Again she pondered my words.

"Why don't you talk like a colored?" she asked.

"My mama was raised with Katie's mother, so she spoke better. And Katie helped me after I came to Rosewood, and I practiced at it because I wanted to learn. Katie taught me to read better too, and now I can read pretty well."

"You're lucky, being friends like you are."

"And cousins," I said.

"Oh yes, I almost forgot. I never had a friend like that."

"Did you have brothers and sisters?" I asked.

"No, I was an only child," said Mrs. Hammond. "My parents died when I was young and I went to stay with an aunt in Charlotte. When she died I received a small inheritance, just enough to open this store."

"When did you get married, Mrs. Hammond?"

An embarrassed look came over her face. "I've never been married," she said. "I just called myself Missus when I came here so that people wouldn't think I was alone . . . or maybe so I wouldn't feel so alone myself."

All of a sudden we were interrupted by Katie's steps running up the stairs from the shop.

"Mayme, Mayme . . . guess what!" she cried as she reached the top. "There's a letter from Emma and Micah!"

Suddenly Katie realized what she'd done, running right into Mrs. Hammond's bedroom like it was her own. A timid look came over her face.

"I'm sorry for yelling, Mrs. Hammond," she said. "I was just excited."

"That's all right, Kathleen. It is nice to hear happy sounds. My house is always so quiet. Who is this letter from?"

"Emma, the black girl who was living with us— the one with the son . . . who was drowned . . . she had escaped from the McSimmons plantation right after the war."

"Oh . . . oh, yes—that unpleasantness."

"She married Micah Duff, the black buffalo soldier who came to town a while back. I think you were the first person he saw in Greens Crossing. You sent him to Henry, and Henry sent him to us, and he and Emma fell in love and got married and are now on their way west to Oregon."

"Open the letter!" I said excitedly. "I wonder where they are."

Katie tore open the envelope, took out the single sheet, and began to read.

"Dear Katie and Mayme and Templeton and Ward and Josepha and Henry and Jeremiah,

"Emma and I are well and happy. We made it to Independence, Missouri, and there bought tickets on the railroad to California. Emma misses you all dearly and sends her love. Sometimes she doesn't know whether to laugh for happiness at our adventure together or cry for the memory of how much she loves and misses William and you all. She does quite a bit of both!"

I glanced over at Katie. She wiped a tear or two from her eyes and blinked several times to keep reading. I was fighting back the tears too!

"We are in Ogden, in the salt country of the Mormon settlers in the Utah Territory. We got off the train for a few days to rest. We must now decide whether to continue to California when the next train comes through, or to buy supplies and join a wagon train for Oregon. The railroad from here goes southwest, while the Oregon Trail moves north toward the Columbia River. The railroad is easier and faster, but as you know I had my heart set on Oregon.

"Whatever we decide, we ought to be over the mountains and to the Pacific well before the winter snows. A few early snows on the Rockies, though pretty, remind us that we are at the mercy of the elements and that we must continue to press on.

"I hope this letter arrives safely and that Mrs. Hammond gets it to you. I know she never—"

Katie paused and glanced at the bed.

"Go ahead, dear," said Mrs. Hammond. "Whatever he says, I won't mind."

"—I know she never thought much of me," Katie went on, "but there is a soft spot in my heart for the dear lady, because, as circumstances work themselves out, had I not gone in to see her when I first arrived in Greens Crossing, who can tell, I might never have met you all . . . and my dear Emma."

I glanced unconsciously toward Mrs. Hammond. She was looking down at the bedcovers with kind of a sad look on her face.

"We long for news of you all, but know we will have to wait until we are in the West for you to be able to write to us. We both send our love. You are dear to our hearts."

A bell sounded from below.

"Uh-oh—a customer!" said Katie. "I'm almost done.

"You are dear to our hearts," she read again.
"We miss you and thank you for everything.
  "God's best to you all.
  "Micah Duff"

Katie dashed downstairs, leaving me alone again with Mrs. Hammond.

꘎ ✳ ꘎

A Visit
31

*B*y late afternoon of the second day we had spent with her, Mrs. Hammond was feeling so much better that she told me she was ready to go downstairs to the shop. We went down together, and she told Katie that she was feeling better and that we should get on our way home before it was too late. She could handle things alone for the last hour or two. The color had returned to her face and she seemed to have most of her energy back. She assured us that she would be fine for the rest of the week.

She thanked us again and we set out for Rosewood. I thought about waiting for Jeremiah and riding back with him, but realized it probably wasn't such a good idea to stay in town alone.

Everyone back at Rosewood was just as excited as we had been about the letter from Micah and Emma. It got read two or three times and there were more tears in that house than just Katie's and mine!

We had helped Mrs. Hammond on Wednesday

and Thursday. We heard nothing more from town until midway through Sunday afternoon several hours after those of us who had gone to church—Katie and me and Papa—had returned to Rosewood.

A buggy pulled by a single horse approached. Uncle Ward, who was the only one outside, was surprised to see Mrs. Hammond driving up toward the house.

"Mrs. Hammond, good day to you," he said, taking the reins of her horse and helping her down from the buggy.

"Thank you, Mr. Daniels," she said.

"Are you sure you're well enough to be out riding?" he asked as he tied the reins to a hitching rail.

Mrs. Hammond smiled. "I needed some fresh air, and well . . . I just felt like—"

"Come in," he interrupted, "—everyone else is inside."

She followed him, carrying a small bag. He led her into the kitchen, where Josepha and I were cutting up some vegetables for a stew.

"Look who's here," said Uncle Ward. "We've got a visitor!"

"Mrs. Hammond!" I exclaimed.

"Hello, uh . . . Mary Ann," she said, then glanced nervously toward Josepha. "I came out just to . . . to thank you again for helping me like you did."

"Let me go get Katie," I said and ran out of the kitchen.

"Katie!" I yelled up the stairs. "Mrs. Hammond's here!"

Katie walked into the kitchen just as my papa and Henry came in from outside.

"Uncle Templeton," said Katie, "Mrs. Hammond came for a visit."

"I can see that.—Hello, Mrs. Hammond," said Papa, walking toward her with a smile and his hand outstretched. "Welcome to Rosewood!"

"Thank you, Mr. Daniels," she said, more nervous than ever to be suddenly the center of so much attention. She had heard so many rumors about the strange goings-on at Rosewood . . . now here she was right in the middle of them . . . whites and blacks mixed up together like nobody could tell the difference!

"Josepha," said Papa, "put on a pot of coffee.— Let's go into the sitting room."

We followed him into the parlor, all except Josepha, and sat down.

"I said to Mary Ann a moment ago," said Mrs. Hammond, "that I came out to thank you two girls again—"

She glanced over at Katie.

"—for your . . . for your thoughtfulness and for helping me like you did."

"We enjoyed it, Mrs. Hammond," said Katie.

"Why, they came back here," said Papa, "raving about what a time they'd had being shopkeepers!"

"You are very kind," said Mrs. Hammond. "But you two girls did far more for me than I can ever repay, especially because I know I haven't really ever done anything to deserve your kindness."

She glanced toward Katie and me and smiled.

"And I . . ." she went on, hesitantly but somehow determined to continue, "I am . . . what I am trying to say, though this is very difficult for me—"

She drew in a breath, glancing down at her lap, where she was holding the small bag she had come with.

"—and that . . . well, I . . . I am sorry for the way I've been to you all."

"Oh, Mrs. Hammond," said Katie, standing and hurrying over to where she sat on one of the couches. Katie sat down beside her and placed a hand on Mrs. Hammond's arm.

It was quiet a moment. Slowly the rest of us realized that she was crying softly. Katie continued to sit with her.

At last Mrs. Hammond drew in a few deep breaths, sniffed a couple of times, and looked up and tried to force a smile.

"And I also wanted to . . ."

She glanced around the room.

"Where is the colored lady?" she said.

"Josepha?" said Katie.

"Yes . . . Josepha—wasn't she from the Mc-Simmons place too?" she asked, looking over at me.

"Yes," I nodded. "But she didn't come till after I was already here."

"Yes, well . . . I wanted to thank her for the delicious soup and bread."

"Josepha, let the coffee wait," called Papa. "Come in here a minute."

A *few seconds later, Josepha appeared at the door, though she wasn't smiling.*

"Mrs. Hammond has something she wants to tell you," said Uncle Ward.

"Yes . . . well," said Mrs. Hammond, glancing toward Josepha, "I was just telling the others that I was sorry I hadn't been as nice as maybe I ought to have been. A lady living alone all her life like me, with nobody to keep her company but herself . . . she can get kind of crotchety and I'm afraid I have . . . and I remember one time when you were in the store with Mrs. McSimmons, God rest her soul, and I'm afraid I spoke rudely to you. I want to apologize for that . . . and to thank you for the wonderful soup and bread the girls brought me this week. I, uh . . ."

She opened the bag on her lap and reached inside.

"I brought you some chocolates," she said. "I hope you will enjoy them."

She looked up toward Josepha and forced a timid smile.

The room fell completely silent. After everything Josepha had said in the last day or two, the significance of the moment wasn't lost on any of us, and I don't think on Josepha either.

Mrs. Hammond got up and walked over and handed the box of candy to her.

"Thank you," she said again. "That was really the best soup and bread I have ever had, and I didn't deserve them."

Josepha took the box, mumbled a few words of

thanks, then said something about having to check on the coffee, and disappeared back into the kitchen. Mrs. Hammond went back to the couch and sat down again beside Katie.

By the time Josepha appeared with a tray of coffee things, Papa had got Mrs. Hammond talking, like he is so good at doing. With the rest of us joining in, she was asking questions about Rosewood and all of us, and we were talking and laughing like she'd been part of it all along. Henry and Jeremiah even got a chance to tell her a little of their stories, and she listened just as interested and attentively as she had to the rest of us.

Henry spoke so graciously to Mrs. Hammond. You could see from the look in his eyes and the tone of his voice that he really had compassion for her. It was as if he felt the pain of her loneliness himself. It made him love her and care about her all the more. I think she felt it too. Though she had always looked down on Henry, after that day I think there was some kind of special bond between them that Mrs. Hammond herself probably didn't even understand.

But love is like that. You can never tell how it is going to change you inside.

When Mrs. Hammond left an hour later, we all knew that Rosewood had a new friend.

⁀ ❋ ⁀

HARD TALK
32

*J*osepha was quiet for a day or two after that. And I thought a little grumpy too. I wasn't sure, but I had the feeling it had something to do with Mrs. Hammond's visit.

Remembering what she'd said about her promise to my mother, the thought struck me that maybe I had a responsibility to Josepha too.

I got up my courage to have a serious talk with her.

"Josepha," I said the next day, "can I talk to you?"

"Sure, Mayme, chil'," she said, "what 'bout?"

"You know that promise you made to my mama?"

"I's never forget it."

"You know how much I appreciate all you've done for me, and for being such a friend to my mama?"

Josepha nodded.

"But now the time's come when I'm almost grown up, almost as old as my mama herself was."

"And a fine han'some young lady you is too. Yo mama'd be proud."

"What I'm trying to say is—I've been wondering, now that I am almost grown up, if maybe that promise you made goes both directions."

"How you mean—bof directions?"

"That maybe I have something like a responsibility toward you too, Josepha."

"You mean—like you needin' ter take care er me too, like I said I'd do ter you?"

"Maybe a little like that," I said.

"An' you has, chil'. You an' Miz Katie took me in an' you's given me a home like I never had before. An' I'm mo grateful den you kin know. Why, you done more fo me den I kin ever hope ter repay."

"I'm glad, Josepha," I said. "But that wasn't exactly what I meant."

"What, den?"

"Well, I . . . I have something to say to you that I only say because I love you so much and care about you, and I . . . I hope you won't take it wrong, but—"

"Go on, chil'—git out whatever it is you gots ter say."

"It's just . . . I think you have been a little hard on Mrs. Hammond with some of what you said about her. I think she was trying to reach out to us all . . . and you too, and . . . well, Josepha, I thought you were pretty cold to her."

I let out a long breath. That was really hard to say!

It was quiet and awkward for several seconds.

"So you think I oughter show da lady mo kindness, is dat it?"

"I suppose so," I said.

"Well, maybe you's jes' too young ter know how it is between whites an' coloreds," said Josepha.

I could tell from her tone and the flash of her eyes that she was angry.

"How many years wuz you a slave? You wuz jes' a girl—what cud you know? How many people dat you loved did dey take away from you? You had a family, an' now you gots Katie an' yo papa an' Jeremiah. Who I eber had 'cept a friend dat died when he wuz too young? What kin you know 'bout what I's feelin' inside an' what it's like ter be all alone an' lonely wiff nobody ter look after you an' nobody ter care for you! You ain't got no call ter talk ter me like dat!"

She turned and stalked out of the kitchen and away from the house. I stood staring at her back in shock. My heart was breaking!

How could this have gone so terribly wrong? I sat down and began to cry.

That's where Henry found me five minutes later. I looked up and there he was. I didn't know where Josepha had gone. She hadn't come back.

Henry sat down.

"You want ter tell yo ol' friend 'bout it?" he said.

I started crying again. Then I gradually told him what had happened.

Henry sat for a long time thinking about what I had said.

"Growth's a fearsome thing sometimes," he said
at last. "Some folks ain't used ter soul-growin' inside
demselves. When da trunks er dere souls start ter git
wider an' stretching out, an' when dere roots start ter
go deeper, all dat growin' an' stretchin' hurts an' dey
don't like it."

Henry sometimes had such a simple but pro-
found way of putting things!

"But a tree can't grow wiffout its ol' bark
stretchin' an' crackin' an' splittin'," he added. "You
eber look at one er dem pine trees yonder in da
woods?"

I smiled and nodded.

"What's dere bark like? It all nice an' smooth?"

"No," I answered. "It's rough and cracked."

"Dat's what growth does ter make room fo da
insides er dose trees ter git bigger. Da skin's gotter
break fo da inside er dat tree ter grow. Da tree gits
stronger, but da bark's gotter break. People's jes' da
same. Ef we's gwine grow bigger inside, somethin's
gotter stretch. An' sometimes dat ol' soul-skin's gotter break. Breakin' hurts, but sometimes breakin's da
only way ter grow."

"But I didn't want to hurt Josepha."

"'Course you didn't. But maybe it's her time ter
do a little growin'. Maybe it's time fo her soul ter git
a little bigger. Maybe some ob da ol' bark's gotter
break."

"But I hurt her, Henry. Now she's angry at me."

"She won't be fo long. Da lady's got too much
love in her heart ter stay angry at you. But most folks

don't like it much when other folks shows 'em places where da trunk er dere tree's growin' a mite crooked. Seems like we'd want other folks' help, 'cause we need each other. But folks is funny dat way. Dey don't want no help wiff dere growin'."

"What should I do, Henry?"

"You let me hab a little talk wiff her, dat is if you don't mind me tellin' her what you tol' me."

"No, of course not."

꒰ ✳ ꒱

A Coat of All Sizes and Shapes
33

H ENRY FOUND JOSEPHA OUT IN THE VEGETABLE garden with a hoe in her hand. From the way she was attacking the weeds, he knew she was still agitated.

"I came on Miz Mayme cryin' in da kitchen," said Henry. "She tol' me what happened."

"Did she tell you what she said ter me?"

"Dat she did."

"Da nerve ob dat girl! What she thinkin' dat she kin talk ter me like dat!"

"It didn't sound ter me like she said anythin' mo den what da Lord himself might say ef He wuz talkin' ter you."

"What you sayin', Henry Patterson—dat da Lord'd treat me wiff dat kind er disrespect?"

"It din't soun' ter me like Mayme treated you wiff disrespect. Ain't it da highest kind er respect ter try ter help a frien' be mo like da Lord hisse'f?"

"Not da way she done it!"

"An' ain't it da Lord hisse'f dat tol' us ter forgive our

enemies? Ef you figger she dun you wrong, den you gots ter forgive her."

Henry's words stung. Josepha had no immediate reply except another whack at the ground with her hoe.

"An' I'm thinkin' maybe ol' Mrs. Hammond deserves da same."

"Mrs. Hammond ain't my enemy," snapped Josepha.

"Ain't dat all da mo reason?"

"I don't like her, dat's all, an' I don't figger it's none er Mayme's business, an' none er yers neither!"

"She's a lonely woman dat ain't got no frien's in da worl'."

"An' I still say it ain't none er yo affair!"

"Who's business is it ef it ain't da business er folks dat loves you? Mayme loves you, Josepha. Her heart's like ter break right now."

"What right she got ter say dat ter me?"

"Da right er love."

"Love . . . hummph!"

"She loves you an' wants you ter be da bes' person you kin be. An' she knows it ain't bein' yo best fo you ter harbor sour feelin's in yo soul. You's a better person den dat, an' Mayme knows it. She's seein' da bes' Josepha, but right now you's not bein' da bes' Josepha."

"Now dere you go getting' all high an' mighty an' talkin' ter me like you wuz my daddy or my master! What gib you da right ter git dat way wiff me?"

"Maybe da same right as Mayme's got."

"Hummph! Mayme's jes' a girl!"

"But a mighty wise girl. An' she ain't a girl no mo, Josepha, she's a growed-up young lady. It sounds ter me

like you's got a dose er pride dat ain't altogether been dealt
wiff."

Josepha bristled and her eyes flashed.

"What dat surposed ter mean?" she shot back. "Pride!
Whatchu mean, pride!"

"Jes' what I said. Soun's ter me dat Mayme picked at
somethin' dat you need ter take a look at."

Josepha hit the ground with a vengeance.

"Da devil's got a coat er pride jes' made ter fit each one
ob us," Henry went on. "It fits so nice an' snug, we gits
so's we like wearin' it. We don't eben know we's got it on
cuz it feels so good an' warm. It comes in all shapes an'
sizes. Dat's what pride does. But it's da devil's coat."

"Why you know so much 'bout dat ol' coat?"

"Cuz I got my own dat I had ter git rid ob. I had ter
learn da hard way. My own pride might er cost me my
family. I'll neber know. But even tryin' ter stand up fo truf,
I had a streak er pride. I tol' you 'bout it before. Dat wuz
my coat er pride, made ter fit nobody but me."

"An' you figger I's too proud ter be nice ter Mrs. Hammond?"

"I don't know," said Henry. "I can't rightly say what
you's thinkin'. But it seems a mite like you think you's better'n her. An' dat's pride, pure an' simple."

"Dere you go agin! What business is it er yers ter say
dat ter me?" said Josepha, more angrily this time.

"Maybe none, but I figgered it oughter be said."

Josepha stared at Henry another second or two, then
threw down the hoe at his feet and turned and walked away
in a huff.

Dejected and even more heartbroken than Mayme,

Henry returned to his cabin, sat down on his bed, and buried his face in his hands.

Josepha, meanwhile, was in a turmoil of emotions. She walked across the field toward nowhere, stomping at the ground as she went. When she came to herself she was standing beside the river, tears streaming down her cheeks.

Her anger had subsided, replaced by grief for the things she had said to the two people she loved more than any other two people in the world. But now it would take twice the humility and courage to get rid of the coat as before, because now she had to say she was sorry, a thing that's sometimes hardest to do to those we love the most.

Josepha's heart stung her for her outbursts. Mayme was right. Henry was right. They had both been right. Her anger only showed how right they had been. Her pride had gotten the better of her, just like Henry said.

She sat down at the river's edge, remembering the happy time she and Henry had spent in this very spot, playing in the water like two happy children.

How quickly it had all changed.

Again tears welled up in her eyes, and slowly her body began to shake with heart-wrenching sobs.

Henry had seen Josepha walk away and knew she couldn't go far. He had been watching from his cabin window for her return. At last, some thirty or forty minutes later, he saw her ambling slowly toward the house.

They had been thirty or forty minutes of the hardest thinking and praying Henry Patterson had ever done in his life. The turbulence of the exchange with Josepha had sent unexpected emotions and thoughts rising in his brain and heart.

It was not just the last thirty or forty minutes. Henry now realized that it had been growing invisibly within him for the better part of a year.

And now that he saw it for what it was, what ought he to do about it?

He left his cabin and went out into the grassy pasture where a few horses were grazing.

He needed to go for a walk and fetch a few things.

An hour later Henry appeared at the kitchen door. What he had to say was for Josepha alone. He was relieved to find her by herself in the kitchen.

She answered the door. He knew instantly that she'd been crying.

"I brung you dese," said Henry, holding out the small bouquet of wild flowers he'd picked in the field.

A look of confusion spread over her face. No one had ever given her flowers!

"I wants ter apologize fo bein' so hard on you," he said. "Maybe I didn't hab no right ter say dose things."

"You had every right, Henry Patterson," said Josepha emphatically, "cuz every word wuz true."

She took the flowers, wiped at her eyes and held them to her face, then drew in a breath and smiled.

Suddenly Henry stepped toward her, leaned forward, and kissed her. Josepha's eyes opened wide and her heart started beating so fast it felt like it was going to jump right out of her chest.

But already Henry had turned and was disappearing across the yard.

Two Hearts
34

HENRY WAS LYING ON HIS BED STARING UP AT THE ceiling, wondering if what he'd just done was the stupidest thing he had ever done in his life.

He did not hear Josepha's approach. She crept up the steps almost on tiptoe and timidly knocked. Not suspecting who it was, Henry rose and went to open the door.

There stood Josepha, still holding the simple bouquet, a sheepish look on her face.

"Nobody eber gib me flowers before," she said. "I wanted ter thank you proper. I wuz so speechless I didn't know what ter say."

Henry gazed into her face just a moment, then opened his arms, stretched them as far as they would go around Josepha's waist, and drew her to him. The bouquet of flowers was crushed between them.

"Oh, my goodness, what's dis all about!" exclaimed Josepha.

"I ain't too shore, Miz Black," said Henry, "but I's afraid dis ol' heart er mine's losin' itself fo da second time in its life. I hope you don't take no offense at da affections ob an ol' colored man.''

Gradually Josepha relaxed and slowly returned Henry's embrace.

"Maybe it ain't too late after all," she whispered.

"What dat you said?" asked Henry.

"Oh, nuthin' . . . jes' thinkin' out loud."

"Happy thoughts, I hope."

"Yes, sir, Mister Patterson—dey's happy thoughts indeed."

ANOTHER LETTER
35

*O*ur aunt Nelda from Philadelphia—where Katie's mother and uncles, and my family too, were from—had never seemed to have much use for any of us, at least not for her two brothers, because she seemed to think they had wasted their lives. But gradually over the last couple of years there had been more letters back and forth between Pennsylvania and North Carolina, and she had gradually been taking more and more of an interest in Katie. I think at first Papa might have been a little annoyed by it, thinking that maybe she was trying to work her way into Katie's good graces and thinking that the company of her two rough and wayward uncles wasn't good enough for her. But by this time we were all so close that nothing anybody did or said—not even an aunt—could get between us. So Papa didn't seem to mind so much now. Aunt Nelda's letters always came either to Katie or to all three of them— Katie and Papa and Uncle Ward, and usually it was

Katie who wrote back. I don't know if they had told her about me. I mean, she knew that Katie had a black friend called Mayme and that we had survived together. Whether she knew that I was kin and that she was my aunt too, that much I didn't know. Papa was still guarded and private about what he said about him and Mama.

The most recent letter had come to Katie, and in all the hubbub about Mrs. Hammond and then Micah and Emma's letter, she hadn't said anything about it. So it was a surprise at the dinner table several days later when she announced:

"Aunt Nelda said she would like to come for a visit."

We all looked around at each other. Papa and Uncle Ward wore questioning expressions.

"What did you tell her?" asked Uncle Ward.

"Nothing yet," answered Katie. "I wanted to see what you thought first."

"Hmm . . . well, I reckon you might as well tell her to come whenever she likes—what do you think, Templeton?"

"Sure, why not?" said Papa, though he didn't seem completely enthusiastic.

And so Katie wrote back the next day, and three weeks after that came another letter telling us that she would arrive by train in Charlotte two weeks later.

I think maybe we were all more than a little nervous before her visit. We didn't have any idea what to expect. After all Katie's anxiety years earlier about us being found out by her kin and her telling me her Aunt Nelda had never liked any of them that much, I couldn't help wondering why she was coming and what she would think. Papa was jittery too, and that was a mite peculiar for him. He was so friendly with everyone. There wasn't anybody he didn't like. But maybe it's different with kin.

As the day drew closer everything around Rosewood got quieter. No one knew what to say. We were all just waiting. Neither Papa nor Uncle Ward had seen their sister for years. Why was she coming for a visit? No one knew. Then suddenly we got nervous and the quietness turned into a flurry of cleaning and baking and washing, straightening up all the rooms, making sure everything would be just right.

All four of us went in to Charlotte to meet her train.

The train stopped at the station. People began to get out. Papa was always kind of the leader in situations like this because of his friendly personality. The moment he saw his sister, he stepped forward and greeted her warmly.

"Nelda," he said, "welcome to Charlotte!" He didn't exactly give her a hug or a handshake, but placed his hand on her shoulder.

"Hello, Templeton," she said.

He led her over to where we were waiting. Uncle Ward stepped forward.

"Hello, Ward," she said.

"Nelda . . . it's nice to see you again. It's been a few years."

"Thank you. It's good to see the two of you too. I cannot in all honesty say that you haven't aged a day since I saw you. You are older—of course, so am I. But you . . . you look well, both of you."

"Come and say hello to Kathleen," said Papa, leading her to where Katie and I stood.

"Oh, Kathleen," she exclaimed, "I would know you anywhere. You are the picture of your mother!"

"Hello, Aunt Nelda," said Katie. "I'm glad you could come. It is nice to see you at last."

"And this must be Mayme," she said, turning toward me with a smile.

"You remember Lemuela," said Papa.

"Of course."

"Mayme is her daughter."

"I see. How wonderful. She's almost family, then."

I saw Katie and Papa exchange a brief glance. It was their place to tell her more when the time came, not mine. I knew they wanted to let it sink in slowly to her that I wasn't just *almost* family, I *was* family.

Aunt Nelda stayed at Rosewood a week, and it was a better visit than any of us had expected. Enough time had gone by that the old antagonisms of the past had faded away. Most evenings Katie and I lay in bed upstairs in our rooms drifting to sleep, listening to the talk and laughter from downstairs of the two brothers and their sister catching up on their lives and sharing story after story from their younger years, memories of their parents, and of Katie's mama.

One night they began reminiscing about their grandparents.

⁓ ❋ ⁀

"How well do you remember Grandpa Daniels?" asked Ward when they were talking.

"You mean Grandpa William and Grandma Sarah?" asked Nelda. "—I don't remember them at all. I think they died when I was two or three. Do you really remember them, Ward?"

"Just faintly. My only recollection is that they were religious—seemed too religious even to a little tyke like me."

"Quakers, weren't they?" asked Templeton.

"That's what Mama always said," replied Nelda. "It's strange, now that I think of it, how the Daniels family was Quaker for so many generations, ever since old Elijah Daniels came over from England with the Woolmans and the Bortons . . . but then it died out with our folks."

"Yeah, well, Papa was the Daniels, and I don't think he cared too much for all that. Mama was religious enough, but she was no Quaker."

"I do remember her telling us about the Woolmans and the Bortons," said Templeton, "and that we'd come from an important line of people and were related to the famous John Woolman."

"Papa was funny about his heritage," said Nelda. "Everything I know about our family's Quaker roots I remember Mama telling me, not him. She must have gotten it all from Papa's parents before they died. What about the old homestead—did you ever see it, Ward?''

"Mama took me and Templeton out to see the farm once. But that was after Grandma and Grandpa were gone and the place had been sold."

"She took Rosalind and me out to see it too. We were probably ten or twelve."

"Anybody living in it?" asked Ward.

"A man and his wife, I think. Actually I've forgotten. All I remember is that it was run-down and old-looking even back then."

"Yeah, that's how it was when we saw it too."

"And why not?" added Templeton. "The first house was built there in the 1700s when the first Daniels came to Pennsylvania as part of William Penn's Quaker experiment, as Mama told it. It's amazing anything's still left of it."

"There might not be by now," said Ward.

"Be nice to see it again though, wouldn't it?"

"If we could find it," Templeton agreed. "I don't know that I could. You know where it is, Nelda? You were there more recently than us."

"I don't know . . . somewhere near the Maryland border . . . what was the name of the town it was by . . . Hanover, that's it. Hanover, Pennsylvania."

"Funny, when you think if it," said Templeton. "Here we've been living in the South, and Rosalind spent all her adult life in the South, but we're not really Southerners at all. Kathleen's the only true Southerner in the whole family. But our roots are really in Pennsylvania."

"Quaker roots," said Ward thoughtfully. "Kind of strange to think of it like that. But I suppose it explains how we were raised. Mother wasn't a Quaker, but she tried to teach us the Bible. Kind of wish I'd paid more attention to things she taught us and what they said about the old days and how our people came here and all. But when you're a child you don't think of that.''

⤳ ❋ ⤶

"Did you hear that, Mayme?" whispered Katie as we lay listening. I had been reading in bed with Katie before I went back to my room. But by then our books were on our chests and we were just dreamily listening to the conversation downstairs.

"What?" I said. I had almost been asleep.

"They're talking about some place their grandparents used to live, an old family homestead or farm or something. I just heard Aunt Nelda say it was just outside Hanover. That's where Rob might move to!"

I was still too sleepy to understand what she was getting so excited about.

"I don't remember," I said.

"I told you that he wrote to say that Sheriff Heyes was going to move from Ellicott City to take a job as sheriff in Pennsylvania and asked Rob to go with him. Now Uncle Ward and Uncle Templeton and Aunt Nelda are talking about the same town. Isn't that an amazing coincidence?"

"Maybe it isn't a coincidence," I said, though I don't even know why I said it. "I'm sleepy. I'm going back to my room."

That's how it was most nights during Aunt Nelda's visit. We never tired of listening to them, but usually were off to our beds while they were still going strong. It was really wonderful to see them laughing and talking like that. I know everyone was relieved and happy. It's not right when parts of a family aren't together like they ought to be, and this was just like what Katie had said about people growing together. Aunt Nelda had probably been nervous to come too, just like the rest of us had been nervous about seeing her. But everybody had grown together a little bit at a time.

When Papa finally told Aunt Nelda that I was his daughter, she didn't seem altogether surprised.

"I wondered," she said. "I knew that you and Lemuela had been fond of each other. I thought I could see a little of the Daniels look in Mayme's face."

The evening before she was scheduled to leave, Aunt Nelda said she wanted to talk to Katie and me about something. We sat down in the parlor with Papa and Uncle Ward because we wanted them to hear whatever she had to say.

"This wasn't really the purpose of my visit," she began. "I just wanted to see you all and to see how you, Kathleen, were getting on and whether you needed . . ."

She paused as if rethinking what she had been about to say.

"A woman's influence!" said Papa with a grin.

"Well, you can hardly blame me," said Aunt Nelda. "I didn't know. You two were . . . different back then."

"Wild, you mean!"

"Well . . . different. And with Rosalind gone . . . I have wondered if Kathleen needed an aunt. But I can see that you are all happy here and doing well and I have no wish to interfere in any way. However, with you girls—both of you," she said, glancing toward me, "growing into such fine young ladies . . . I have been thinking . . . well, there are good schools in the North, two in Philadelphia, for young ladies of good breeding. And now," she added, again looking in my direction, "one of these has begun accepting young Negroes. There are so many more opportunities now than there used to be—good opportunities for education and advancement . . . that it simply seems to me that this might be something for you all to consider."

"What's wrong with plantation life like this?" asked Uncle Ward.

"I am not saying that there is anything wrong with it, Ward. The girls have become accomplished and capable young women. It's only that the girls ought to have the opportunity to see more of the world if they want to—to travel and get more of an education and meet people. Then they can decide what they want to make of their lives. Women didn't used to have the opportunities they do today, and it seems that the girls ought to take advantage of some of them."

She paused a moment.

"You know, for all your reckless ways," she went on to Papa and Uncle Ward, "the two of you did see a lot more of the world than I ever did. I'm not saying it was right or wrong or anything because I don't know. I'm only saying . . . I don't know, it's hard to admit this, but . . . well, in a way Rosalind and I were always a little envious of that. We never saw anything of the world."

She took in a breath and tried to smile.

"The girls are young," she went on, "and these are changing times. They will have opportunities we never had . . . any of us. Just think about it, that's all I ask . . . for the girls' sake."

She looked around at the rest of us. Papa glanced our way too, then nodded.

"We'll do that," he said.

Katie and I looked at each other and nodded too.

The next day we took Aunt Nelda back to Charlotte and to the train. The subject of Katie's and my going north did not come up again . . . at least not then.

~ ✳ ~

FATEFUL DAY
36

After Mrs. Hammond's visit our trips into town were different. We were now eager to stop in and see her. The difference was remarkable. She was so friendly to us now. I'm sure we were changed too. When relationships with people get better it usually is a two-way street. I realized that I needed to try harder too, just like I'd said to Josepha. All of us were changed by what had happened.

Josepha was a little nervous the first time she went in. But she was determined to see Mrs. Hammond face-to-face and make amends.

We went in together, Katie and Josepha and me. I saw Mrs. Hammond hesitate slightly as she glanced toward Josepha. But Josepha didn't beat around the bush. She walked straight up to the counter and looked Mrs. Hammond in the eye.

"I want ter thank you for dem chocolates, Mrs. Hammond," she said. "Dey wuz wiffout a doubt da bes' chocolates I eber had in my life."

"Well, thank you . . . uh, Josepha," replied Mrs. Hammond, a little taken aback at Josepha's unexpected friendliness. "I, uh . . . am certainly glad you enjoyed them as much, I hope, as I did the soup you made for me."

"An' dere's one more thing I gots ter say," said Josepha, "an' dat's ter gib you my apologies fo bein' a mite surly when you wuz out ter our place. I reckon whites an' blacks has gotter bof learn dat dere ain't no difference in da color ob dere insides—blacks jes' as much as whites. I'm tryin' ter learn dat myself too. So my apologies. Dat wuz right neighborly ob you ter call like you done."

"Well . . . uh, thank you," said Mrs. Hammond, struggling to smile. For someone like her, I suppose receiving an apology was just as hard as giving one. "Think no more about it," she said. "We'll just consider ourselves friends from now on."

Katie asked Mrs. Hammond about our mail, and I think both she and Josepha were glad for the interruption. Josepha and I turned and wandered about the store.

But though things with Mrs. Hammond were better, things were getting worse throughout the rest of town. Henry heard more than one muttered threat at the livery stable, and Jeremiah said that except for Mr. Watson most of the men at the mill refused to talk to him.

Henry got up as usual at daybreak that fateful morning the following week. When he came in, the rest of us in the Rosewood family were already talking around the breakfast table about going into town too. It had been nearly a week since we had seen Mrs. Hammond. But as Henry and Jeremiah both had to be at their jobs early, they were the first to ride away from the house about half past seven.

The rest of us all arrived in town sometime after eleven o'clock and went about our own business. Papa and Uncle Ward went to the bank. Josepha was in Mrs. Hammond's general store picking up Rosewood's mail and a few supplies. Katie and I had gone to the shoe and boot shop.

The thundering approach of the white-sheeted riders, coming from the end of town where the livery stable was located, didn't at first alarm us or attract the attention of the townspeople of Greens Crossing.

But inside the livery, the moment Henry heard the angry shouts he sensed trouble. He started to walk outside. Several gunshots at his feet stopped him.

"Get back inside, Patterson," called one of the hooded riders, "or you'll be a dead man!"

The livery was quickly surrounded by the horsemen. The first torch landed on the roof and was quickly followed by many more. Within seconds, the small building was completely on fire.

Henry ran to the stalls where three or four horses already smelled the smoke and were whinnying and rearing in terror.

With effort, Henry got them loose, then unlatched the rear door and kicked it wide. A blast of heat from five-foot flames sent him staggering backward. He shouted and kicked and whipped at the terrified horses, until they bolted through the smoke and flame to safety.

"Don't let him through!" shouted another rider. "Shoot him if he tries to make a break for it!"

The instant the horses stampeded past them, the riders closed ranks, guarding every inch of the perimeter.

The explosions of gunfire, followed so quickly by a plume of smoke rising from the tinderbox of straw and dried wood, brought everyone running out of stores and homes. Mr. Watson was one of the first men into the street. Glancing toward the livery, he shouted for the fire brigade. Several men ran to where the hose and pump were kept, while a dozen more hurried toward the livery.

In the bank, someone shouted, "The livery's on fire!" Papa and Uncle Ward looked at each other, then bolted outside.

At Watson's mill, Jeremiah heard the shouts and was only seconds after his boss into the street. Papa and Uncle Ward ran to join him from the direction of the bank. Jeremiah sprinted ahead of them toward the livery.

Inside the burning building, the dense, suffocating smoke was so thick that Henry could see nothing. All was blackness about him. He grabbed a bucket of water from near the anvil and doused it over his head and shirt, then dropped to the floor, avoiding the smoke and trying to breathe the little air coming through what openings it could find beneath the flames. He knew any possible route of escape was gone.

Flames rose crackling into the sky. The building was too far gone for the makeshift fire brigade, rolling the pump on its wheels along the street, to hope to accomplish much. The men of the brigade slowed as they drew closer, no doubt intimidated by the circle of hooded men surrounding the blaze. All they could attempt to do now was keep the fire from spreading.

As more and more people reached the scene, no one held out much hope that life would be found inside once the flames began to subside.

～ ✳ ～

Josepha was in the general store visiting with Mrs. Hammond when the commotion began. Shots and gunfire brought them both to the front porch of the shop. They saw the first of the smoke rising into the air. With a terrible feeling of dread, Josepha ran back inside the store, looking around hurriedly, with Mrs. Hammond on her heels.

"Where you keep yo guns?" she cried.

"What are you going to do?" asked Mrs. Hammond in alarm.

"Never you mind, I'll pay you fo everythin' later—where's da ammunition!"

A minute later Mrs. Hammond's heart was pounding as she ran from her store trying to keep up as Josepha hurried along the boardwalk as fast as she was capable of moving, stuffing shells into the chamber of one of Mrs. Hammond's most expensive items of inventory.

They arrived in time to see Mr. Watson pulling Jeremiah feet-first away from the edge of the burning building. He had made a mad dash to try to rescue his father, but the smoke had quickly overtaken him and his clothing had caught on fire. Two other men ran over to help Mr. Watson drag Jeremiah to safety, then helped beat the fire off him. The young man lay on the ground, unconscious, his arms and face singed, his shirt and trousers still smoldering.

Whatever the white-hooded clansmen surrounding the burning livery had expected, it was not the lone black woman now hurrying toward the scene to oppose them single-handedly. Had they seen her coming, armed as she was, any one of them would have shot her dead in an instant without the slightest qualm. But they were so preoccupied with the fire and jesting about young Patterson's fate, that they did not see her approach behind them. They were taken off guard when two quick shots rang out from the rifle she was carrying. By the time they turned around in their saddles, the barrel of Mrs. Hammond's gun was pointed straight at the chest of one of the men, and from a distance of only about ten feet. The gleam in her eyes left no doubt that she would shoot if she had to. From such a short range, the man under the sheet did not like his chances.

"All right, git outta here!" she yelled. "All ob you—git goin' or I's start shootin'. You kin kill me, but I's take you wiff me, mister," she said to the man as she stared at him down the barrel. "Den I'll shoot whatever ob da rest ob you I kin afore I's dead."

As Ward and Templeton and several others from the mill reached the scene, they saw the standoff. Without pausing to consider the consequences, Templeton ran straight into the middle of it. He grabbed the man's rifle where it hung clutched in his hand at his side, yanked it out of the man's grasp, then turned it toward the others.

"You heard the lady," he said. "Get out of here!"

A shot rang out from Josepha's gun, narrowly missing the man's head. Whether it had been accidental or intentional, he wasn't sure he wanted to wait to find out.

He swore loudly, vowing to kill them all. Everyone within earshot recognized the sound of Sheriff Sam Jenkins' voice. But Sam was not prepared to die quite yet.

He lashed his horse, and the rest of his gang followed and were soon disappearing out of town.

⤴ ❋ ⤵

That's when Katie and I ran up. I was frantic with terror to see Jeremiah lying on the ground. But things were happening so fast I hardly had time to think.

Josepha had thrown the rifle to the ground and was running straight toward the blaze.

"Josepha . . . stop!" Papa called after her.

"I stood watchin' an' did nuthin' da las' time when I wuz jes' a girl," she yelled back at him. "I ain't gwine lose dis man da same way!"

"She's running straight for the fire!" someone cried out.

"Get that pump over here!" yelled Uncle Ward, sprinting toward the men who had been pushing the small water tank up the street. "Give me that hose! The rest of you start pumping!"

A few trickles began to squirt out the nozzle. The men rolled the pump to within thirty or forty feet of the blaze, then started pumping in earnest. Suddenly a large stream of water poured out. Grasping the nozzle like he held a snake's head in his hands, Uncle Ward aimed the spray over Josepha as she ran, dousing her head and shoulders and back as it poured against one of the burning walls of the stable. Holding it steady, he managed to extinguish a small portion of the burning wood.

While Uncle Ward did his best to keep that portion of the wall wet, I grabbed a bucket of water from near the horse trough and ran to where Jeremiah lay, gently pouring some of the water onto his face and arms. He groaned, but did not open his eyes. Every few seconds, I glanced over at the scene behind me.

What Josepha had been planning to do, no one knew. But now, dripping from head to food as the water continued to spray over her head, she picked up a pitchfork from the ground and set about attacking the side of the wall with a vengeance. The smoking boards broke and splintered and when she had whacked through enough of an opening, she dropped to hands and knees and crawled through, flames surrounding her on all sides.

"She'll kill herself!" cried someone from the crowd.

"Josepha!" called out Katie, trying to stop her.

At last seeing what she was trying to do, Papa darted after her. Before he could reach the hole, the surrounding wall flared up in flame again. He leapt back from the sudden blast of heat.

"Douse it, Ward!" he cried. "Pour as much water as you can . . . get it through that opening! We've got to keep her from catching fire!"

"Pump, men!" Uncle Ward shouted.

Again the spray blasted against the wall and within seconds the charred smoking wood around the hole was dripping and the flames beaten back, though the entire rest of the livery was an inferno.

Uncle Ward then managed to force some of the stream through the hole and inside where Josepha had disappeared. None of us knew whether it would do any good.

The crowd quieted. All we could do was wait. The only sounds were the roaring rush of flames into the air, the crackling of burning wood, and the spray of the hose water against it. All our eyes were glued to the three-foot hole that Josepha had bashed through the wall that Uncle Ward was now trying desperately to keep wet.

"Wait . . . hold it a second, Ward!" cried Papa. "I think I see something!"

He ran forward and knelt down and peered inside.

"It's Josepha! Keep the water coming, Ward . . . all around that hole!"

A black head appeared. Josepha was crawling

and wriggling on her stomach back toward the outside, pausing every so often to reach back and drag Henry's unconscious body after her.

The instant he was able, Papa squeezed in, reached past her, and grabbed hold of Henry's shirt at his shoulders. Josepha let go and crawled out, her dress smoldering and muddy, smoke pouring from her whole body. Her hair was singed and her dress had burned in spots, but she was soaking wet. Uncle Ward's efforts to keep her doused had no doubt saved her life.

A great cheer went up from the crowd as she crawled out. Uncle Ward now sent a spray pouring onto her, just to make sure. It knocked her to her knees just as she was trying to crawl back to her feet.

Papa now wriggled out and dragged Henry free from the blaze. Henry was as smoky and wet and muddy as Josepha, but unconscious. A quick douse from Uncle Ward's hose over both men saw to it that none of their clothing caught fire.

As soon as Papa had pulled him safely away from the building, Josepha knelt down beside Henry and kissed his face and forehead and cheeks. By then Jeremiah was coming back to himself. While I was relieved he hadn't been seriously hurt, I worried his father hadn't been so fortunate.

"Don't you die on me, Henry Patterson," said Josepha, half crying, half praying. "After all I done ter git you outta dere, don't you dare go leavin' me now! Ef I's got ter be da bes' Josepha I kin be, den you's got ter be da bes' Henry you kin be, an' we ain't neither ob us had da chance ter be dat together yet."

A few more kisses, then a groan sounded. Finally came a sputter and a cough. It was followed by a fit of coughing, for his lungs were still full of smoke.

"He's alive!" someone shouted to the onlookers.

Slowly Henry began to breathe easier, then rolled over and looked up to see a dozen faces, white and black together, staring down at him.

"Hit's a mighty warm day," he said, still coughing and sputtering. "Yes'sir, I'd say hit's a mite too warm fo comfort."

Everyone laughed. But the fire remained dangerous.

"Let's get the pump to Watson's mill!" cried one of the men. "We've got to get water up on the roof!"

As the crowd hurried down the street to make sure the fire didn't spread, Henry still lay struggling to fill his lungs. He looked up to see Josepha's face about a foot away, beaming with happiness and with tears streaming down her face.

"How'd I ever git out er dat place?" said Henry. "An', Josepha, what's you doin' lookin' such er mess?"

"She saved you, Henry!" exclaimed Katie, as she, Papa, and Uncle Ward slowly gathered round. "She ran straight into the fire!"

"Dat right, Josepha? You do dat fo me?"

"I reckon I did. I didn't stop ter think 'bout it."

"Well, den, I'm mightly obliged ter you. I's gwine hab ter fin' some way ter repay you."

Where I was kneeling beside Jeremiah, I turned

and saw Mrs. Hammond approaching, the only one of the townspeople remaining with the little Rosewood family. The others made room for her beside Henry as he sat up on the wet ground.

"I, uh . . . I am so glad you are all right, Mr. Patterson," she said.

"Thank you kindly, Mrs. Hammond," replied Henry, slowly kneeling, then getting up to his feet. I helped Jeremiah get up as well and we walked over to join the others.

"I's sorry 'bout stealing dat gun from yer store," said Josepha. "I'll pay you fo it when I can."

"Nonsense, Josepha!" said Mrs. Hammond. "Stealing! Good heavens, that wasn't stealing. You were just running off those ruffians. That was about the bravest thing I have ever seen a woman do in my life."

"Dat's right kind er you ter say. But I didn't think 'bout being brave, I jes' had ter git dis man outta dat fire."

We all laughed, then turned back toward the destroyed building, sobered to realize how close we had come to losing our friend.

Out of the corner of my eye, I saw Henry's arm slowly reach around Josepha's waist as they stood side by side, wet and smokey and muddy and with some of their clothing singed. He pulled her toward him.

"Why don't you all come back to my place and clean up," said Mrs. Hammond. "Kathleen . . .

Mayme, you take them all upstairs while I see if anyone is in the shop. You know where everything is . . .
make yourselves at home."

꙳

AFTERMATH
37

A LL OF GREENS CROSSING AND THE SURROUNDING
towns were stunned by the livery fire. The area's
blacks were frightened. The clansmen and their sympathiz-
ers were emboldened in the knowledge that they could
probably get away with anything, and in broad daylight.
Everyone knew that the local sheriff and several of the largest landowners in Shenandoah County were part of it. Who
was going to stop them?

Times were changing. No one could turn the clock back
now. What Abraham Lincoln had set in motion was rolling
full steam ahead into the future, and it didn't look like
happy times were ahead for the nation's former slaves.

Two days after the fire, Mr. Watson came out to Rosewood to talk to the two Daniels brothers. They knew from
the expression on his face that whatever might be on his
mind, it was serious.

"You boys know that I admire what you've been doing
here," he said. "I've been pulling for you all along, and I'll
keep pulling for you. But I've been getting threats too, on

account of Henry's son working for me. The boy's a hard worker, one of my best. But I just can't take any chances. I've got to let him go. I hope you can understand."

Templeton nodded. "Yeah, we do," he said. "These are bad times. We've all got to do what we've got to do. We'll get by. You want me to talk to him? After all, he is going to be my son-in-law one of these days."

"No," said Mr. Watson. "It's only right that I tell him. But I wanted you two to know how it was, that it's nothing personal."

"We understand," said Templeton.

"I'd watch yourselves too," added Mr. Watson. "You do know whose rifle you took and turned on that bunch?"

"Yeah, I know. Sam already doesn't like us much."

"This won't help matters."

"We'll be careful."

They rose and shook hands.

"Where can I find the boy?" asked Mr. Watson.

They walked outside and pointed out the way to Henry's cabin.

As Mr. Watson made his way toward the small house, a single-seat buckboard was just leaving Rosewood on the road into the countryside with Jeremiah's father at the reins. Beside him, in her finest dress, sat Josepha, feeling happier than she had ever felt in her life.

From an upstairs window where they had earlier that day helped Josepha get ready for her picnic with Henry, Katie and Mayme watched them go with expressions of youthful glee on their faces. They were almost as excited for the two older people as Henry and Josepha were for themselves.

"Well, Miz Josepha," said Henry as they rode, "what-chu think 'bout all dis?"

"All dis what, Mister Patterson?"

"Dese coupler ol' colored folks behavin' like dey wuz still as young as Miz Mayme an' Jeremiah, goin' fo picnics together, goin' ter da river together, goin' fo walks together, da man takin' his lady friend flowers? All dese carryin' ons got tongues waggin' an' wonderin' what dey's gwine do next! So what are we gwine do?"

Josepha laughed. "I don't know, Mister Patterson. Dat's likely up ter you."

"Dey's all mighty curious what we's up to," chuckled Henry.

Josepha laughed again. "Dem two girls back at da house, dey don't know what ter do wiff me dese days! So what is we up to?" she added, trying to swallow a giggle.

"I's goin' out fo a ride an' a picnic wiff a lady I's grown mighty fond ob, dat's what," replied Henry.

"Jes' like a coupler white folks. Who'da thought a black man an' a black woman would hab da freedom ter go out ridin' in an expensive carriage like dis? I neber been ridin' like dis in my life."

"Not me neither. But times is changin', I reckon fo da better an' da worse in some ways. But dis part ob it's fer da better, an' dat's a fact. Dis shore ain't nuthin' we'd ever be able ter do back in da ol' days. What master would gib us a carriage ter use like it wuz our own?"

A few minutes later, Henry pulled the carriage off the road and guided the single horse across a smooth field of grass where daisies and a few yellow wild flowers were growing, then reined in.

He got down and secured the carriage, then offered his hand to Josepha. She stepped to the ground, not quite daintily but with a lightness of step that was almost elegant for a woman her size.

"What you got in dat basket?" Henry asked.

"Ef you'll jes' hand it down ter me," replied Josepha, "we'll find us a place on dis nice grass ter open it an' fin' out."

"Soun's good ter me," said Henry.

Two minutes later they were walking across the grass hand in hand, the picnic basket swinging at Henry's side.

Half an hour later, Henry and Josepha sat on the blanket Josepha had brought, quietly talking as they finished up their outdoor lunch.

"I don't know exactly what you's thinkin' 'bout all dis," said Henry. "I reckon it's a mite unushul, so I thought I oughter explain myself as best I kin. Back in da ol' days, some things wuz simpler. Coupler folks like us, we jes' did what da master tol' us. But now we ain't got nobody ter tell us what ter do, 'cept da Lord, ob course, but His voice is a mite hard ter hear sometimes. So a body's jes' gotter make up his own mind what's right.

"What I's tryin' ter say is dat I don't know exactly *what* we oughter do. You's workin' fo Miz Kathleen in da house, but now all ob a sudden I's outer work an' ain't got but fifty dollars ter my name. Dat soun's like a lot, but it won't go far when no more's comin' in. I don't see much likelihood er gettin' no work roun'about here no time too soon. So I's kind ob a man in er fix."

Suddenly Josepha looked across at him with fear in her eyes.

"Henry Patterson," she said, "you's not tryin' ter tell me you's leavin' Rosewood!"

The serious expression on Henry's face told her that the thought had crossed his mind.

"I wouldn't be altogether tellin' da truf ef I said I hadn't given dat thought some consideration. A man's gotter hab work, an' it wudn't be right er me ter presume on Miz Kathleen's an' Mister Templeton's an' Mister Ward's good graces. Dey's right generous folks, but a body can't expect other folks ter take care ob him. I's been givin' dem half my wages from da livery fo da little cabin dey let me an' Jeremiah use, an' fo da food dat we all enjoy eatin' together, an' Jeremiah's been doin' da same. Dey don't like takin' our money, but it ain't much, an' it's da right thing 'cause dis is a big place an' dere's lots ob us ter feed an' we all gots ter do our part, jes' like you do in da kitchen, an' it ain't as ef da crops make all dat much money. Da cotton hasn't been too good dese last coupler years. But now wiff me an' Jeremiah bof out er work, things is boun' ter change—an' so we gotter figger out what ter do."

Josepha's worry was growing. She didn't like Henry's serious tone!

"I reckon it'd be different fo white folks," said Henry. "Dey could jes' go off an' git new jobs. But who's gwine hire a fifty-year-ol' colored man roun' 'bout dese parts?"

Henry paused and took in a long breath.

"So I had me a little talk wiff Mister Ward and Mister Templeton," he went on, "an' I laid dis troublesome situation before dem an' asked what dey thought I should do, since neither me nor Jeremiah got no mo wages comin' in. An' dis is jes' between you an' me, an' you gotter promise ter say nuthin' 'cause he's gotter tell Miz Mayme in his own way, but Jeremiah's considerin' goin' up norf fo a spell ter see what kind er work he kin find, like what you said. Dat's why I said I'd considered da same thing myself."

Again Henry paused briefly, then continued.

"An' da long an' da short ob it," he said, "is dat Mister Templeton an' Mister Ward tol' me dey wanted me ter stay right here where I wuz an' dat I'd be workin' fo dem from now on an' dat we'd all git by jes' fine, an' dat wiff three men we'd be able ter git da cotton back ter like it wuz before da war, an' den dey said dat ef I tried ter leave ter fin' work dey'd hog tie me an' keep me here.

"So I reckon I ain't gwine be leavin' anytime soon, an' so dat got me thinkin' long an' hard 'bout you an' me, an' since we's bof here an' I got my situation kind er figgered out, I's finally ready ter ask you ef you'd maybe do me da honor er bein' my wife fo however many years we got lef'."

Josepha gasped in shock. Whatever she had been expecting, it wasn't this!

"You's always sayin' somethin' ter take my breath away," she said.

"So what you think? Wiff Jeremiah goin' norf, da little cabin he and I share can be our cabin now. 'Course you'd still have ter go ter da big house ter fix everybody else's meals, but it'd be kind er like havin' our own place."

"I figgered you an' me, dat we'd jes' ..." Josepha began.

Her brain was reeling, and words were coming out in a jumble.

"I don't know what I figgered," she went on. "I's up dere in da house, an' you's . . . but you's down dere in da cabin . . . I jes' didn't never think . . . you . . . you's sayin' you want . . . ter marry *me*!"

For answer Henry leaned over and kissed Josepha.

"I reckon it came on me slow," he said after a moment, "realizin' dat you wuz becomin' mighty special ter me, an' dat fo da second time in my life I knew dat I loved a woman. I hope you don't mind ef you's da *second* woman I kissed."

"I don't reckon I mind," said Josepha. "I ain't neber been kissed by a man before you in my life, so I don't reckon I kin begrudge Jeremiah's mama dat you loved her afore me. What wuz her name?"

"Lacina."

"Dat's a pretty name. She muster been a fine woman."

"She wuz. But now I reckon dere's room where she lives in my heart ter share wiff you, effen you don't mind."

"I don't reckon I think much ob a man havin' two wifes at da same time. But I don't mind sharin' her memory wiff you. Dere's jes' one mo thing."

."What's dat?" asked Henry.

"I'd like it ef you'd call me Seffie. I ain't been called dat in a lot er years, an' it's a special name ter me."

"So what's yo answer, den, Miz Seffie?" said Henry.

"I reckon, Mister Patterson, dat my answer's yes."

⤙ ❊ ⤚

At supper that evening when we were all at the table together, not even news of Jeremiah's talk with

Mr. Watson could dampen the joy we all felt when Henry told us about his talk that afternoon with Josepha.

Katie and I shrieked with joy and jumped up to hug Josepha. Papa and Uncle Ward and Jeremiah gathered round Henry with back slaps and handshakes.

It was almost more than we'd dared dream of!

⁊ ✻ ⁌

THREE CONVERSATIONS
38

*T*he conversations that took place four days later were all ones that influenced our lives in unforeseen ways. The first was between Jeremiah and me.

I knew that Mr. Watson had let him go at the mill, but I didn't know what he was thinking of doing about it.

He asked me if he could talk to me after lunch. He took my hand as we walked out toward the woods. I knew it was serious because he said nothing for a long time. We were all the way to Katie's secret little meadow in the woods before he said a word. By then I was really getting worried!

"You know 'bout Mr. Watson an' da mill?" he said.

I nodded.

"You know how me an' Papa hab been givin' some ob our wages to Mister Ward and your daddy," Jeremiah went on. "It ain't as if it's dat much, but Papa says dat now dat we's free, we's got ter prove dat we's worthy er freedom by workin' hard an' payin' our own way an' not lookin' fo nobody ter pay our way fo us like da white masters used ter do. Dey used ter do everything fo us. Now we's got ter do fo ourselves an' Papa says we gotter show dat we can, dat we kin work hard. Mister Lincoln's dead an' now we gotter prove dat he wuz right. Dat's what my daddy says. An' da way we do dat is ter work hard an' not expect no hand-outs from nobody.

"Now your papa an' Mister Ward, dey's 'bout da finest two men I eber knowed besides my papa and Micah Duff. An' dey said da same thing ter me as dey did ter my daddy, dat I could stay on wiff him an' dey'd fin' plenty er work fo us bof. But I been thinkin' 'bout it, an' it ain't jes' da danger ter blacks here, I figger too dat it don't seem right fo you an' me ter git married when we's beholdin' ter folks fo everythin', even folks as generous as Miss Katie an' Mister Templeton an' Mister Ward. An' now wiff my daddy plannin' ter marry Josepha, an' dem both bein' here wiffout other jobs, it seems dat maybe I needs ter be helpin' out wiff some real money so dat things don't git bad like dey was a while back for you an' Katie. I saw yer papa an' Mister Ward go into da bank da day ob da fire, an' dey ain't sayin' nuthin', but I heard 'em once talking 'bout taxes an' where dey wuz gwine git da money ter pay 'em."

Jeremiah stopped and drew in a long breath. That was a lot of talking for him to do!

"I gotter work," he went on. "I need ter be earnin' money so's we kin git married an' not be beholden to nobody. An' I figger I gots ter help my papa a little too 'cause he can't be dependin' on your papa every time he an' Josepha wants ter buy somethin'. So I's decided dat I need ter fin' me another job an' put some money away fo you an' me, an' fo my papa an' maybe fo dose taxes too. But since dere ain't likely ter be no work roun' here, I's decided ter go up norf fo a spell an' git me a job."

"Oh . . . oh, Jeremiah!" I said, drawing in a breath of shock. I couldn't help it, I felt tears filling my eyes. I clutched his hand tight and looked into his face.

"I don't like da thought ob leavin' you any more den you does," he said. "But it won't be fo too long. Dey say dere's jobs in da harbors an' in da factories an' wiff train buildin', an' dat even a black man kin make better money up dere den a white man does down here. We's be together agin soon, an' by then maybe I'll hab enuff saved dat will last us awhile an' things'll git better here, an' I'll be able to git another job, an' maybe den da time'll be right fo us."

I sat down on a log, still stunned. But as heartbroken as I was, I admired Jeremiah all the more for wanting to work hard for himself. Somehow inside I knew it was the right decision.

But I couldn't help crying. The thought of him leaving Rosewood was almost more than I could bear. We'd been waiting, for one reason or another, for so long!

*While we were off talking in the woods—with me
crying!—my papa and Uncle Ward rode into Oakwood.*

≈ ❊ ≈

People were used to the two Daniels brothers by now,
but they still turned a few heads wherever they went. And of
course word had spread about the fire and what had happened. Most folks didn't approve of the KKK's tactics. But
to turn a gun on a white man in defense of a black man, for
whatever reason, was a sin that most Southerners would
never forgive. The fact that Templeton Daniels carried a rifle
across his saddle as they rode into town drew even more
looks than otherwise, and stares followed them as they rode
down the street, then stopped in front of the sheriff's office.

They dismounted and went inside, Templeton still
carrying the gun.

When Sam Jenkins looked up, hatred filled his eyes.

"I believe this is yours, Sam," said Daniels, setting the
rifle down on the sheriff's desk. "You left it behind when
you and your cowardly scum rode off the other day."

"How dare you talk to me like—"

"Shut up, Jenkins!" interrupted Ward. "Now you just
sit there and listen. My brother's right—you're all nothing
but a bunch of yellow cowards, going about like little boys
dressed up in sheets. You don't have the guts to own up to
what you're doing. My brother came to return your gun—
he's a little more neighborly than me. I came to tell you
this—I've been in jail a few times, I'm more than fifty years
old, I've already lived longer than I probably have a right

to, and so there's not much I'm afraid of. I'm not afraid of jail, I'm not afraid of dying, I don't think I'm even afraid of hanging, though I don't relish the thought. But one thing I'm especially not afraid of is you. I'm sorry about your boy. Nobody ought to have to lose a son like that. I'd hoped maybe you'd learned from it a bit about hate, but it doesn't seem that you have. I think you're a coward, Jenkins—a coward and a hypocrite . . . sitting there with that badge, then going out and hiding behind a mask when you try to kill people. No true man would do that, only a coward. So I'm telling you that if you lay a finger on any of our family, black or white, or so much as set foot on Rosewood without our permission . . . I'll personally kill you, Jenkins. They may hang me for it, but you won't be there to watch. Don't push me, Jenkins. I mean what I say. I'll kill you if you give me cause."

Ward turned and walked out. Sheriff Jenkins stared after him, his face trembling and so white with rage that he couldn't even manage a word. Templeton followed a few seconds later, almost as shocked at what his brother had said as the sheriff.

⌒ ❁ ⌒

The third conversation that day took place later, after Papa and Uncle Ward were back from Oakwood. They didn't tell any of us right then what had taken place in the sheriff's office. It would come back to haunt us one day, but not for a while.

The rest of the day had been sad and thoughtful for me after my conversation with Jeremiah. Katie and I had talked. I'd told her about Jeremiah's decision and cried again. Later, while Katie helped Josepha get supper ready in the kitchen, I went up to my room to rest. I was trying to get ready to put on a smiling face when I went down to supper. I couldn't act all glum for Jeremiah's sake. He felt right about his decision and I had to show my support by acting like I felt good about it too.

After a while, I got up from my bed and wandered to the window. In the distance I saw my papa and Henry and Uncle Ward walking away from the house.

⌒ ❋ ⌒

"We thought maybe it was time we took a look at the work you've been doing on the cabin," said Templeton. "Why don't you show us?"

"You wuz jest down dere yesterday, Mister Templeton," laughed Henry. "You done as much ob da work on it as I hab."

"Well, we want to see it again," said Ward. "Supper's not quite ready. By the way, Henry, that cabin of yours and Jeremiah's is pretty small for a married man, and it's got no kitchen. How's Josepha going to manage as a married lady without a kitchen?"

"We figgered she'd still be cookin' for you all at da big house," said Henry.

"I'm glad to hear that!" laughed Templeton. "But what if she wants to make a special cake or batch of biscuits just for you? What's she going to do then?"

"I hadn't thought er dat, Mister Templeton."

They reached the new house and walked inside.

"You do beautiful work, Henry," said Ward. "Look at this, two big rooms, and this big kitchen with that new counter you put in, the sink with an inside pump, and the place there for a cook stove—you've turned a small cabin into a spacious home, Henry. Nobody'd ever know it used to be a slave cabin."

"Thank you, Mister Ward—I's pleased how it all's turnin' out," said Henry, still a little bewildered by the gist of the conversation, since all three of them had been working on the house together.

"By the way, I'm not sure whether Templeton told you, but last time we were in town we ordered the new cook stove, made to fit right there—brand-new, coming from Richmond. And while we were at it, we ordered a new bed, extra wide and extra long."

"We figured the new occupants of the house might like it that way," added Templeton with a mischievous wink, though Henry did not understand his meaning.

"Yep," he nodded, "I's sure dey will at dat."

"And we ordered a couple of chairs and a couch. We thought they would look good over here," said Ward, now wandering into the empty space of the living area off the kitchen, "alongside this handsome bookcase you built. I must say—very fine work, Henry!"

"Thank you, suh. But effen you don't mind my askin' . . . I did tell you dat Jeremiah's plannin' ter leave fo a spell?"

"That you did."

"Seems like you's goin' ter considerable expense when

he an' Mayme ain't gwine be ready no time soon.''

"Well, speaking of Mayme and Jeremiah," said Templeton, "we've been thinking about that, and when we heard about what Jeremiah was set on doing, we changed our plans. This house turned out so nice that we decided to sell it."

"Sell it!" said Henry in surprise, unable to keep the excitement out of his voice. "Effen you don't mind my askin' . . . does you hab yorselves a buyer yet?"

"Nope," said Templeton, shaking his head. "These are tough times. The market's a little slow for converted slave cabins."

"Effen you don't mind my askin' agin . . . uh, what wuz you thinkin' 'bout askin' fo da place?" said Henry.

Ward and Templeton looked at each other. "We'd talked about somewhere in da neighborhood of twenty, maybe twenty-five dollars," said Ward.

"Twenty-five dollars!" exclaimed Henry. "Dat can't hardly be. I run up ten or twelve dollars at Mister Watson's on yo account jest' fo lumber an' roofin' an' da new windows. An' dat new cook stove's likely gwine cost ten er twelve mo, den da bed an' dose chairs. It don't soun' ter me like dat could possibly be da price."

"You're probably right," said Templeton. "But the way we figure it, the house is here and isn't doing anything, and if we can just recoup what we've put into it, then that ought to be enough. We're not trying to make a profit on it, Henry, we're just trying to make it available as a nice home to someone, possibly a newly married couple, who could be happy there. Do you know anyone who might be interested?"

"Well, beggin' the two of you's pardon," said Henry, "but does you think you'd be willin' ter sell ter black folks?"

"Hmm . . . that is an idea," nodded Templeton. "I don't see why not, since we had planned it for Mayme and Jeremiah. Why . . . you have someone else in mind?"

"Well, effen you don't mind da presumption . . . I's thinkin' dat perhaps, effen you wuz willin', dat maybe me an' da future Missus Patterson might raise dat money an' buy da house ourselves."

"You and Josepha, why that is a fantastic idea!" said Templeton.

"But dere's jes' one thing," said Henry. "I's afraid I gotter take exception ter dat price er yers. I know what we put inter dis place, an' I know dere's more den dat. An' I wudn't gib you less den forty dollars fo it, an' to tell you da truf, I know it's worf more den dat. But you jes' name your price an' I'll talk ter Josepha, an' we's see effen we kin do it."

"You are a hard negotiator, Henry," laughed Templeton. "Why don't we tentatively agree on forty dollars, then."

"Effen you's shure dat's all you wants ter ask."

"All agreed?" said Templeton, glancing at the other two men.

"We probably should clear it with Kathleen," said Ward.

"Right . . . of course. Forty dollars, then—pending Kathleen's approval."

The three shook hands.

"I'm much obliged ter you bof," said Henry. "Dis is gwine make my Seffie 'bout da happiest black lady in da whole worl'."

HENRY AND JOSEPHA
39

*T*he big day came.

Just like for Emma and Micah's wedding, Reverend Hall came out to the house. We were all thinking of Emma and wishing she could be there with us. The only other cloud on the day was that Jeremiah would be leaving after the wedding. Many mixed feelings were running through my mind.

But I determined not to be sad for myself. This was a day to be happy for Henry and Josepha.

Katie and I helped Josepha get ready upstairs just like we had with Emma. Josepha was as excited as a girl. She had never expected to be a bride. But she was about to become Mrs. Henry Patterson!

What to do for a wedding dress had been our biggest problem right from the start. We'd thought about a trip into Charlotte to buy one, but nobody was anxious to do that, especially now with hotels not allowing blacks and whites to stay together. In the end it was Mrs. Hammond who helped us out of the difficulty. One day Katie and I were asking her about ordering a dress for Josepha.

"I don't know," she said, "for a woman . . . well, you know—so large . . . it can be difficult to get a good fit, and once the dress comes, what can you do? And a nice dress can be quite expensive."

She thought a moment, then a smile came over her face and she began to nod.

"Yes," she said, "I think . . . yes, I think we could do it."

"What, Mrs. Hammond?" asked Katie excitedly.

"Well, what I was thinking . . . was that we could make a very nice dress ourselves."

"Do you really think we could!"

"I used to do quite a bit of sewing when I was young—yes, I am sure we could."

Katie and I took some fabric samples home to Josepha from Mrs. Hammond's supply. Within the week we had several yards of a beautiful light green linen material, and Josepha had begun her fittings with Mrs. Hammond upstairs in her house above the shop.

The four of us had such fun, laughing and talking together, while the dress slowly took shape around Josepha's frame. It turned out that Mrs. Hammond was a much better seamstress than she let on. The dress had all sorts of fancy folds and tucks, so that by the end it was better than any store-bought dress could possibly have been. By then Josepha and Mrs. Hammond had become such good friends that Josepha had asked her to stand beside her at the wedding along with Katie and me.

Then the day came. Mrs. Hammond was the first to arrive. She wanted to make a few last-minute alterations to the yellow bow that went around Josepha's middle. We hurried her inside the house and upstairs to Josepha's room and there the four of us— two young ladies barely twenty and Josepha, who I think was forty-nine, and Mrs. Hammond, who was probably about the same age—carried on like four giggling schoolgirls as we helped Josepha get ready.

Once Josepha had the dress on and everything was in place, we fixed her hair while Josepha held a mirror to see what we were doing. With a few flowers and ribbons, she looked beautiful.

Meanwhile down in what was already being called "the new house," Papa and Uncle Ward and Jeremiah were busy getting Henry ready. Also with Mrs. Hammond's help, they had tailored one of Papa's old fancy gambling suits and ruffled shirts to fit Henry. Mrs. Hammond had let down the legs a couple of inches and taken the waist in about the same amount, since Henry was both taller and thinner than Papa. But the end result, when I finally saw it a little while later, was amazing. Henry looked like a black riverboat gambler!

Mr. Thurston and Reverend Hall and his wife arrived about eleven in the morning. Aleta and her father arrived a little while after that. Since this was the second wedding we had had at Rosewood, we did everything nearly the same as we had before for Emma's. Reverend Hall and Katie talked a bit about arrangements, then she hurried back upstairs where the rest of us were waiting. Josepha had asked both Papa and Uncle Ward to walk her downstairs to give her away to Henry, just the same as Emma had done.

"Everything's just about ready," said Katie as she came in. "What about you, Josepha—are you ready?"

"I don't know, chil'," said Josepha. "I's so happy an' nervous, I don't know what ter think!"

We heard the kitchen door open downstairs.

"That must be the men," said Katie. "It's about time for us to leave you, Josepha."

Katie stepped forward, gently embraced Josepha and kissed her on the cheek. "We love you, Josepha. We're so happy for you."

"Don't do dat, chil', you's gwine make me start cryin' all over again!"

Then she looked me straight in the face with her hands on my shoulders.

"Thank you for being such a big part of my life," I said.

I hugged Josepha and cried. I couldn't say anything more. Neither did she. We didn't need words.

Finally Mrs. Hammond stepped forward, hesitated just for a moment, then put her arms around Josepha. "God bless you, Josepha. You're a sweet and lucky lady."

"Thank you so much fo everything, Elfrida," said Josepha. "You's a good friend."

She stepped back. Both women had wet eyes.

The sound of men's footsteps on the stairs told us it was time to go.

We all took Josepha's hand one last time, gave it a squeeze, and with smiles all around left the room just as Papa and Uncle Ward walked in.

"All right, you all, get out of here!" said Papa. "We'll take over from here!"

"There's a mighty handsome man downstairs waiting for you, Josepha," said Uncle Ward.

"Oh, Mister Ward, don't make me cry!"

"Don't worry about a few tears. There's always more where they came from—good for the soul, they tell me, though I can't claim much personal knowledge.—So, what do you think . . . you about ready to go meet your man?"

"Oh, I don't know . . . I reckon so!"

"You look ready to me," said Papa. "You're a beautiful bride, Josepha. We're all very proud of you."

"Thank you, Mister Templeton. You hab bof been so good ter me."

"There's Katie at the piano!" said Uncle Ward. "Sounds like it's time!"

They opened the door and began slowly to descend the stairs, Josepha on the arms of both men. She was beaming as she came down into the room. The moment she saw Henry standing there smiling, so handsome in Papa's ruffled shirt and tie and dark blue suit, I could see that the sight of him took her breath away.

Mrs. Hammond and I were standing on one side

of Reverend Hall. Jeremiah was standing on the other. Henry's face was so proud as he watched Josepha in her new green dress descend into the room. It was obvious he loved her so much.

They came down and stopped in front of Reverend Hall. Katie played a little more, then reached the end of the music and stopped. She stood up from the piano and came over and stood next to me.

"Dearly Beloved," said Reverend Hall. "We are gathered here this day to unite this man and this woman in holy matrimony. If any man should show just cause why they should not be so united, let him speak now or forever hold his peace."

After a brief silence, he went on.

"Who gives this woman to be married to this man?" he asked.

"We do," said Papa and Uncle Ward.

They both stood aside and went to stand with Jeremiah as Josepha stepped forward and took her place at Henry's side.

As she did, she thought back to the day she had left the McSimmons plantation and had gone to Greens Crossing in search of Henry.

⤚ ✳ ⤙

She remembered ambling toward the livery stable, weary from her long walk in the hot sun. She had immediately recognized the man behind the fence holding a pitchfork, but wondered if he would remember her.

"You be Henry, effen I'm not mistaken," she had said.

"Dat I is," replied Henry.

"I'm Josepha, from da McSimmons place."

"I knows who you is," Henry had chuckled. "You don't think I forgot our first meetin'. Why I owe you dis job er mine. But whatchu doin' so far from home, an' on what looks ter be sech tired feet?"

"Ain't my home no mo," she had said. "I's a free woman, so I done lef'. I ain't gotter take dat kin' er treatment no mo from nobody. An' now I'm lookin' fer Miz Mayme, an' I'm hopin' you might be familiar 'nuff wiff her ter be able ter direct me ter where I kin fin' her."

At that, Henry had chuckled again. "I reckon I kin do dat all right," he said. "Why, I might jes' take you dere mysef', effen you ain't in too much a hurry. Hit's a longer walk den I think you wants ter make, an' effen you kin wait till I'm dun here, I'll fetch you dere in dat nice buckboard ober dere dat I's repairin' fer Mister Thurston. I reckon hit's 'bout ready fer me ter take ter him, an' Rosewood's right on da way. I don' think he'll min' a passenger ridin' 'long wiff me."

Henry had been so kind to her, even then.

Josepha had sought out Henry Patterson to find Lemuela's girl Mayme. How could she ever have imagined that one day she would be standing beside him like this!

⤳ ❋ ⤲

"Do you, Henry Patterson," said Reverend Hall, "take this woman to be your wedded wife, to have and to hold from this day forward, for better, for worse, for richer, for poorer, in sickness and in health, to love and to cherish, till death do you part, according to God's holy ordinance?"

"I shore do," replied Henry.

"Do you, Josepha Black," Reverend Hall said, turning to Josepha, "take this man to be your wedded husband, to have and to hold from this day forward—for better, for worse, for richer, for poorer, in sickness and in health, to love and to cherish, till death do you part, according to God's holy ordinance?"

"Dat I do," said Josepha. "An' God bless him fo lovin' da likes er me."

A few laughs went around the room. We couldn't help it!

⤳ ✳ ⤳

As the laughter quieted, Henry's mind flitted back to the day he had first seen Josepha.

He'd had no premonition at the time that the Mc-Simmons' cook might become his future wife. But the impression she made on him was a lasting one. Yet the deeper love he now felt had blossomed slowly within him, taking him over so gradually during their time at Rosewood that he never saw its approach until suddenly one day he recognized it for what it was. By then he knew that he loved her. But he did not know when he had *begun* to love her. Yet when it comes to love, perhaps beginnings do not matter so much as endings.

And so now here he stood, as surprised as she. His happiness was different, for it must make room for a memory. But it was just as complete.

꜒ ✳ ꜖

"Inasmuch as you, Henry, and you, Josepha," Reverend Hall was now saying, "have declared before God and these witnesses your wish to be united in marriage, and have pledged love and fidelity each to the other, I now pronounce you man and wife.—Ladies and gentlemen," he said, turning to the rest of us, "may I have the honor to present to you Mr. and Mrs. Henry Patterson!"

Cheers and clapping broke out. Then we all rushed to hug Josepha and Henry, and the men shook hands. There were kisses and congratulations and Mrs. Hammond was right in the middle of it, happy and smiling with the rest of us. I think she had almost by then become color blind like everyone else at Rosewood.

I looked for Jeremiah and walked over to him. As we stood side by side, he put his arm around me. I know we were both thinking the same thing—we hoped our own day wouldn't be too far away.

Since we had invited the Halls and Mrs. Hammond and Mr. Thurston and Aleta and her father for lunch, it didn't take long before the talk turned to food and coffee and the cake we had made.

That was all Josepha needed to hear. Pretty soon she was in the kitchen and putting on a clean apron over her new green wedding dress and getting ready to continue preparations for the great wedding feast we had planned. It was a kitchen, after all—the place where she was happier than anyplace in all the world.

⤳ ❀ ⤶

PARTING
40

*E*ven before we had all completely finished the wedding feast, Jeremiah slipped out of the house. I watched him through the window as he went into the barn. My heart sank. I knew what he was doing. The moment had finally come that I'd been dreading. I knew he was planning to leave after the wedding, though he hadn't said much to me about it recently. I suppose I had secretly been hoping that he'd changed his mind. I think we were both too sad to talk about it.

As we ladies were cleaning up in the kitchen, Jeremiah came back into the house and said he wanted to talk to me. As we left the house I saw his horse tied to the rail beside the barn. It was saddled.

Jeremiah took my hand and we walked out toward the woods where we had often walked together. We were quiet most of the way. Both of our hearts were heavy.

"Jeremiah," I finally burst out, "why do you have to go?"

He let out a long sigh. We stopped and sat down on a fallen log.

"I jes' think it's best," he said after a minute. "I don't like it no better'n you. But I gotta do somefin' ter make some money, an' Mister Watson done gib me a letter an' tol' me about a place in Delaware where dey likely can use a young man like me. It won't be fo long."

"How long?" I asked.

"I don't know, maybe a few munfs—till I kin save some money so dat we kin pay our fair share here, an' till it's safe roun' here agin. Da way things is, it's too dangerous. Dose blame white boys hate me, an' ef dey know I's gone, dey's not gwine be thinkin' 'bout Rosewood quite so much. Especially now dat Papa ain't workin' in town no mo', I's hopin' dey forgit 'bout us altogether."

"I still don't like it," I said.

"Neither do I. But da time'll go by an' den we'll be together again."

I felt tears beginning to drip down my cheeks.

"But why do you have to go today?"

"I reckon I don't. But my daddy's married now an' dis is da day he's makin' a new beginnin', an' it seems like it's a good day fo me to make my new beginnin' too. I talked to my daddy 'bout it. I wudn't leave if it wud make his special day sad fo him an' Josepha. But he said dat maybe it wuz fittin' dat he an' me start new on da same day. So he said I cud go wiff his blessin' an' it'd jes' be dat much sooner I'd be gettin' back."

It was quiet for a minute or two.

"I got somefin' for you," said Jeremiah, "—kind er like a present ter help us remember."

I glanced over at him as he stuffed a hand into one of his pockets. I hadn't noticed him carrying anything. What could it be?

"I know it ain't da same or as fancy as da one you call da Tear Drop dat your mama had. But I figger it'll help you remember me an' remind us bof dat we'll be together agin soon enuff."

He held out his hand and gave me a little silver cufflink with the letters JP on them.

"Oh, Jeremiah, it's pretty!"

"I axed Mrs. Hammond ter order dem fo me. I ain't altogether even shore what cufflinks are for, but dey's always two ob 'em, so I figger we cud each keep one, kind er like a promise ter each other."

"This is even more special to me," I said. "The Tear Drop was my mama's to remind her of my papa. I treasure it because it reminds me of her and Papa. But this is my very own and will remind me . . . of the man I love."

"An' da man dat loves you. An' I do, you know, Mayme. I do love you more den anyone in da world. You always been da only girl fo me."

"Thank you, Jeremiah," I said.

I scooted closer to him on the log. He put his arm around me and we sat for a long time like that together, not saying a word.

When we got back to the house, the men were outside talking and laughing with Henry, a few of them smoking cigars, and the women were just finishing up inside. Henry and Papa and Uncle Ward saw us walking toward them hand in hand, but they didn't call out to us. They too knew that Jeremiah was planning to leave Rosewood that same afternoon.

Jeremiah went to get the last of his things.

When he was ready, the rest of us gathered with Jeremiah by his horse, where the few things he was taking, and as much food as Josepha and I'd been able to pack for him, were tied behind his saddle.

"You take care of yourself, you hear," said my papa, shaking Jeremiah's hand.

"Yes, sir, Mister Templeton. I will."

Then he shook Uncle Ward's hand. Katie stepped forward and gave him a big hug. When she stepped back, she was crying. Josepha nearly swallowed him up in her embrace. She was crying too.

When she stepped back, Jeremiah looked at his father standing beside her.

"You two look good together," he said. "Congratulations agin. I hope you's bof be real happy."

He took a few steps forward, and the father and son embraced. Henry whispered something I couldn't hear. Jeremiah looked up into his eyes, wet like the rest of ours, and smiled and nodded, then stepped back.

Finally Jeremiah turned to me. By then I was

bawling like a baby! He took me in his arms and we held each other tight.

"I love you, Mayme," he whispered.

"I love you too, Jeremiah," I said. "And you better do like Papa said and take care of yourself!"

"Don't you worry none . . . I will."

He gave me one final squeeze. He nodded to Papa, and Papa reached his left arm over my shoulder and shook Jeremiah's hand again. Jeremiah stepped back, looked around at everyone else again with a last smile of farewell, then mounted his horse.

We all stood watching as he rode off in the direction of Mr. Thurston's. He looked back as he came to the bend in the road, waved one more time, then disappeared from sight.

I turned my face to Papa's chest and cried again while he held me close.

⤙ ❈ ⤚

Endings
41

*P*apa and Uncle Ward had tried to talk Henry and Josepha into going on a honeymoon. But the thought of having their very own house, paid for in full with their very own money at a final price of fifty dollars, was more exciting to them by far than a honeymoon trip somewhere else.

When Josepha heard of the negotiations over the price, if negotiations they could be called—with the sellers trying to lower the price and the buyers trying to increase it—she insisted on paying her fair share along with Henry. She had saved nearly thirty dollars of her own since gaining her freedom—which she kept beneath the mattress of her bed in her upstairs room in the house. She insisted on contributing at least ten dollars toward the house.

So the price eventually went from twenty-five to forty and finally to fifty, and the newlyweds began their life together with a new house and thirty dollars between them.

For two former slaves, it was wealth untold! If any two people in Shenandoah County, North Carolina, not to mention the whole country, were happier than Henry and Josepha Patterson, I don't know who they were.

There was nothing they were more anxious to do than to stay right at Rosewood and spend their first days together under a roof they could call their own.

Everybody stayed at Rosewood most of the afternoon after the wedding, and except for Jeremiah's absence, we had such a good time. I felt both happy and sad together. That evening we all left the house and walked Henry and Josepha down to their new house like an old-fashioned wedding processional.

The whole week before the wedding they had made final preparations to get the house finished and ready. The bed had arrived along with most of the other furniture. There were kitchen supplies and rugs and food and so many other things to think of that they could use. A lot of it Papa and Uncle Ward had bought from Mrs. Hammond, and they took quite a bit from the big house too—extra tables and chairs and a sideboard and wardrobe that weren't being used, and we had more than enough pots, pans, and plates and knives and forks to share. The new house, being small, filled up pretty fast. And just seeing Josepha at the kitchen counter—her very own kitchen counter!—and Henry sitting at the table . . . well, it was as homey as if they'd been there all their lives.

As we walked them down to their new house we

all were talking gaily. Then somebody started singing and pretty soon we were all loudly singing "Jimmy Crack Corn."

We reached the new house and everybody quieted down.

"Well, Missus Patterson," said Henry, "welcome ter our new home."

Again, one by one, everybody shook Henry's hand and gave Josepha one last hug, then stepped back.

Henry turned to us all.

"We's bof mo grateful ter you all den we kin say. You's all da bes' frien's a man an' woman cud hope ter hab."

Then he turned and led Josepha inside.

Epilogue

S EVEN OR EIGHT MONTHS LATER, WHEN THE
visitor arrived at Rosewood and was invited into the
house for a serious talk with Ward and Templeton Daniels,
it was a conversation that would, in the months that followed, change the lives of everyone in the Rosewood family
forever.

Their visitor from town sat down. They offered him a
cup of coffee, but after a brief sip and imperceptible grim-
ace, he set the cup aside.

"So, those two girls of yours are gone, eh?" he said.

"Yeah, and it's too quiet around here!" laughed Templeton.

Behind them the door opened.

They glanced up to see Josepha walk in, followed by
Henry.

"Are we glad to see you!" said Templeton. "We need
a fresh pot of coffee. We've been drinking what's left from
breakfast and it's not too good."

"Hello, Henry," said Mr. Watson.

"You didn't gib Mr. Watson my ol' stale cold coffee?"

asked Josepha, glancing at the cup in front of their guest as she walked toward the cook stove.

Ward nodded. "It was all we had."

"Well, you jes' wait a minute or two till I put on a new pot.—You didn't by chance bring any mail from town fo us from dem two girls?" she asked, turning toward Mr. Watson.

"No, I'm sorry, Josepha," he replied, "I didn't think to check."

"Still no word yet!" she said, half to herself. "It been too long. Dey shoulda wrote by now."

"I'm sure they're fine," said Templeton. "Probably just busy, that's all."

"I still think it's been too long. I don't like it."

"From that look on your face, Herb," said Ward, "I'd say you got something serious on your mind."

Herb Watson tried to laugh with him, but without much humor in his tone.

"I suppose you're right," he said.

"Anything you got to say, you can say to us all."

Watson nodded. He might as well just get down to the business of his call.

"I'd hoped, as much as I didn't want to do it, that letting your boy go," he said, glancing in Henry's direction, "would take care of things. But I'm still getting pressure. And unfortunately, with the law on their side . . ."

He did not finish. Except for Josepha at the stove, the kitchen fell silent.

"Come on, Herb, out with it," said Templeton at length. "How bad can it be?"

"It's bad, boys. I can hardly bring myself to say it."

"Come on, just give it to us straight."

Watson sighed.

"I guess what I'm trying to say is that maybe it would be better for everybody if you'd get your lumber and supplies elsewhere—just for a while, until things settle down."

"You don't want to sell to us?"

"Come on, you know it's not like that. But I'm being pressured, and . . . well, why should we intentionally alienate them? There are other places."

"What about our cotton, Herb?" asked Ward.

"I don't know—that's still several months off. It's only May—let's worry about that when the time comes."

"If we don't sell this crop of ours this fall, we'll never meet our taxes," said Templeton. "We were a little short last year and they gave us a year's extension. But they won't look kindly on us being short again."

"Yeah, I know that. But like I say, maybe things will have cooled off by then."

Ward shook his head and drew in a deep breath. "They're trying to squeeze us out," he said. "It's beginning to look like, after all we've put into this place, they might finally do it."

"I'm sorry, boys," said Watson. "I'll think on it and see if there isn't something I can come up with."

He rose to leave.

"Don't you want a cup er hot coffee?" asked Josepha.

"Thanks, but I've got to be getting back. Sorry to put you to the trouble, but this wasn't a very pleasant errand. I feel like a scoundrel having to say what I did."

"It's not your fault, Herb," said Ward.

"By the way," Watson said, "how is your boy doing, Henry?"

"Doing good," answered Henry. "Though he ain't much ob a letter writer."

"He's found himself work in Delaware," added Templeton. "He's making pretty good money, trying to save enough to marry that daughter of mine."

"I'm glad to hear it. Give him my regards when you hear from him."

"We'll do that."

"Sometimes I think we all ought to pack up and join him," sighed Ward. "Probably save everybody a lot of trouble."

"We can't give in, Ward," said Templeton. "We've got to fight this. We've weathered plenty of crisis times before now."

"We always had the cotton to bail us out. And I'm not sure it's worth it if it gets someone killed."

"Well, thanks for letting us know, Herb," said Templeton. "I'm sorry our troubles keep landing on you."

"Nothing's landed on me yet. I just hope we can figure out a way to keep this mess from landing on anybody."

As Herb Watson headed back to town, and Henry and Josepha made their way back to their own house, the two brothers sat back down in the kitchen that had once been so full of life and activity. The whole house seemed far too big, far too silent, and far too empty for just the two of them. It seemed deserted.

More had changed around here than just the attitude throughout the South toward Negroes. Rosewood had changed too. They weren't so sure they liked it.

AUTHOR BIOGRAPHY

MICHAEL PHILLIPS BEGAN HIS DISTINGUISHED WRITING career in the 1970s. He came to widespread public attention in the early 1980s for his efforts to reacquaint the public with Victorian novelist George MacDonald. Phillips is recognized as the man most responsible for the current worldwide renaissance of interest in the once-forgotten Scotsman. After partnering with Bethany House Publishers in redacting and republishing the works of MacDonald, Phillips embarked on his own career in fiction, and it is primarily as a novelist that he is now known. His critically acclaimed books have been translated into eight foreign languages, have appeared on numerous bestseller lists, and have sold more than six million copies. Phillips is today considered by many as the heir apparent to the very MacDonald legacy he has worked so hard to promote in our time. Phillips is the author of the widely read biography of George MacDonald, *George Mac-Donald: Scotland's Beloved Storyteller.* Phillips is also the publisher of the magazine *Leben*, a periodical dedicated to bold-thinking Christianity and the legacy of George MacDonald. Phillips and his wife, Judy, alternate their time between their home in Eureka, California, and Scotland, where they are attempting to increase awareness of Mac-Donald's work.

MORE FROM
MICHAEL PHILLIPS

If you enjoyed this book, you will be sure to enjoy the companion series to CAROLINA COUSINS—SHENANDOAH SISTERS, the four books about Katie and Mayme and their scheme at Rosewood. The first book in the series is entitled *Angels Watching Over Me*.

For more exciting stories about the Underground Railroad and how Amaritta helped runaway slaves get to freedom, don't miss Michael Phillips' other newest series: AMERICAN DREAMS—*Dream of Freedom* and *Dream of Life*.

To read about Alkali Jones and the adventures of the Hollister family in California during the gold rush, read THE JOURNALS OF CORRIE BELLE HOLLISTER starting with book one, *My Father's World*.

For contact information and a complete listing of titles by Michael Phillips, write c/o:

P.O. Box 7003
Eureka, CA 95502
USA

Information on the magazine *Leben*—dedicated to the spiritual vision of Michael Phillips and the legacy of George MacDonald—may also be obtained through the above address.